PROMISE OF PLEASURE

Erik stopped pacing and fisted his hands at his waist. "That Greek ox wants you."

Valdis laughed despite the heat she felt creeping up her neck. "How absurd. He's a eunuch."

"There are ways for a man to have a woman, ways to pleasure her that your master is fully capable of and he knows it." A small muscle tensed in his jaw.

"You almost sound jealous," she said. "Does the bull wish to trade places with an ox?"

He scowled at her. "I'm only trying to warn you."

"Well, now you've tickled my thoughts," she said.

If she didn't know better, she'd think he was beginning to feel possessive of her. "Just how might our 'ox' pleasure the cow without any 'bullish' attributes?"

Erik's eyes darkened as he walked toward her. "Are you sure you wish to know?"

She held his gaze for a moment, then glanced away lest he see how his intense look unsettled her. Her heart fluttered like a snared bird against her ribs. She drew a deep breath and gathered her courage.

"Are you offering to show me?"

MORE PRAISE FOR DIANA GROE!

MAIDENSONG

"Groe brings both Scandinavia and the exotic eastern city known to the Vikings as Miklagard to life through her strong characters. Readers will watch for Groe's next historial romance."

—*Booklist*

"From the ice-swept plains of Scandinavia to the blistering heat of the Byzantine slave markets, this steamy love story calls to mind the great mistresses of the genre: Small, Henley and Mason. Filled with forbidden love, betrayal, redemption and hope, Groe's strong start will leave readers eager for more."

—*Romantic Times BOOKreviews*

"Ms. Groe is a fresh new voice in Romance. Dramatic and stirring, *Maidensong* will leave you clamoring for more of Diana Groe's work."

—Connie Mason, *New York Times* Bestselling Author of *A Taste of Paradise*

"This story is fast-paced and extremely enjoyable. It is clear that the author knows her stuff, and the Viking world vividly comes to life in a way rarely seen done well in a romance novel. If you enjoy a passionate tale told across the tapestry of a well-woven historical backdrop, then you must pick up this book!"

—Historical Romance Writers

"*Maidensong* is a beautifully written epic tale of love, honor, and sacrifice....With heart-stopping action and tear-dropping emotion, Diana Groe makes her debut on the scene with a keeper!"

—Romance Reviews Today

"*Maidensong* takes us on a whirlwind journey to new lands with unique characters and a heart-stopping adventure....Diana Groe's debut novel shows an incredible amount of storytelling talent. Take this wonderful journey—you'll be glad you did."

—Fresh Fiction

SILK DREAMS

DIANA GROE

LEISURE BOOKS   NEW YORK CITY

For Brian, always...

A LEISURE BOOK®

July 2007

Published by

Dorchester Publishing Co., Inc.
200 Madison Avenue
New York, NY 10016

Copyright © 2007 by Diana Groe

ISBN-10: 0-8439-5869-3
ISBN-13: 978-0-8439-5869-0

The name "Leisure Books" and the stylized "L" with design are
trademarks of Dorchester Publishing Co., Inc.

Printed in the United States of America.

Visit us on the web at www.dorchesterpub.com.

SILK
DREAMS

CHAPTER ONE

The Byzantine slave market buzzed like a swarm of drones in search of a new queen. The fresh shipment of potentials docked at the Imperial Shipyard in the sheltered recess of the Golden Horn. The women were driven from the relative safety of the caïque that had borne them to Constantinople, to be pinched and prodded up the winding alleys toward a pristine marble colonnade. Mindful that even drones have stingers, Valdis Ivorsdottir resisted the urge to scream when a bystander's inquisitive fingers brushed her body as she walked the narrow way.

The Frankish girl in front of her wobbled on her feet. Valdis reached out a hand to steady her. Last night the Frank's twin sister had died, whether from sickness or merely from willing herself to leave their floating *Hel*, Valdis could not be certain. When their Moorish captors consigned the dead body to the deeps of Middle Earth's great inland sea, the living twin had to be physically restrained from following her sister into the water. One of the traders seemed content to let her go, Valdis surmised from his animated speech, since her value as half of a matched set was severely diminished. But cooler heads prevailed, and the girl was kept from harming herself.

Now the Frankish maiden stumbled toward the auction block, pale and drawn, obviously wishing for death, the poor remainder of a pair of pretty playthings. Valdis pitied her, but though she shared the girl's fate, she would not emulate her.

Valdis wanted her freedom, and to win that she had to live.

"Courage," she whispered, knowing the girl couldn't understand her. The Moorish traders had purchased Valdis on the wharf at Birka in the far North, and then wended their way along the continental coast, cherry-picking other pale blossoms as they traveled south. Her captors forcefully discouraged conversation among their prisoners. Still, a silent bond was forged. Tremulous smiles and small kindnesses knit the band of women together in their captivity.

After the first degrading intimate inspection to determine her purity, no one molested Valdis. Her captors provided opportunities for her to regularly wash herself and offered abundant food and drink. In fact, several women noticeably gained flesh during the long passage to Miklagard.

Valdis did not.

When she realized they were trying to round her sharp angles, she refused any more than was necessary to retain her health. If they compelled her to eat, she later slid a finger down her throat and emptied her stomach into the waves, letting her captors blame her illness on the pitching sea. As a daughter of the seafaring Norse race she suffered no such infirmity, but she would not allow herself the burden of excess.

The leanest runner travels swiftest.

But there was no place to run. All her life, she'd heard of the glories of Miklagard, the fabulously wealthy city in the sybaritic south. Now she saw only its squalor. Strange scents from the cramped streets of the Byzantine capital suffocated her, as the cloying sweetness of a decaying corpse mixed with the spicy pungency of Asiatic cooking. Bewildering sounds pierced her ear, the cacophony of endless tongues wagging in a babble of languages and the braying of Imperial horns.

Worst of all was the press of people.

She never imagined so many existed in all the nine worlds, let alone within the confines of this fortress city. Men of every imaginable color, black as jet, pale as moonstone, and every hue in between; turbaned, shaved bald as a brown egg, dark eyes overhung by brows that met in the middle, jaws fringed with curly beards dyed impossible shades of scarlet, or male faces as smooth and hairless as her own—there were too many variations to count. She confined her gaze to the slender back of the Frankish girl in front of her, but the bizarre images wormed their way into her mind through the corners of her eyes.

Valdis was hemmed in on all sides, kept wearily in line with the others.

There will come a time to run, she promised herself. Valdis let her eyelids sink briefly and imagined she was back in the Northlands, a fresh breath of snow from the mountaintop washing over her and the blue fjord shimmering in the land's deep green embrace. Perhaps Ragnvald's dragonship would be sliding into the harbor. . . .

Her toe caught on a paving stone and she stumbled. Valdis snapped her eyes open. No more dreaming. It might bring on another fit, another nightmarish interlude in which she knew not where or who she was. She dared not risk it. By the Thunderer, the last one up-ended her life.

Ragnvald would never come for her again.

She took the Frank's icy hand and squeezed. The girl smiled thinly at her, gripping her as if Valdis were her only tenuous hold on this world. Valdis gained strength from bearing up her weaker companion and slid an arm around the girl's shoulders as they neared their destination. The women were bundled into the colon-nade, separated into groups and penned like beasts with females from other vessels. Fat, smooth-faced keepers with curved blades dangling from their hips stood silent watch over them.

The Frankish girl was forced to the block first. Valdis hoped she wouldn't faint dead away. The trader rattled off a stream of words in praise of her charms, but he had to shout to be heard over the din. One after an-other, the women were sold like prize heifers at market.

Valdis couldn't watch. She sank in a heap and let the cool marble seep into her bones. If she allowed herself, she would weep for days at the shame of it.

No, she told herself with sternness. When her captor motioned her to the dais, Valdis straightened her spine. Whatever happened, she must be strong. She must not let anyone see. Her strange weakness had expelled her from her home.

If it were discovered here . . . she didn't think there was much farther a body could fall.

Damian Aristarchus flicked the lion-tail whisk across his broad shoulders. It was a good thing the market opened early. By midday, the biting flies were vexing this close to the wharves.

He looked around at the other buyers, calculating the

probable weight of their remaining coin. He'd made a few bids early on to drive up the prices without burdening himself with an actual acquisition. A signal from the emperor's chief eunuch excited other buyers and made them image qualities in the merchandise that weren't readily apparent. Damian merely wanted to lighten their purses so he'd have less competition by the time the auctioneer trotted out his most valuable specimens.

"See anything you like?" Publius asked, fingering the black pearl that bobbled from his left ear.

Publius kept watch over the harem of Habib Ibn Mahomet, a wealthy silk merchant from Cordoba who was visiting his wives and concubines at his sumptuous house in Constantinople at present. In the past few years, Mahomet had achieved a near monopoly on the lustrous fabric throughout the Empire and amassed the attendant prosperity such a coup brings. The silk magnate bore close watching.

What other intrigues has the Cordoban spun for himself? Damian wondered.

As serpentine as Mahomet's plans might be, Publius, by contrast, was easy to decipher. The fat eunuch always sought to ingratiate himself with his employer by procuring a new diversion for him.

Damian edged away from Publius. Even though Damian was himself a eunuch, he had little use for the unfortunates he dubbed "fat aunties." So often, those who'd been stripped of their manhood let the satisfaction of their bellies substitute for the lost pleasures of the love-couch. Each time he saw Publius, it seemed the man had ballooned even further. Publius was so grotesquely fat, Damian suspected he'd never be able to find his balls even if he still possessed them.

It had been ten years since Damian fell under the

castrating knife, but he'd been a soldier before his un-manning. He prided himself on maintaining rock hard musculature and a flat belly. He knew it was a senseless conceit, especially as it took more effort with each passing season, but it appeased his vanity. If Damian couldn't act the man, at least he could still look it.

"The Nubian's a pretty piece," Publius said, working his way close to Damian again. "I'm surprised you didn't bid on her. You've been free enough with the emperor's coin today, though I notice you haven't actually bought anything yet."

"Don't worry," Damian said. "When the right one appears, I will." The stock was thinning, so he was sure the best was soon to come.

When Damian looked toward the dais again, the dusky Nubian was being led away with a majestic roll of her monumental hips. It might have been a mistake to miss her. Women of that country were reputed to possess unusual amatory skills, sly tricks of tiny muscles that could drive a man to his knees.

A new girl took her place.

"Too tall," Damian murmured. She'd easily be able to look him in the eye.

She towered above the Arab auctioneer, but despite her height, there was a fragile quality to her slender limbs. Her pale arms were already pinking in the hot sun.

"Too skinny. There's not enough flesh on that one to tempt a half-starved stray," Publius said with a snort.

"That's easily remedied." Damian shouldered past him to get a closer look. Straight as a horse's tail, the girl's hair fell to her waist, a cascade of ripened wheat. That alone accounted for her favored placement in the lot.

Experts could lighten a woman's hair, of course, but the result was usually a brassy hue that fought with the woman's skin tone and no matter how often she

washed, Damian always fancied he caught a whiff of
sheep urine wafting about the coiffure.

But this woman's hair was obviously natural, for it
perfectly complemented her ivory skin and pale brows.
Her face was far too angular to meet the standards of
feminine beauty popular in Byzantium, but her features
were at least harmonious and well-balanced. Her eyes
were downcast, seemingly fascinated by her own long
toes peeping from beneath the thin linen palla.

Then she suddenly raised her head and he was startled by her eyes. She looked out on the world through
one eye as dark as the Nubian's, while the other was a
pale blue tinged with violet.

Two souls in one body? Damian wondered. He'd
heard of such things, but this was the first woman he'd
seen with this unusual feature. Light and dark, angel
and demon, such a one might be just what he required.
From the corner of his eye, he caught Publius making
the sign against evil.

That settled the matter. He would have this one, whatever the cost.

Erik Heimdalsson leaned against the marble column,
bored with the market. Though it would be some time
till the sun reached its zenith, he was already thirsty. It
had taken him a while to develop a taste for the Christians' strong red wine, but now it called to him with reg-
ularity. He frowned with impatience at his friend. Erik
and Hauk had squired the emperor around his hold-
ings near Thessalonica for the past month, always on
the alert for a threat against the divine presence. Now
that Erik was back in the city, he had some serious
drinking to catch up on. He resented Hauk for dragging
him to this interminable auction.

"Why do you want to spend your silver on a woman,

Hauk?" Erik demanded. "A whore is much cheaper, and you're not taxed with her keeping once she's fulfilled her purpose."

"Mayhap I'm tired of whores." Hauk signaled his willingness to part with more bezants for the girl than Erik would pay for one of those blooded Arabian stallions he'd been considering. "Besides," Hauk said with a shrug, "that one has the look of the fjords about her."

Erik cast a glance at the tall girl on the dais and then looked away. Against his will, his gaze was drawn back to her willowy form. The palla draped about her was thin as a butterfly's wing and the morning sun rendered it all but transparent. She stood ramrod straight, her high breasts full, nipples showing taut through the linen. There was a pleasing contrast between the girth of her waist and hips, and the outline of her long legs was shapely. He could see why Hauk was willing to part with his hard-earned coin for her.

His lips drew together beneath his pale mustache. A bed-slave might be fine for Hauk, but Erik had learned the hard way that a permanent attachment to a woman was a weakness a man could rarely afford. It had certainly cost him dearly.

"Careful, friend," Erik cautioned as Hauk's bid soared higher. "Better a clear, no-nonsense agreement with a willing woman of light virtue. No one gets hurt and everyone emerges from the tussle with exactly what they bargained for."

Hauk shook his head. "There comes a time in a man's life when he wants something more."

Erik had once had more. Or thought he did. Whenever Erik was tempted to try for more again, he remembered who he was and why he was in Miklagard.

He was Erik Heimdalsson, convicted murderer and banished son of the North. In this southern city, through his own valor he'd risen from the status of lowly *tagmata* to the rank of centurion in the Varangian Guard, the Byzantine emperor's elite force. Erik feared no man.

And trusted no woman.

Someone in the throng called out that the girl's high price demanded proof that her hair color was genuine.

"Oh, no, girl," Erik said under his breath as the young woman gripped the edges of her garment and struggled away from her captor. "Don't fight them."

The auctioneer reached again to remove the girl's palla and met with strenuous resistance. She back-handed the little man and sent him staggering. Erik smiled despite himself. Whether in warhorses, fierce hunting dogs, or the beautiful and cruel kestrel he'd bound to his fist and bent to his will, he admired spirit wherever he found it.

But this girl's spirit was going to earn her a beating. Erik's jaw tightened as a pair of eunuchs grabbed her arms and bore her away for discipline.

"A thousand pardons," the auctioneer stammered to the assembled buyers. "I beg your indulgence while this ungrateful odalisque is brought to a more biddable frame of mind."

The crowd fell into light gossip, awaiting the first blow, the first delicious shiver from the first spine-tingling scream. The traders wouldn't countenance their merchandise being spoiled by the lash, but cruel practice had presented them with a punishment designed to inflict maximum pain without damaging the appearance of the victim. Erik heard the stinging slaps of the bastinado and the grunts of the eunuchs who delivered the blows to the bottoms of the girl's feet. From the girl herself, he heard not a peep.

Erik ground his teeth as the punishment wore on. He'd seen grown men reduced to incoherent sobs by

this type of beating, but the girl still didn't cry out. Erik
fingered the handle of his battle-ax and imagined feed-
ing the spineless worms who were abusing her to its
sharp edges. The thought gave him pleasure, but the action would land him in prison. And a Miklagard gaol
was far worse than banishment.

"Cry out, girl," Erik muttered. "It's what those cursed
fuologi are waiting for."

The sounds of leather on flesh ceased and Erik
guessed she'd passed out. A gasp rose from the assembly when the girl reappeared, visibly shaking, but walking under her own power. She mounted the dais,
leaving a trail of slim bloody footprints on the rose-
veined marble. White-lipped, she resumed her position
in the center of the dais.

The auctioneer moved toward her, but she stopped
him with a glare, her dark eye spitting fire and the pale
one cold venom. He stutter-stepped back. Erik could almost imagine the girl a practitioner of *seid* craft, the
way she shoved the man away with just a look. Then
she turned her gaze on the crowd. Her contempt rolled
over them in palpable waves.

She drew open her palla and let it float to the ground,
pooling on the dais by her tortured feet. Her pale arms
raised in a gesture that didn't have a smidge of submission in it. She dared them to look on her.

So Erik did. She was well worth seeing. From the
crown of her head to the curve of her ankles, he found
no blemish. Of course, the Byzantines liked their women
rounder, but the triangle of pale curls on her mound
would be novelty enough to pique their interest.

She certainly piqued his.

He forced himself to ignore the way his body quickened to her. No good could come of this, he told him-

self. Then she looked directly at him and held his gaze for the span of several heartbeats.

"Help me," she mouthed in the tongue of his homeland.

The slave market faded around him and he felt himself pulled into those mismatched orbs of hers. He breathed in the green scent of the fjords in spring, heard jackdaws chattering in the forest, and felt the caress of a snow-tinged breeze—snippets of the home he'd never see again. Then she broke the spell and bent down, her breasts falling forward in a way that made his hands throb to hold them. She pulled the palla back up around her and stared straight ahead with studied indifference.

The Greek who'd been vying with Hauk for her raised his bid without prompting.

When the auctioneer recovered his power of speech, Erik's hand flew up to best the Greek.

"What are you doing?" Hauk demanded.

"Probably doing you a favor," Erik said, signaling again as the bid volleyed back and forth across the colonnade. "She's a witch, I'll warrant. I'm saving you from her curses. Anyone with eyes can see this girl is trouble."

"A man can always do with that kind of trouble." Hauk crossed his beefy arms over his chest and raised a russet brow at his friend. "If you wanted her, all you had to do was say so."

Erik barely heard him. He edged closer to the dais, one hand on his ax handle, the other hefting his money pouch, trying to calculate how much of last month's pay still resided in the leather bag.

The Greek raised the bid again.

Erik narrowed his eyes at the man. He'd seen him before at the palace. A eunuch, he was sure. Nearly all the officials who kept the Byzantine Empire humming were members of the "third sex." Even though the Greek's frame had the wiry toughness of one who'd seen combat, Erik fancied he could smell the man's perfume from across the colonnade. His lip curled in dislike.

Could the Greek be trying to acquire the girl for his employer? Not likely. The emperor was a follower of *Kristr*. His Imperial Greatness kept a discreet mistress or two, but no harem. That was the province of the few followers of the Prophet who made Miklagard their home.

"Lend me the rest of your bezants," Erik hissed to Hauk as he signaled once more to the auctioneer. Hauk pressed his purse into Erik's hand.

The girl still stared straight ahead, as if unaware that she was the vortex of the market's swirling excitement. Her eyes seemed to lose their focus and her lids fluttered rapidly for a few heartbeats. Then she gasped as if she'd been holding her breath, her gaze darting about like a starling in a net. She gave herself a brief shake and continued to stare into the distance.

Is she spelling me, even now? Erik wondered. It didn't matter. For one brief moment, when she looked at him, he'd tasted home. He had to have it again. Erik nodded at the auctioneer and glared over at his competitor.

The Greek's dark eyes met Erik's, then slid over him in that damnably condescending way the Byzantines had. Something in their very stance shouted how superior they felt themselves to the *barbaroi*—the barbarian sobriquet with which they tarred the rest of the non-Byzantine world. Even this eunuch, this limp-sword, this half-man felt himself better than Erik.

The Greek flicked his fly-whisk again and, even counting Hauk's coins, the girl's price climbed beyond Erik's reach.

Impotently, Erik watched as the eunuch paid the

auctioneer and signaled for a sedan chair. The Greek bundled the girl into the enclosed seat and climbed in with her.

The knot of buyers dissolved around Erik, scurrying off to the next venue where the finest examples of human flesh might be offered for sale.

"What does a ball-less wonder want with a woman?" Erik asked. *And why that one?*

"Who knows? I've little luck when it comes to understanding the way these Greeks think. Guess you won't be needing this," Hauk said as he snatched his purse back from Erik. "You were probably right about her. A permanent woman is more trouble than she's worth. Let's go see if we can wake up those little dancers at the tavern by the Xenon." Hauk strode from the colonnade.

Erik glared at the empty dais. She'd shown such courage, his chest ached. The outlines of the girl's bare feet still showed, pink-tinged on the marble. He was nearly overcome with the urge to plant kisses on the slim imprints.

Bah! That cinched the matter. She was undoubtedly an adept at the dark arts of *seid* and he was well clear of her. The last thing he needed in his life was a woman. A witch would be even worse.

He needed a drink, that's all. He followed his friend away from the market, congratulating himself on his narrow escape. After all, he'd nearly beggared himself for her and she didn't even look back.

"The beauty of a truly artful plan is its seeming art-lessness."
—from the secret journal of Damian Aristarchus

CHAPTER TWO

As if through a gauze panel, Valdis watched the soldier advance. He was dressed in the style of the Varangians—a long byrnnie draped over his muscular form, his calves bared above regimental hobnailed boots, an ax tilted from a shoulder baldric, its razor edge thirsty for blood-wine. She couldn't see his face beneath his conical helmet. Only his eyes blazed above the bronze cheek pieces, pale and glittering with the early stages of the madness called berserkr.

Even though the man moved with the sturdy grace of a blooded warrior, Valdis sensed danger hovering about him like a silent corbey circling a carcass. He slid catlike along the corridor, appearing and disappearing as he stepped from fading sunlight to shadow. The space he traversed had many windows on one side and was indented with several niches on the other, the homes of secret trysting places for lovers. On came the soldier with single-minded doggedness. Valdis's chest tightened.

He doesn't know, she realized. *He doesn't feel death*

*stealing over him. Valdis sensed the gaping blackness
reaching for him.*

*A dark figure emerged from one of the niches and
clubbed the warrior from behind. He crumpled to the
flagstones with a clatter of mail. The blow was hard
enough to knock off his helmet.*

*Valdis pushed back the gauze obscuring her sight and
looked at his face.*

I know this man, she thought.

*His eyes stared sightlessly at her, the pupils so en-
larged they nearly swallowed the icy gray of his irises.
Then she remembered who he was and gasped.*

The sharp intake of breath woke her. For a moment
she hovered in the thin veil between the waking world
and the land of shadows. Valdis lay still, trying to orient
herself. This was the third time the same dream had
plagued her since her arrival in Miklagard. She looked
up into the swirl of gossamer curtains splayed over and
around her sleeping couch.

It made no sense. She'd only seen the man during the
brief time she'd stood on the slave market dais. She didn't
even know his name. Why should she dream of the
Varangian? Even though two men vied for her, the Byzantine was the one who bought her and now frustrated her
days with his attempts to teach her the Greek tongue. Why
could she not banish that Norse soldier from her dreams?

And why was she tormented by his danger?

The soft brush of sandaled feet brought Valdis to full
wakefulness. The Greek, or one of his many servants,
was stirring. She parted the bed curtains with one finger and peered out from her filmy cocoon.

It was the Greek himself, newly risen from his sleeping couch in the adjoining chamber. Even though he'd
made no sexual overtures toward Valdis, she knew he
slept in the nude not a stone's throw from her. He

seemed unaffected by their proximity, and if he cast
furtive glances in her direction, she'd yet to catch him
at it.

He was turned from her, his tight buttocks dusted
with fine dark hairs. A body slave scurried to his side
and lifted a linen robe of obvious quality over the
Greek's head. The soft fabric draped his broad shoulders and tapering torso, falling in creamy folds till the
hem brushed his ankles. When the man turned to perch
on the bed so his servant could lace his sandals, Valdis
let the curtain drop.

While she was grateful the Greek hadn't forced himself on her, she was puzzled by his indifference. She
knew she was desirable. Early on, her parents marked
her as comely, the one whose unique beauty would secure the family's fortune. She was destined for a grand
match, her mother always told her. When she caught
the eye of Ragnvald, the *jarl's* oldest son, her father
spent himself into poverty preparing for her wedding.

Then the unthinkable happened.

Even now, she was unable to conjure her parents'
faces without seeing pinched expressions of confusion
and suspicion. She had no clear memory of that awful
morning before the assembled gathering at the *jarlhof.*
She could only trust the account of her younger sister
Jana before she was bundled off to the flesh market at
Birka.

Some malevolent spirit had taken hold of Valdis and
thrown her to the ground, thrashing and raving. She
was obviously cursed. The *jarl* was relieved the malady
had shown itself before his noble house was ensnared
in a misalliance. Her parents claimed to know nothing
of the ill wish stalking their daughter.

Only Valdis suspected it wasn't the first time evil had
swirled his bony finger in her brainpan.

The spells had started in conjunction with the appearance of her woman's moon. Valdis hadn't taken much notice of them in the beginning. They were flickers of inattention, she told herself. Then she realized she would fade out of normal family conversations, losing snippets of stories told by firelight and coming back to awareness only at the end of jokes, when everyone else was doubled over with mirth and she was left to wonder what she'd missed. Once, her mother scolded her for batting her eyes too much. She hadn't realized she'd done so.

Then there was that day in the forest when she was herding geese one moment and lying in a tangle of gorse the next, bruised and disoriented, her chin wet with her own spittle.

She was undoubtedly witched.

The Greek was talking now, low-pitched instructions to the body slave, who responded in deferential tones. Valdis watched them through the thin curtain, hazy forms without distinguishing features.

Just like my dream, until the last terrible moment.

She pushed back the sheet and reached for her own palla before the body slave could hustle over to assist her. She hadn't been dressed by another since she was toddling. It made no sense to revert to such helplessness now.

Once she was clothed, the Greek approached her, bearing a silver tray. He set it down on the low table near her sleeping couch. The ebony table was inlaid with ivory and far finer than anything in Ragnvald's *jarlhof*.

Valdis was still in awe of the Greek's grand apartments. Sleek marble floors of moss green, thick damask wall hangings depicting jewel-toned birds whose fanlike plumage was surely an artist's fantasy, and everywhere the imperial golden eagle of Byzantium—on the caps of columns, on the strange two-tined implement with which the Greek encouraged her to eat, and on the gold signet ring that never left the man's right fore-finger. Sometimes, the grandeur became more than Valdis could bear and she was forced to squeeze her eyes shut to let her mind rest.

"Day-mee-uhn," the Greek said, his long-fingered hand splayed across his chest. He gave her a hopeful nod.

Valdis just looked at him. She knew he was telling her his name and encouraging her to reciprocate. But why should she? The longer she kept him from realizing she was picking up much more of his language than she voiced, the longer she'd be able to live in this silken gaol without any other duties than to eat and sleep un-molested while she uncovered a method of escape.

The Greek didn't seem to want her body. Why then did he want her to speak to him so badly? And if all the man wanted was conversation, why hadn't he bought a Greek girl?

She picked up a slice of fruit and bit into it, the un-usual combination of tart and sweet making her mouth water.

"Orange," he said.

She filed the information away, but didn't repeat the word as he clearly wished for her to do. She swallowed the delightful bite and grinned at him. There was no need to be unpleasant just because she was being un-cooperative.

A muscle twitched along the Greek's smooth jaw, but though he scowled darkly, Valdis knew she was in no danger. A man capable of doing a woman real harm had a hardness about his eyes, a glint of steel protrud-ing from his soul. Though her captor carried himself like a warrior, something in his face spoke of an inti-mate acquaintance with suffering. In some men, pain begat cruelty; in others, an empathetic spirit. The Greek would not beat her. However, the guards stationed outside the door of his chambers assuredly would if he gave the word.

But this man would not give such an order.

Valdis took another bite of the orange, licked her lips, and smiled once more.

Damian let the door slam behind him. How could he have miscalculated so badly? He was sure he'd found the right woman for the task, certain he'd seen the requisite spark of intelligence in her unusual eyes. He treated her with kindness, almost deference. How could she be so slow in grasping his desire that she master his language?

It was probably not a mental defect, despite that moment on the dais when her eyes seemed to glaze over strangely. No doubt she suffered from shock after the bastinado was applied to her feet. The rapid fluttering of her eyelids made her mismatched eyes seem all the more supernatural. It was just the thing to convince the superstitious that she communed with the spirit world. It would certainly increase the plausibility of the ruse he intended.

She was being stubborn, as only those cursed *barbaroi* could be.

He could be just as stubborn. Though he'd hoped not to involve another party, he was going to have to bring in a third. Quintilian was sending over the best Greek speaker from among his Norse officers first thing this morning.

He could see no other course. Even so, it galled Damian to have to use a Varangian. He was enough a student of history to mistrust them. After all, years ago a flotilla of five hundred dragonships attempted the sack of Constantinople itself. Even with the advantage of the weapon known as Greek fire, the ferocity of the Northmen nearly prevailed. The emperor, in his divine wisdom, had deemed it expedient to hire the *barbaroi* and incorporate the Norse pirates into the body politic of the Empire. Since the first Northman donned a *byrnnie* stamped with the Imperial eagle, the Varangian Guard had pledged their honors and their lives to the service of the Byzantine Emperor.

But Damian was a skeptic at heart. Loyalty bought with *bezants* couldn't compete with the devotion of a native-born Roman. Technically, he admitted to being Greek, as nearly everything in the great city was, from the culture and architecture to the people themselves, but in his heart, he was Roman—a defender of the glory of the fallen West, a jewel of hope for mankind that still glistened in this eastern setting.

And wasn't it the same sort of godless barbarians as the Varangians who toppled the first Rome?

Damian followed the labyrinth of corridors to his office, deep in the bowels of the Imperial Palace. Even in this remote place, far below ground where it was unlikely any foreign dignitary would ever tread, the love of beauty led the designers to fashion a pleasing space. Damian slid the key into the lock on the silver-plated door and let himself in.

The scent of leather bindings and musty parchment greeted his nostrils. Light shafted from a row of clerestory windows. The wells that brought sunshine to his lair were narrow and deep and grated at the surface with iron bars. No one could venture down the constricted tunnels to gain entrance to his vault by that route, and Damian possessed the only key to the argentine door.

It was good that the door was kept locked. One entire wall was honeycombed with cubbyholes filled with scrolls and bound manuscripts. If Damian were the type to be motivated by greed, he possessed enough secret information in this small space to blackmail most of the Byzantine nobility into threadbare poverty.

But his concern was not gain. It was for the emperor's safety and continued reign. To ensure that end, he was not above using either subtle means or brute force.

A fist pounded on the door, demanding entrance.

"Speaking of brute force," Damian muttered, then raised his voice. "Come."

The Varangian swung open the door and stomped in with typical *barbaroi* disregard for decency and decorum. Better to let this underling know his exact position from the start, Damian decided.

He didn't spare the man a glance, making a great show of studying the missive spread before him. It was an inconsequential report. He employed numerous spies throughout the great city and frequently paid for drivel, but one never knew when a nugget of pure gold might be found among the dross.

Damian heard the creak of hardened leather from the Northman's chest piece as the *barbaroi* shifted his weight from one foot to the other. Damian shuffled a paper or two and signed his name with a flourish to the last one before deigning to look up.

He recognized the man immediately. It was the Varangian who drove the girl's price so unconscionably high. Obviously, the Northman remembered Damian as well because that same sneer creased his lip.

"There's been some mistake," Damian said. "What are you doing here?"

"I am under orders," he answered in flawless Greek. The man handed over a scroll bearing the seal of the general. "I was told to report to the office of the chief eunuch. However, if there's been a mistake, I'll be more than happy to return to my unit. I've fought many campaigns to win my centurion eagle. This reassignment is likely to cost me my command."

Damian returned the Northman's scowl and ripped open the scroll. He ran his gaze over the familiar, precise curlicue script and read:

> Hail Damian Aristarchus,
>   Greetings.
>   Before you stands Erik Heimdalsson, a centurion under my command. In truth, I am loath to lose him, but you demanded our best Greek speaker from among the Tauro-Scythians.

Damian was mildly surprised to see the leader of the Varangians use this epithet for his troops. *Tauro-Scythian* was even less kindly meant than the term *barbaroi*. Then his time in armed service rushed back to him and he remembered his old commander swearing the air blue and denigrating the heritage of his favorites. He read on.

>   I assure you that Heimdalsson is the best. He has an infallible ear for languages and can ape several different accents, from Cretan to Paphlagonian. He is quick-tempered and should be deemed dangerous, but there is no officer among this pack of wild dogs I'd rather have at my side in battle. Tell him I'll have him hung upside down in the barracks if he fails to please you.

Damian smiled at the image of the smug warrior in such a demeaning position before he returned to the letter.

*There is one stipulation on the transfer of Heim-
dalsson to your command. I understand your desire
to have him gelded before he enters your Imperial
service, but let me assure you, such a course would
render the man useless. While there is no stigma attached to the condition of a eunuch among us—
indeed, as you yourself have experienced, it is often
the path of preferment to high office—but among
the Varangians, it is a source of such shame, the
man would probably fall on his own sword.*

Written with the callousness of an intact man, Damian
thought with bitterness. He shifted in his seat. How often had he contemplated the very course? The idea of
suicide held real appeal for him during the excruciat-
ing period of recovery after the hot knife severed his
ballocks from his shocked body. Sometimes, when he
woke in the night, drenched in old woman's sweat,
Damian still weighed the value of a gladius thrust to his
heart. He read on:

Heimdalsson may be a hell-bound barbaroi, *but
he has taken the Varangian Oath. Among the
Northmen, a pledge binds a man more effectively
than the promise of gold, which I'll not deny they
covet beyond the degree of most. Erik is the emperor's pledge-man. He will serve you well.*

The document was duly signed and embossed with
the general's signet. Damian rolled up the scroll and
tapped the end absently on the enamel desktop.

This was an unexpected turn. He'd tried to find a fe-
male Norse-speaker for the task, but it seemed the *Tauro-
Scythians* preferred to keep their fair-haired women in
their distant frozen vastness. If Damian had to employ a

Northman at all, common decency required he be a eunuch since the man would be spending copious amounts of time with a virgin. Quintilian had ruled that out and Damian could not afford to feud with the man who controlled a force of *berserkrs* a thousand strong. Now Damian would have to monitor the time the girl spent with her language tutor—time he could put to use elsewhere, but her purity must be without question for his plans to succeed.

Damian would have preferred a Northman without a personal interest in the girl. Of course, given her unique appeal, any man would soon acquire an interest.

Even a half-man, he admitted to himself. When he was first gelded, he continued to wake each morning with a painful erection for some months, an ache that could not be assuaged. Then he schooled himself to thrust that part of his nature aside, to cultivate the life of the mind to compensate for the loss of the flesh. But since the girl had taken up residence in his apartments, his phallus stirred to life once more with frustrated lust.

He studied Heimdalsson's rough-hewn face, meeting the Northman's icy gaze without a blink. Damian read a certain undisciplined intelligence in the *barbaroi's* features.

But could he be trusted? Perhaps it didn't matter. Just because he made use of the man, the *Tauro-Scythian* didn't have to be privy to all Damian's plans.

"Very well, Northman," he finally said. "I'm told the Varangians are prepared to die for the emperor if needs be. Is this true?"

"I am the Bulgar-Slayer's pledge-man," Heimdalsson answered. "My blade and my body are the emperor's to command. My heart's blood is his. What does my lord the emperor require of me?"

"Nothing so dramatic, I fear. You'll be back leading

the charge at the head of your one hundred ruffians in no time." One corner of Damian's mouth lifted in a wry smile. "You only have to tame and teach a willful woman."

CHAPTER THREE

A tingle of fear pierced Valdis's groin. She stood on the edge of a cliff, albeit a man-made one. She leaned over the balustrade of the balcony and peered at the *tag-mata* exercise yard below. The Imperial forces struck terror in the hearts of all peoples who lived along the coasts of the inland sea, but the fighting men far beneath Valdis's feet looked small and insignificant from this height.

So must all humans appear to the Court of Asgard, she reasoned. No wonder her Norse gods took so little interest in her plight. Perhaps the distance was so great, this sun-baked land so far from the North, Odin the one-eyed All-Father was unable to see her at all.

Damian's apartments in the Imperial Palace faced the rising sun. Valdis shielded her eyes against the glare of mid-morning and gazed upon a forest of stone men and women mounted on tall spires. Yesterday when Damian caught her looking at them with interest, he tried to tell her about them, but she could attach little meaning to his words. "Acropolis" was a word he repeated several times, so she assumed that was what the congregation of granite was called.

The statues were so beautiful she at first surmised that they must be the gods of this southern city. Only the trio of giants at the Great Temple in Uppsala could compare with these stone renderings. Then she remembered that the citizenry of Miklagard were followers of *Kristr*. If at one time the statues of the Acropolis were venerated as Odin and Thor and the stiff-phallused Frey were in the North, that time was long past. Stately robed courtiers wandered among the stone gods without leaving a single offering.

There were, however, a few broad pedestals where a living man resided, hunkered against the wind. "Stylites," Damian had named them.

Valdis thought them mad.

But the common folk of Miklagard revered the stylites, bringing them food and drink, which was lifted to the filth-encrusted hermits in wicker baskets.

How strange the people of this city are.

Her gaze swept further north, beyond the gates that marked the Imperial Palace as a city within a city. Domes and *stele* and minarets stabbed the sky as Miklagard flowed over its seven hills. There seemed no end to the packed tenements and opulent palaces, and everywhere were the ornate houses of the Christians' three-headed god.

But she knew the city eventually found its boundary in a series of walls so tall and thick she hadn't believed the tales when she first heard them as a girl.

She believed them now.

Valdis turned back into the Greek's apartments, discouragement sagging her shoulders. Even if she could escape the Imperial grounds, and that was no mean feat, where would she go?

Perhaps it was time to begin limited cooperation with her captor. If she could speak the language, she might be able to find her way back to the wharves. Then she could barter passage on one of the many ships she watched slipping from the Golden Horn into the deep blue water sparkling beyond.

The eagle-embossed door to the apartment swung open and the Greek entered with a courteous-sounding greeting, as if he hadn't stalked out in a furious boil not long ago. An amused smile played about his full lips. Behind him, Valdis saw another man pause at the threshold before following Damian in.

It was the Varangian from the slave market.

Odin was crossing their paths once more. This must be why she'd dreamed of him. Surely this countryman of hers would come to her aid.

She could have wept at the sight of him, rough-edged and big, despite the polished leather chest piece and kilt that marked him as a Varangian. His face spoke to her of home. His brows were so pale as to be almost invisible above his North Sea eyes. A small scar lifted one of them in a perpetual question. His flaxen hair brushed his broad shoulders. Some warriors followed the fashion of fussily braiding their long beards, but this man's facial hair was neatly trimmed and brushed free of snarls. His upper lip was hidden by a mustache, but what she could see of his mouth made her run her tongue over her own lips. High, flat cheekbones and a sharp nose made his face too raw-boned for Grecian ideals of masculine beauty, but Valdis's breath quickened as she drank in the sight of him.

He was out of his element in the Greek's elegant

chambers, yet he took possession of the space as if by
right. Despite the high airy ceilings, he charged the
rooms with a crackle of power. Here was a man who
could meet any challenge flung at him, and Valdis
doubted many would dare oppose him.

If only she could bend him to her will . . .

"Thanks be to Odin," she murmured.

Damian spoke a few words to the Northman, who continued to look around the lavish space. Like Valdis, he was
clearly in awe of the magnificence of their surroundings.

"The eunuch says he's glad to learn that you're not
mute after all," the man said.

Valdis frowned. *Eunuch?* She lifted a brow at
Damian. Birka's skald had ventured to Miklagard once
and brought back many amusing and scurrilous tales
about the eunuchs of the great city, aping their mincing
gait, corpulent forms and feminine voices. The darkly
handsome Greek before her displayed none of the af-
fectation she'd heard attributed to members of the
"third sex."

But it explained much. No wonder Damian was unaffected by her presence in his sleeping chambers. He
was not a true man.

The Varangian certainly was. He strode toward her
with the confident awareness she expected in a male.
He stopped an arm's length away from her and let his
gaze slide over her in deliberate study, as though he
hadn't been at the slave market and already seen her
unclothed.

"Who are you?" he asked.

"Have you been gone from the fjords so long you've
forgotten whatever manners you might have had?" she
returned with tartness. "You might at least give me the
favor of your name before demanding mine."

"Erik Heimdalsson, from Hordaland," he answered.

"I'm a centurion, and a soldier quickly loses patience with the niceties of polite society. Now, as to your name, your host demands it, not I."

Valdis cast a glance at Damian, who was looking at her expectantly. "He's not my host. He's my gaoler. And he seems to think he owns me."

"He doesn't just think it, he knows it," Erik said. "If it's any comfort to you, he paid handsomely for the privilege. You at least owe him your name."

"I owe him nothing, but I'll give my name to you. It's Valdis," she said. "Valdis Ivorsdottir of Birka."

Erik relayed the information. Damian flashed his row of even teeth at her and repeated her name with the beguiling hint of an accent. Then he withdrew to his room, busying himself with correspondence at a small desk but keeping a discreet eye on Valdis and Erik.

A self-appointed chaperone.

"A soldier, you say." Valdis draped herself across the gold brocaded divan and motioned for Erik to sit on the ottoman opposite her. "Rather an odd choice for an interpreter, don't you think?"

"I'm not here to translate. I'm here to teach you their language and I expect you to learn quickly." He ignored her offer and stood over her, hands fisted on his waist.

She smirked up at him. If he intended to intimidate her, he'd have to try harder than that. Damian's protective presence insulated her from this big man's threatening stance.

"You seem intelligent enough. The eunuch admitted he tried to teach you. Why have you resisted learning?"

"Because whatever he wants me for must require it."

"Are you always this stubborn?"

"What would you have me do?" She rose to meet his challenge. "I am not accustomed to life as a thrall. I'm the freeborn daughter of a landed *karl*. Unlike you, I've no ax to wield or I'd have done it. Would you submit willingly to an iron collar?"

"I see no collar." He looked down at her and Valdis felt his gaze traveling further south than her neck. Her nipples tingled under his scrutiny. She turned from him and strode to the open balcony.

"Mayhap not in truth, but it's there all the same. I won't bear the weight of it." She glanced over her shoulder, mildly disappointed he hadn't followed.

Erik was looking around her gilded chamber. "*Ja,* I can see how life on a cushion would gall a body. You are clean, well-clothed, fed and housed as if you were the goddess Freya herself." He moved toward her, then walked past her to lean on the balustrade. "Has the Greek made any other demands on you besides learning his language?"

"No."

"Then consider yourself fortunate in your lot. Everyone in this city is a thrall, one way or another."

Valdis frowned at him in confusion.

"Every soul in Miklagard serves the emperor. From the boy who sweeps the camel dung from the Mese"— he extended an arm to point at the wide major thoroughfare that knifed through the city—"to the *tagmata* in the yard below, to your perfumed master in the next room. They all live or die, are exalted or abased, by the one who wears Imperial purple."

"I suppose that includes you as well."

"It does. I am oath-sworn to serve the Bulgar-Slayer as long as I live," Erik said.

"You never intend to return home?"

A shadow passed behind his eyes. "I'm not here to talk about me. I'm here to teach you to speak the language of the Christians."

"Only because of your oath to the emperor?"

"Why else?"

She peered at him from under her lashes. "You bid on me at the market. You might have another reason besides your devotion to the emperor."

"I have repented that foolishness. Believe me, your master did us both a favor when he outbid me."

She decided to toss the knucklebones of fate and hope for the best. Valdis leaned toward him and rested her fingertips on his forearm.

"I asked for your help at the slave market and you did what you could then. Now you're in an even better position to aid me."

"I'm a soldier under orders. Nothing more." Despite his words, he looked at her with the same hungry longing she saw in him when she was on the dais.

"No wonder you encourage me to accept thralldom," she said with bitterness, hoping to goad him into helping her. "You've accepted the collar readily enough. You even take orders from a eunuch."

He snatched her hand in his and gripped it tightly. "Don't confuse honoring an oath with slavery. Do you think I enjoy serving under your master? I only do it because we are both pledged to the emperor's interests. But you're right. It makes as much sense as . . . as yoking a warhorse with a mule."

She pressed her advantage. "Neither of us belong here. Don't you want to hear Norse instead of the babble of tongues in this place? Don't you wish to see lights dance on the Northern horizon again? Or raise a horn of mead instead of the Christian's sweet wine?" She lowered her voice to a feverish whisper. "Please, Erik. Let us find a way to leave this place and go home."

She thought she had him until she said the word "home." He jerked away from her as if she were an adder.

"Never speak to me of that again," he said. "I cannot go home."

"Then at least help me leave the palace, to—"

"And just where do you think you would go?" He folded his arms across his broad chest. "Women may own property and choose their own men in the Northlands, but let me assure you that is not the case here in Miklagard. If you venture abroad in the city without an escort, you'll find yourself in a brothel by nightfall, spreading your legs for all comers."

"I asked for your help and you bid on me," she said. "How did you intend to help me then?"

He raised a hand to stroke her cheek. "I intended on helping myself, Valdis. I'd have taken you to my bed and enjoyed the forbidden pleasures of the North for the brief time I held you." His face hardened like an ice-choked fjord. "Right now I'd like nothing better than to bend you over this balcony rail, pull up your skirt and rut you blind. You should thank the gods the Greek won you instead of me."

Valdis backed away from him, shocked by the man's raw suggestions and even more shocked at the heat between her legs. A sharp edge flashed in his pale gray eyes. She was suddenly thankful Damian was within easy call.

"So you must regard me as your teacher, not your champion. The first lesson I have to teach you is the place of a woman in Miklagard," Erik said. "The best a woman can hope for, Valdis, is the protection of a good man."

An unpleasant smile spread over his face. "And as you've already discovered, I am not a good man."

"Fortune favors the bold. She also favors those who know how to manipulate the bold."
—from the secret journal of Damian Aristarchus

CHAPTER FOUR

"Kharan' ligo—" Valdis said flatly, leaning her cheek upon her palm.

"Lego," Erik corrected for the third time. *"Lego,* not *ligo. Kharan lego soi.* Try it again."

"Kharan lego soi," she repeated.

"Good. Now what does it mean?"

Her brows knit together and she gnawed her bottom lip. Finally she shook her head. "I can't remember. None of it makes any sense. It's all gibberish."

"No, that's not the right answer," Erik said, being purposely obtuse. *"Kharan lego soi* means 'I wish you joy.' Now say it again."

She mouthed the syllables in a tone that suggested she wished him snatched bald-headed or roasted on a spit—anything but joy.

"Good. Now count to one hundred like I taught you yesterday," he demanded.

"Pax!" she shouted at him.

Enough. At least she'd used a Greek word correctly.

He grinned at her. She was even more comely than usual when color worked its way up her neck and onto her cheeks. Perhaps that was why he enjoyed driving her to irritated outbursts.

She really had done well in the weeks they'd been working together. She could name all the pieces of furniture in the Greek's apartment and correctly give the plural, as well. Days of the week, months, colors, articles of clothing—individual words seemed to stick in her mind, but the complicated grammar eluded her completely. Grecian word order seemed to make no sense to her Nordic brain. Valdis's frustration reminded him how bewildered he'd felt when he first came to Miklagard five years earlier.

He forced the grin from his lips and regarded her with sternness. *Idiot!* he berated himself. If he lowered his guard by so much as a finger-width, her hypnotic eyes would lance him to the heart. He wasn't sure which one of them troubled him most—the sensual dark or the ethereal violet. He was never certain which eye to focus his gaze on, and indecision kept him strangely off-balance.

Erik continued to be grateful to Odin or *Kristr* or whichever god had conspired to assist the Greek to outbid him for her. If she'd been his, he'd have lost all sense of duty to his regiment. He lived each day for the time he could escape her presence. Valdis was a siren, he told himself, a slow poison seeping into his veins, leeching his resolve to rebuild some semblance of a life.

Sometimes though, he allowed himself to fantasize about doing as she begged, about stealing her away from the Imperial Palace and whisking her out of the city.

But where could they go?

Not to the North. No one within three hundred *landmiiller* of the fjords would offer him rest or shelter, food or fire.

After what he'd done, he couldn't blame them.

It was just as well that he held himself aloof from her. If he didn't allow her close, he couldn't hurt her. But he did wonder from time to time, say every other breath or so, how her silken arms would feel wrapped around him and if her mouth tasted as delectable as it looked.

No, he told himself with vehemence. Nothing good could come from wanting what he couldn't have. He already knew he was cursed where women were concerned, so he protected Valdis from himself by scowling at her every chance he got.

"Mayhap the eunuch will take pity on you and let you practice the alphabet for the rest of the afternoon." Erik didn't know how to write Greek himself, but Damian Aristarchus seemed to want Valdis to learn. If her master took over her lessons, it would afford Erik a chance to escape to the exercise yard below. He seriously needed to work off the frustration brought on by the lust being around this woman caused him. "Where is that tablet and stylus?"

Valdis crossed her slender arms on the table before her, buried her head in them and wept. Erik was dumbfounded. How could a woman who refused to scream when the bastinado was applied to her bare feet erupt into tears over a language lesson?

"What's this?" Damian demanded. "What have you done to make her cry?"

Erik caught Valdis stealing a sly glance at him through her parted fingers. Was the woman born with the ability to dissemble or had she practiced on other unsuspecting men?

"I've only carried out your orders," he told Damian gruffly.

"I didn't tell you to vex her beyond bearing." Damian

slid next to Valdis and put a brotherly arm around her shoulders.

Erik narrowed his eyes at the eunuch. The intent look of interest on Damian's face was anything but brotherly.

"That's enough work for one day." Damian rubbed his palm up and down the smooth skin of her bare arm in a way that made Erik's fingers itch to strangle him.

"Good," Erik said, turning away. He needed to escape before he acted on his desires.

All of them.

"I didn't say you are excused. I still need your services as a translator, but Valdis will not be forced to speak another syllable of Greek for the rest of the day if she has no wish to do so," Damian declared, fawning over her like a lovesick swain. He made a circular motion with one hand, a signal for Erik to relay his message.

Valdis rewarded the eunuch with a coquettish smile that would have done credit to the love goddess Freya herself. Irritation boiled in Erik's chest. He wished it didn't bother him so that the smile wasn't directed at him.

"Come." Damian raised her to her feet. "We are going to the Hippodrome. The Blues are taking another pass at the Greens, much good it may do them. Chariot races. I think you'll enjoy this."

Valdis watched his lips as if the meaning of his words might be divined by close scrutiny, a tiny smile of triumph tugging at the corners of her luscious mouth. Erik realized she understood far more of the Byzantine's tongue than she could speak.

"You too, Northman," Damian said without taking his dark gaze off Valdis. "I need you to be my mouth."

You're eating the woman alive with your eyes. Next you'll want me to be your cock as well. Erik bit back the thought sullenly. His member rose merrily at the barest thought of bedding this bewitching Norsewoman.

The eunuch offered his arm to Valdis and she took it without hesitation. Erik was left to trail after them like an Alsatian guard dog as they wended through the corridors and past colonnaded fountains and statuary. They strolled between rows of cypress lining the walkway like crisp green spears and finally through the heavy gilded gates that marked the end of the protected confines of the Imperial grounds.

On race day, the city gave itself over to every conceivable excess. At one crossroad, Valdis saw a girl doing handsprings on the cobbled pavement. Each time her lovely legs waved in the air, her palla slid down and bared the lower half of her lithe body, offering a glancing peep at the triangle of curly black hairs at the apex of her legs. When a *tagmata* tossed a silver *nomismata* to her, she did a handstand and let her garment drape down to her armpits for several heartbeats. Her little breasts puckered under the soldier's scrutiny like ripe figs.

Valdis suddenly felt better about being considered Damian's property. Though her freedom of movement was curtailed, Erik was right. Her cosseted existence in the Greek's plush chambers was far better than what awaited an unprotected woman on the streets of Miklagard.

"Look out!" Erik grabbed her as a heavy, wheeled cage rumbled past. He pinned her against a whitewashed building, placing his own body between her and the crowded street. Over his shoulder, Valdis saw a pair of gigantic striped cats snarling from behind the bars of the cage. One swipe of a set of cruel claws missed Erik's head by finger-widths. A carnivorous stench wafted behind the cats even once the carriage turned the corner.

Valdis found she was shaking. Truly, danger came in many forms in this vast city. She looked up at Erik, surprised that he troubled himself to shove her from harm when he took such pains to keep his distance as he tutored her. The hard lines of his face softened as he gazed back down at her.

"Are you all right?" His voice was husky, his pupils dilated to reduce the gray of his irises to slender rings.

She nodded, not willing to trust her voice. His body was warm and hard and she could feel his heart hammering against her breasts. Her own pulse beat a brisk tattoo in concert. Even though Damian treated her well, since she'd been sold into slavery the only man who had protected her from anything was this unlikely Northman.

"Thank you," she finally managed to say. One corner of Erik's mouth lifted in a half smile even as his eyes narrowed in speculation. He showed no sign of releasing her. Valdis wondered if, in his own way, the big Varangian wasn't more dangerous than the great cats.

Damian gave an order and Erik slowly stepped back. She tucked her hand into the crook of the eunuch's elbow, feeling as if she'd escaped peril twice in as many heartbeats.

Street vendors hawked their wares with singsong cadence as the crowd surged toward the Hippodrome.

"Hold a moment," Erik said when they passed a particularly aromatic stall. "Palace food will keep a body and soul together, but you've not known the taste of Miklagard till you've tried *pastfeli*."

The eunuch made complaining noises.

"He's concerned we'll arrive after the race is over if we stop for every sweetmeat seller on the Mese," Erik explained, then barked a few syllables in Damian's direction. "He wants you to learn. I told him language is more than words. It's a people's whole experience and this is one you won't want to miss." Erik signaled his or-

der to the merchant and fished the appropriate payment from his leather pouch. He offered her a glistening bite. "Try this, Valdis. After that scare, you look pale.
You need to eat something."

She hesitantly parted her lips and when he placed
the *pastfeli* on her tongue she felt as though a ray of sunshine had dissolved in her mouth. She savored the
sweetness of honey and detected the flavor of sesame
seeds and orange as well. She licked her lips and asked
for more.

"In Greek," he said, cocking his head at her.

She stumbled through the correct phrase and was rewarded with a square of *pastfeli* served on a broad
grape leaf. A bit of the treat slipped through her sticky
fingers and dropped to the paving stones. A small furry
body darted through the forest of legs and slurped it up
before the honey could settle into the cracks. It was a
scruffy little black dog, its snarled hair falling in wisps
around its thin body. The tiny creature reared up on its
haunches and pawed the air like a miniature stallion,
begging for more.

"Looks like you've attracted a talented rat," Erik said
with a laugh at the dog's antics.

"It's not a rat." Valdis frowned at him, then knelt and
let the animal lick her fingers clean. It shied when she
tried to pet it. "But I've never seen such a small dog.
What kind is it?"

Erik shrugged and relayed her question to the Greek.

"A Maltese cross of some stripe. Probably covered
with vermin," Damian said, grasping her elbow with
firmness. "Come."

With reluctance, Valdis let herself be led along, but
when she glanced back, the dog followed, skittering between the multitude of feet. Then they entered the

broad gate that led to the Hippodrome and Valdis forgot about the dog.

Even in her dreams she'd never imagined such a massive structure. They passed through a vaulted tunnel and emerged near the low wall separating the spectators from a large oval track. A *spina* ran through the middle of the arena, studded with statuary, bronze equines, ample naked women and well-endowed men, and spiked with obelisks at intervals. From the lowest tiers of seating, Valdis looked up as rank upon rank, the simple benches gave way to porticos and private boxes. Halfway to the heavens, the outer walls of the Hippodrome coliseum curved in, offering shade to the most desirable seating. Pennants stood at attention along the ridgeline. Valdis imagined even Valhalla, the great hall reserved for the glorious dead, would fit snugly into one end of the sand-covered arena floor.

Damian gestured for her to follow and she climbed toward the dizzying heights. The crowd was awash in colors—verdant, cerulean, jet and dazzling white—proclaiming allegiance to one of the four chariot teams that would shortly compete. Damian ushered her into a well-appointed private box.

Trumpets brayed and the clarion call echoed around the oval. The crowd responded with a roar rivaling thunder, a wall of sound that pressed against Valdis's ears till they ached. Then there was silence, as if every soul in the vast Hippodrome dared not even draw breath. Valdis heard the pennants above her snap in the breeze.

Across the wide space, Valdis saw a glittering figure emerge from a dark tunnel to take his place in an ornate, well guarded box. Jewels winked from his stiff vestments and light splayed from the diadem on his head. As one, the crowd fell to its knees.

"The Bulgar-Slayer himself," Erik said under his breath, tugging Valdis down beside him. The small hairs on his bare arms tickled against hers. She resisted the urge to move away, enjoying the heat of his skin so near.

Trumpets squealed again and the emperor raised one hand in greeting. The crowd voiced its delirium at this small gesture with another full-throated roar.

From one end of the arena, a herd of antelope with curved horns was released to spring across the open space. Then a door opened from the floor of the oval and the two great cats Valdis had seen earlier sprang up from the depths to pursue their hoofed prey. Once each cat made a kill, handlers whipped the felines back to their subterranean lair.

One spectacular after another paraded across the broad oval for the crowd's amusement. A girl did acrobatics on horseback that no sane person would attempt on solid ground, leaps and twists and harrowing near-misses as she vaulted from one galloping steed to another. The audience gasped when it seemed she'd fallen, but the equestrian grasped her mount's mane and bounded up to its back once again. The girl was hailed with adulation worthy of a goddess, the roar of approval making normal conversation impossible. The girl circuited the field, turning flips in concert with her horse's pounding hooves. Valdis thought fleetingly of the poor acrobat she'd seen on the streets, baring her body for a slim silver coin.

She noticed that Damian hardly spared a glance for the activity on the arena below. His gaze flicked from one box to the next, watching the wealthy sip their amber-colored wine or indulge in the decadently expensive flavored ices. The luxury item was brought to the great city by runners in straw-packed boxes from the mountain heights.

"Don't mind him," Erik said when she asked him about the Greek's inattention. "The citizens of Miklagard set a great store in being seen in the right places by the right people. If our Greek didn't notice them, it would be tantamount to an insult. Besides, he's probably also calculating who's intriguing with whom. Politics is a blood sport here and the slightest thing can tip one faction ahead of another."

He reached into the pouch at his waist and drew out an odd assortment of leather and clear round glass. He strapped the lenses to either end of the leather tube and held it to one eye.

"You might enjoy this," he said as he handed the strange ocular device to her. "You can see the wart on the emperor's nose from here with that."

Valdis peered through the tube as he instructed and stepped back in surprise. The emperor was practically in her lap. The cunning invention brought the Byzantine leader close enough that she felt she ought to be able to reach out and pluck one of the gems from his hem.

"There's no wart on his nose," Valdis said as she examined the leader of the Byzantines. Though he scarcely moved a muscle, the man's darting eyes held a furtive, sad look. "But he is wearing the most ridiculous scarlet boots."

Damian spoke a few words and she looked over to see he was finally watching the arena, where archers demonstrated their skill with flaming arrows.

"The eunuch wants you to look at the portico draped in purple at the north end and tell him what you see," Erik said.

Valdis swiveled the device in the right direction. "There's a young man there, dressed in white linen with a purple border. Dark hair, neatly curled beard. He's laughing and drinking from a jeweled cup."

"Describe the people who are with him." Erik relayed Damian's new command.

"There's a lovely woman at his side with bare breasts," Valdis said, a blush creeping up her neck. "She must rouge her nipples. They're as scarlet as the emperor's boots. She looks totally unconcerned about her state of undress, but frankly the man seems more interested in what the older man is saying to him than he is in her."

"Damian says the young man is Leo Porphyrogenito, the emperor's nephew. The woman is the Cretan princess. Women of that isle wear a palla that displays their charms. Sensible custom," Erik said. "No disappointments later."

Valdis paused in her voyeurism long enough to stick her tongue out at him.

"What about the older man?" he asked, totally unperturbed by her rude gesture.

"Darker skin. Even though his beard is shot with silver, he's still a hawk of a man. Well dressed in a flowing robe. The way it hangs it must be silk; very fine silk." In the short time she'd been in Damian's household, Valdis learned to appreciate the feel of that lustrous fabric on her skin. "He wears a jewel on each finger of his hand."

"The silk merchant," Damian said under his breath, nodding as if the information Erik repeated only confirmed a suspicion, and then he murmured an order.

Erik took the seeing glass back from Valdis. "The eunuch says that's enough for now. He wants you to enjoy the show."

Below them, a mock battle raged purporting to show the emperor, Basil the Bulgar-Slayer, pushing back the unwashed hordes from the borders of his realm. The "Huns" were defeated with no apparent casualties to the Byzantine legions.

"I'll wager it wasn't as easy as that," Erik said as he watched the set piece with the eye of a warrior.

Valdis cast him a sideways glance. His mouth creased his face in a hard line, his jaw a block of granite. Controlled power rippled through his honed body. Even at rest, Erik was formidable. In the grip of the black *berserkr* rage, he'd be terrifying, Valdis decided.

"Oh!" she cried out. Something brushed against her ankle and she felt a wet tongue on her skin. It was the little dog again. She bent and scooped it up before it could shy away. "What are you doing here?"

"Probably hoping you'll drop something again." Erik didn't reach over to pet the animal, but his face lighted with a quick grin. "Looks like you've made at least one friend in this city."

"Only one?" she asked pointedly. "We've spent weeks together, practically living in each other's pockets. You could have gotten killed saving me from those huge cats today. Are you telling me I may not consider you a friend?"

He leaned toward her, resting one of his brawny forearms on the marble balustrade. What was it she read beneath the ice of his gray eyes? Pain, certainly, but there was something else. Wariness, the caution of a wild creature who dares not approach from fear of what she might do to him.

Or what he might do to her.

With obvious effort, he turned away to peer down at the oval track. "Trust me, Valdis. You do not want to be my friend."

Her chest constricted at his rebuff. She should have known better. Even though he spoke her language, she couldn't trust this Northman. Hadn't he told her so in a dozen ways since he took up the job of teaching her Greek? She could rely on no one but herself.

The little dog wiggled, trying to free itself. Valdis crooned small endearments and held it close. The animal ceased struggling and nuzzled the crook in her arm, obviously deciding she was trustworthy. She'd felt so alone since she was ripped from her homeland, it was comforting to have the warmth of another beating heart close to hers, even if it only belonged to a mangy stray.

A guttural chant started in the lower tiers, where the dust-choked air nearly blocked the patrons' view of what was happening in the grand oval. Even the upper ring of well-heeled watchers took up the echoing cry. The crowd was weary of the preliminaries. They demanded the main event.

From the far end of the arena, four chariots burst into the harsh glare of the afternoon sun. The equines, four to a team, were caparisoned in garish-hued silk with plumes bobbing from headpieces between their pointed ears. The drivers wore matching silk cloaks that billowed out like banners as they circuited the oval, drinking in the crowd's admiration. After one complete circle, the racers skidded to a stop before the emperor's box to make their obeisance to the Ruler of the World. Hostlers stripped the showy finery from the horses, leaving the animals dancing in their traces. The drivers divested themselves of their cloaks and shining breastplates. The men leaped up onto the chariots, oiled skin gleaming, clad in naught but a strip of silk about their loins in the colors of emerald, sapphire, ivory and jet.

"Every guild and faction in the city backs one team or another," Erik explained. "Rivalry is as intense on the field as in the marketplace. Unlike the North, where a man puts his hand to whatever pleases him, the trades are closely regulated here. A linen merchant may not sell wool. A silversmith can lose a hand for working in gold. It's difficult for a man of trade to better himself unless he rises in his guild to a position of leadership. And even so, a cotton-monger will never rise above a silk trader."

"What does that have to do with a chariot race?" Valdis asked as the teams lined up, tensed to start.

"This oval is the most level playing field in the Empire. A man may never best his more fortunate rival in the market, but his chariot team may upset even the emperor's chosen Greens," Erik explained. "A street sweeper will walk with a swagger in his step for a week if his team runs well."

"That's ridiculous," Valdis pronounced.

"Since when are people not ridiculous?" Erik asked. "I'm not trying to explain why to you. I'm just telling you what is, whether it makes any sense or not. Bear in mind, the Greeks think we are just as odd as we find them. I suspect we probably are."

The horns suddenly brayed and the crowd roared. The horses leaped to a gallop, pounding around the oval, the great muscles in their haunches bunching and flattening. With reins lashed to their powerful forearms, the drivers strained to direct their teams in the correct path. The ivory team took the second turn too sharply and the chariot slid around the end of the *spina* on one whirring wheel.

Valdis watched with a thundering heart, totally caught up in the excitement. The golden spokes of the chariots blurred and sent flashes of light with each rotation. A tingle crept up her spine and the little dog in her arms grew restive, squirming to be released. She set the animal on the ground and turned her attention back to the arena, where the race was still hotly contested.

Horses plunged, sixteen abreast, around the broad oval, fighting for supremacy on the ever tightening turns. One team edged ahead of the others.

She tracked the Green leader, her gaze drawn to the rhythmic pulses of sunlight flashing from the gilded chariot wheels. Her whole being throbbed in concert with the repetitive glimmer. Darkness gathered at the edge of her vision, a tunnel yawned before her and she found it difficult to draw breath.

The little dog was yipping, tugging at her hem, demanding her attention. His frantic barks held a warning tone.

"Gods, no," she mouthed, but no sound came.

The glittering undulations intensified and she stood rigid as the Raven of Darkness blotted out her sky. Its talons sank deep into her brainpan with a raucous shriek, rending her from soul to spirit, and she fell into the blackness of her curse.

"An unguarded word will disclose more of what a man thinks than the planned speech of a thousand."
—from the secret journal of Damian Aristarchus

CHAPTER FIVE

"Dyrr." *His voice pierced through the choking mist with a masculine rumble.* "Angan . . . girnd."

Someone was calling to her, beckoning her with honey-tongued words. My precious, my delight, my desire . . . Who was naming her these things? Even if she didn't recognize the speaker, how could she ignore such a well-spoken summons? Valdis struggled toward full awareness as a submerged swimmer claws toward the surface.

A face swirled in her darkness, his features indistinct, his eyes dark with concern. Another voice spoke, barely concealed excitement in his crisp tone. She understood not a word and spiraled downward, convulsing into the void.

Light split the blackness in jagged pulses. She couldn't see him, but she felt someone with her, someone's arms about her, holding her safe from the Raven, keeping the glistening wings at bay.

The phantom carrion bird retreated and she sailed on an obsidian sea, not a flick of silver on the smooth sur-

face. The ship dissolved in the dark water and she sank into the oblivion of forgetfulness.

No light, no desire, no time or space. She winked out of existence as completely as the flame of a snuffed lamp.

"Valdis." His voice reached down to her and lifted her through layers of mist and darkness, kindling the guttering candle of her soul and coaxing it to full brightness. When she came to herself again, she vaguely realized that she was no longer in the Hippodrome, though she could still hear the crowd in the distance, thousands of hearts beating in unison, roaring like a single being, a vast beast too unwieldy for any mortal man to tame.

"Valdis, come back."

She took a shuddering breath and smelled a mixture of horseflesh and leather—a curiously comforting masculine scent. Strong arms banded around her, cradling her head against the solid expanse of a broad chest. The great muscle of her protector's heart galloped like a chariot team, pounding a rhythm of controlled panic in her ear.

"Valdis, *dyrr.*"

Her eyelids fluttered open and she felt cool blades of grass tickling her ankles. The little dog whined and nosed the curve of her calf. She found herself snuggled between someone's splayed legs, being rocked as if she were a child. Then someone pressed his lips to the crown of her head like a benediction.

She sighed. Her whole being roused to life again, her senses stirring one by one. Wherever she'd been, whichever of the nine worlds her wandering spirit had seen, she had no clear memory of it. All she was left was a slight headache and a strangely restful heaviness, as if she'd slept deeply for the space of about a week.

Then she heard the crowd in the Hippodrome again and realized the race was still in progress. Not much time had passed while she traveled along Yggdrasil's outstretched limbs. At least the World Tree's vast trunk and roots had allowed her to find her way back to Midgard, the world she knew. She could have easily wakened in Niflheim, the iciest corner of *Hel*.

Perhaps the god of this city, the Christian's three-headed deity, had spared her. She could only feel gratitude for whoever was responsible for pulling her back from the depths.

She looked up at the man who still held her tightly. Erik's eyes were closed and she suspected he was praying to whichever god he judged most likely to listen.

"I'm here," she said, her throat raw and her voice strangely hoarse. She must have cried out in the throes of the fit. Her sister Jana told her all the horrible things she'd done when the Raven came for her in Birka— ranting and tearing at her hair, spittle flying as she convulsed on the ground. She couldn't really blame her family for looking on in horror along with the *jarl* and his son. A witching is no light matter. The spell could easily travel to another if anyone dared venture too close.

Yet this man Erik held her as she struggled with her curse. Her raving hadn't repulsed him. He stayed by her and protected her, even from herself.

Of course, she wouldn't put any stock in the honeyed words he'd used to call her back, but perhaps she did have another friend in Miklagard besides the little black stray.

"This is even better than I hoped," Damian said as he paced the length of his apartments. "I've heard of the falling sickness, of course, but to see it in full-blown power . . . well, no thespian effort could match it for dramatic impact. Now we just need to teach her to make use of the spells."

Erik watched the rhythmic rise and fall of Valdis's chest, satisfied she was out of danger. She'd been lucid enough when he and Damian bundled her into a sedan chair and hustled her back to the palace before the crowd poured out of the Hippodrome. She even insisted the stinking little dog be allowed to come with her. According to Valdis, the dog tried to warn her of the onset of the spectacular fit. The animal had been bathed and trimmed by one of the eunuch's perfumed servants and was now resting in a sodden heap on the foot of Valdis's couch.

"Wait a moment," Erik said as he tucked the coverlet over Valdis's sleeping form. "You're thinking this . . . this whatever it is, is somehow a good thing?"

"Absolutely!" Damian's face was flushed with excitement. "In the old Rome, some of our most powerful leaders were touched by the same unusual malady and the ancients believed them kissed by the gods."

"Odin spare me from such a kiss," Erik said with heartfelt earnestness. The evil god's kiss had tossed Valdis into a maelstrom, her body convulsing rigidly. He'd never seen the like.

"And in the new Rome," Damian went on, "such an occurrence will cause those who wish to believe in such things to proclaim Valdis a seeress of uncommon ability."

"But she says she sees nothing when the spell comes upon her," Erik protested.

"None but we know that," Damian said. "When the time is right, she will see what I tell her to see and we will make her prophecy come to pass."

"You want her to pretend to foretell the future," Erik said, trying to wrap his mind around the subterfuge. Northmen were no strangers to guile, but Byzantine thought held more crooks and twists than the most serpentine river. Every conversation held a secret meaning and each promise a stinging surprise. "To what possible end?"

"To the greater glory of the new Rome, of course." Damian bared his teeth at Erik in what passed for a smile, but his eyes were guarded. "You needn't concern yourself with specifics. Your only task is to school her to fluency in our tongue as soon as possible."

Erik looked back at the couch, where Valdis lay at peace in a deep natural sleep. He wondered if his harsh tutelage had in any way contributed to the convulsing fit Valdis suffered. If so, he was determined to train her with a lighter hand in the future.

But he still needed to keep her at arm's length, especially now. He was shocked at the endearments pouring from his own lips as he tried to lure her back to the land of light. Just because she roused a measure of tenderness in him didn't mean he'd be any less a danger to her.

"She might learn more quickly if she had an inducement," Erik said.

"She sleeps in silk, eats dainties from the emperor's own table. I've clothed her in a manner befitting a woman of noble birth." Damian ticked off the benefits he provided for Valdis on his slim patrician fingers. "What more could she want?"

"I know what calls to her with more strength than anything," Erik said. "Freedom. Promise to free her and I guarantee she will put her whole heart into the effort."

"Freedom? Bah!" Damian waved a dismissive hand. "My slaves live lives of safety and plenty and, while I demand certain standards, they are not burdened by a crushing load of toil. Isn't that right, Lentulus?" he demanded of his ubiquitous body-servant.

"Yes, master," came the meek response.

"There, you see. Slave and master alike, we all serve

the emperor's pleasure. As a Varangian, you must understand that." Damian turned back to Erik. "You are familiar with the city, are you not?"

Erik nodded.

"Then you know that not all our citizens are as blessed as Lentulus here. In the pestilential district called the Studion, freemen die of starvation every day. Their women dare not walk the streets without an escort for fear of being molested. Ask the poor if their liberty means more to them than a full belly and peaceful security."

"Valdis is a freeborn Norsewoman," Erik said with inborn stubbornness. "She'll not willingly submit to a thrall's iron collar."

"I've put nothing less precious than silver on her neck and she knows it," Damian argued.

"Silver, gold, gems or pearls—it matters not. As long as you count yourself her master, Valdis will feel the weight of iron." Erik glanced toward the woman's still form. "Give her reason to hope. Assure her she can earn her freedom and she'll serve you well."

Damian narrowed his eyes at Erik, weighing his words for veracity. Finally, he nodded. "When we have accomplished the plan I have set in motion, I will free her. You may tell her so when she wakes."

Erik's chest expanded. He imagined her delight at this news and her gratitude to him for bringing it to her. Then he realized he didn't know what the Greek expected of Valdis beyond learning his language. "Just what is involved in this plan of yours? What must Valdis do to win her freedom?"

"In good time, my large, anxious friend," Damian said as he poured wine for each of them. He offered Erik a precious Frankish glass of amber liquid. "Sit and I will tell you as much as you may safely relay to Valdis. She

Erik looked away from her in an effort to hide his smile. Her spirit in the face of her servitude made him admire her all the more. A graceful willow, Valdis might bend in a gale, but she would not break. She was truly a remarkable woman.

"If you complete the task the Greek sets for you, what you say will be true." Erik couldn't resist looking at her in the half-light of dawn. For a moment, he imagined her head on his pillow, hair tousled, her full lips parted in the relaxation of sleep. What would it be like to wake beside this light-gilded creature? He tore his gaze away and leaned down to pat his mount's thick neck. "Once his plan is accomplished, Damian Aristarchus has promised to free you."

Her breath hissed in sharply. "You mean it?"

Erik nodded. "He gave me his word. Now I'll have no more trouble with your lessons, will I?"

"Of course not," she answered in crisp Greek with the barest hint of an accent. Her lips curved upward in a feline smile.

As he suspected, she'd been shamming. In no time at all, she'd know all he could teach her and he'd be able to rejoin his century at the head of his hundred pledgemen. The thought gave him much less pleasure than he expected.

"The problem isn't the language," she went on, her smile now inverted into a frown. "The problem is *seid*. I don't think I can do it."

"No one expects you to truly have the gift, Valdis."

"You don't understand." She bit her lower lip for the space of several heartbeats. "I already tried my hand at spelling in the Northlands. I think that's why the Raven haunts me, why the powers show their anger by tossing me to the ground and robbing me of reason. A *seid*-woman should use her craft to weave spells of protection, to divine propitious events, to help her people." She glanced up at him, then her gaze darted away. "I used the little I knew for my own purposes."

Erik didn't know what to say. Magic was the province of women. Men who sought power in such ways were deemed effeminate, so he kept himself in willful ignorance of those matters. He rode on in silence.

"I spelled the man I was to marry," Valdis finally said.

When she turned her unique gaze on him, he felt himself tumbling into her mismatched eyes. Erik could well believe she'd witched a man.

"It was a small thing, really. He was the *jarl's* son. I was just the daughter of a *karl* and not a very prosperous one at that. When Ragnvald visited our farmstead, he tore his cloak on a nail in the cattle byre and I mended it for him. I used several strands of my own hair in the threads to make him notice me."

"If this Ragnvald was a true man, he couldn't help but notice a woman like you, *seid*-spelling or no."

She smiled at his fair speech. "At any rate, it seemed to work. Even though his father wanted Ragnvald to settle on the daughter of the *jarl* of Kaupang, Ragnvald's heart wanted me." Her smile faltered. "Until he saw the price demanded for my witchery. When the fit came upon me before our wedding, he suddenly recalled his duty to Birka and declared he must wed the pasty-faced girl from Kaupang."

"He was a fool," Erik said.

Her shoulders drooped. "But you see why I can't pretend to have the Sight. If the gods visited me with this affliction just for a love spell, what might they do if I try my hand at real power?"

"What makes you think love isn't real power?" Erik said, kneeing his mount closer to hers. "Think what love drives a man to do. The Greeks tell a tale of one woman,

Helen, who was so desirable she caused a war between the kings who were determined to have her."

Valdis pulled a face. "Why on earth didn't they just ask her which of them she preferred?"

Erik shook his head, the bitterness of memory clouding his vision for a moment. "Sometimes love takes such a hold on a man, what a woman wants is the least of his concerns."

"Then what the Greeks celebrate is not love—it's dragonlust, the craven desire to possess at all costs." She sighed and lifted her heavy hair with one hand so the breeze could tease the baby hairs on the back of her slender neck. The sight of that tender skin made Erik's soft palate ache with longing to taste her nape with a kiss.

"You may be right," he agreed. "But I don't think your malady was caused by the gods. If you had the power to hex someone with it, would you?"

She shook her head. "I wouldn't wish the Raven that stalks me on anyone."

"We must hope the gods are at least as gracious as their creatures. Sometimes, things just happen for no particular reason. I think your falling sickness is one of those things." Erik pondered the matter as he tugged the stallion's reins, making sure the spirited beast knew who was master. "Now, as to whether or not you should feign an ability you don't possess, if that were a crime, most of the nobility and all the bureaucrats in Miklagard should be imprisoned. But even the gods are not above guile when it suits their purposes. Odin outwits his enemies. Loki changes shape to confound his foes."

At the sound of his name, the little black dog poked his head out of Valdis's saddle bag. She'd named him Loki, after the trickster godling, because he was such a clown, dancing on his hind legs for treats. The dog hadn't warmed to anyone else. In fact, he nipped Erik when he tried to pet him once, but Loki was clearly devoted to Valdis.

"The Greek has promised your freedom if you pretend to have the Sight," Erik continued. "Don't you think your liberty is worth the risk?"

"*Ja,* I suppose it is," she finally said. "Though truth to tell, I'm not sure what I'll do with my freedom. At first, all I could think of was running away to the North. But I can't go home. My family doesn't need another mouth to feed. That path is closed to me. Mayhap I'd go to the Danes or Iceland." She cast a questioning glance at him. "Why ever did you come here to this blazing heat when you could go anywhere in the wide world?"

"The Northlands are closed to me as well," he said softly.

"Why? Because of your oath to the emperor?"

"No," he admitted. He hadn't wanted to tell her, but perhaps it was best she know. If he was going to be damned, better to be damned for the truth. "I can't go home because I've done murder."

*"The law is inviolate for the masses. For the few, it is
a malleable list of suggestions."*
—*from the secret journal of Damian Aristarchus*

CHAPTER SIX

Murder. The word careened around her mind, leaving a
shiver of revulsion in its wake.

When Valdis was growing up, the lawspeaker made a
long circuit among the villages nestled in the fjords and
on the outlying islands of the North Sea, visiting once
every three years to remind folk of the "oughts" in Norse
society. The law united the people and gave them
boundaries so they could live, if not in harmony, at least
in respect of each other's rights. Of all the crimes the
lawspeaker recited against, only oath-breaking was
considered more heinous than murder. It was one thing
to issue a defiance and kill a man in fair combat; it was
quite another to take a life by stealth without giving the
victim a chance to defend himself.

Erik, a murderer? Valdis swallowed her surprise. He
didn't seem the type to stoop to so cowardly an act. Her
natural impulse was to put as much distance between
them as possible.

Then she remembered how he'd held her through

the madness of her latest fit. Everyone else in her life had turned away from her in fear or disgust. She couldn't withdraw from Erik despite his astonishing confession.

"You can't be a murderer," Valdis said. "The law demands the life of the killer for the life of the slain. If you were truly guilty, you'd have met your end on the wings of a blood-eagle or the garrote."

He looked at her and shrugged, his mouth stretched in a tight line.

"Did you flee south to escape justice?" Valdis finally asked when his silence wore her to the breaking point.

"No," he said. "I came before the lawspeaker willingly and admitted my crime, but he banished me instead of giving me the death I deserved."

There must have been unusual circumstances. The lawspeaker rarely strayed from the prescribed punishments meted out in the oral code he was entrusted with keeping. "Who did you kill?"

Erik glanced at her, then looked away, frowning at the memory. "My brother."

Valdis stared at the road rising before her. Of all the betrayals in the Middle Realm, the ones that hurt most came from those closest to a body. *Murder of his own blood.* At least her family had only sold her into slavery. Still, bitterness welled within her. It was an ache that would never go away.

"Do you want to tell me about it?" she asked in a small voice.

"Not particularly." Erik rose in the saddle, craning his neck to see. The head of the long column disappeared around a hillock. He settled back down. "But I suspect I'll have no peace till I do. A woman is like a leaky roof when she wants to know something."

"I told you why I was sold south when you asked," she reminded him.

Erik nodded, conceding her point. "*Ja,* but that wasn't your fault. Your tale only included a minor attempt at witching, not an admitted crime."

She fastened her gaze on him. "I'm prepared to hear your side. You must surely have one since the lawspeaker amended your punishment to mere banishment."

"Banishment is no light matter." He met her pointed stare. "The lawspeaker only thought he was being merciful. Until I worked my way to Miklagard and found a place for myself among the Guard, I thought I'd never belong anywhere again."

"So you feel at home in the great city?" Valdis asked. "It's so noisy and smelly and . . . foreign. How can you?"

"I have my century, my pledgemen to lead. I have friends," he said.

"But no home, no family?" She wanted to ask him if he had a woman somewhere in the sprawling metropolis, but knew he must. A man with his rough, hard-bodied appeal would turn feminine heads wherever he went.

"No," he admitted. "Mayhap a man with my past shouldn't have a family."

At that moment, Damian came galloping back to them and rattled off a string of orders. Valdis was able to make sense of most of it. Her master demanded that she join him at the head of the long column of carts and baggage animals. She urged her horse into a trot after the eunuch, leaning forward over her mount's neck to encourage him up the incline.

Valdis sighed. Damian hadn't bothered with her all morning. Of all times for her master to suddenly command her presence. She felt sure Erik had been at the point of telling her about the murder of his brother. As revolting as murder was, she wanted to hear his tale. It might help her understand the man.

She heard Erik's horse snorting behind her, straining to burst into the lead. Not being the type to trail another animal willingly, the stallion preferred the head of the herd. She suspected the man on his back felt the same, but Erik muscled his spirited mount into submission, just as he bridled himself to duty.

They crested a rise and Valdis saw a lovely villa at the end of a cypress-lined lane. The house was long and low, with a gray lead roof and white marble columns bright against the green lawn.

"It's beautiful," she said. Damian's smile told her he understood her sentiment if not her words. "Does the emperor have many houses like this scattered about his empire?"

"This doesn't belong to the Bulgar-Slayer," Erik said in Norse. "There'd be a guard of ten with a decurion in command if it were a residence of the emperor. No, this belongs to the eunuch himself."

Valdis never thought of Damian as a landholder. As a eunuch, he seemed more a glorified servant, albeit one held in high esteem. Now it was clear he was a man of property, wealthy in his own right.

"You see why noble families geld their spare sons in hopes of preferment," Erik continued in Norse. "Eunuchs tend to rise high in Byzantine society."

"Parents do that to their own sons?" She was astounded. The mutilation still struck her as too bizarre to contemplate. "Do you suppose that is what happened to Damian?"

"No," Erik said. "He's what they call a late-made eunuch. Those that are cut in their early years never develop a beard or have their voices drop. Some grow unnaturally long arms and legs. It's almost as if their

bodies don't know what to do with what's become of
them. They tend to carry extra flesh and some even
grow breasts like a woman." Erik shook his head. "It's
not a life a man would choose willingly."

Valdis sensed Erik's revulsion with the practice. However ordinary neutered males were in Byzantine society
and however highly regarded some came to be, she
suspected Erik would die before he was forced to live
as less than a man.

Damian was talking again as they rode three abreast,
obviously untroubled by the Norse conversation she had
shared with Erik. She was grateful her master didn't seem
to realize he'd been discussed so intimately. Valdis rode
between the two men, puzzling over which secret vexed
her most—the tale of Erik's murder of his own brother or
the manner in which Damian fell under the castrating
knife. She promised herself to discover the truth of each
tale before she parted company with these men.

For she did still intend to shake the dust of Miklagard
from her feet somehow. Freedom called to her from the
distant mountain peaks, whispered to her on each
breeze and sang a siren's song with each blue wave
cresting on the distant sea.

Damian pointed to the villa nestled in the sheltered
valley. She could see more details now as they looked
down on it from the heights. It was fashioned in the
shape of a square with a wide columned portico
wrapped around each side. The tip of a cypress stabbed
the sky from the open courtyard in the center.

"Your room is on the east corner, he says," Erik relayed Damian's message. "It catches the morning light
but is spared the afternoon heat." Erik's brows knit together as he listened to Damian's next words. "Your master says your room is right next to his—not adjoining,
but close . . . as a mark of his favor and his protection."

"Protection?" Valdis asked. Other than workers toiling in the surrounding fields of grain, she didn't see another soul. "What do I need protection from?"

"From me," he admitted. "Aristarchus is very pointed about protecting your virtue. He seems to regard all Varangians as rutting beasts who can't be trusted further than he can throw them."

Valdis lifted a brow at him.

Erik cast a wolfish grin back. "He could be right."

She laughed. His rough good humor warmed her. Being with Erik was like being whisked back to the fjords. His speech, his face, his way of looking at life all spoke to her of home. But in some ways he was even more of a safe haven than the fjords had ever been. Erik accepted her unusual malady without a qualm.

As they neared the villa, a gaggle of servants scurried from the wide carved double doors and formed a line of greeting. Damian dismounted and strode to confer with his head caretaker, leaving Erik to help Valdis to the ground.

"I can dismount a horse on my own," she said as he eased her to earth.

"Mayhap I wanted the excuse to span your waist with my hands," he said, leaving his palms on the curve of her waist longer than necessary. He leaned close enough for Valdis to breathe in his distinctive masculine scent. Her chest constricted strangely.

Damian saw him and hurried back to grasp Valdis's hand with a pointed glare at Erik.

"Perhaps he is right to mistrust Northmen," she said.

Erik chuckled. "And maybe I just want to irritate your master."

Damian led her from the mounting heat of the day into the dim coolness of the interior of his villa. In the grand entrance, an amazing mosaic left Valdis wide-eyed. It was a life-sized portrait of a handsome Greek man, his dark hair and eyes gleaming, an enigmatic smile lifting the corners of his sensual mouth and an erection as long as his arm protruding baldly from under his short tunic. Valdis was reminded of the statue of Frey in the great Temple of Uppsala, his outsized phallus proudly erect. She had no idea the god of increase was worshipped here in the south as well.

"Your master apologizes if the mosaic shocks you," Erik translated. "He recently acquired this property and hasn't had time to redecorate. Apparently the previous owner commissioned it as a portrait of himself. I can only guess the artist intended to flatter him."

"I'm not shocked," Valdis said. "I assume that's the way all men see their own member."

Erik laughed again, the deep rumbling sound sending shivers of pleasure over her. Damian frowned at him and barked an order.

"Greek only from now on," Erik said.

Valdis nodded and followed Damian down one of the long corridors of green stone. Thessalian marble, Damian explained. Arches opened on either side—to the open air courtyard on her left and into sumptuously appointed rooms on the right. When they came to an angle in the hall, Damian pushed open a door and held it for Valdis to enter.

The polished floor gleamed in shades of pink-veined stone and one wall glittered in a mosaic of nymphs and dryads capering about a vat-sized wine bowl. A sleeping couch occupied the center of the large room. White silk draped round the bower, fluttering like butterfly wings. But as luxurious as the appointments were, the row of long windows paned with delicate green glass and the open door leading to the shaded portico made Valdis suck in her breath in surprise. Not only was she given a heart-stopping view of the Empress City, glittering in the distance against the deep azure of the sea, but there was no guard at her door for the first time since she was named a slave.

She still had no place to run, no way to take advantage of this new development, but the mere appearance of freedom set her heart dancing.

"Thank you," she said, turning to smile at Damian.

"I'm glad this room pleases you," he said. "But do not imagine we are here to enjoy ourselves. Your training will commence immediately and you will work hard every day."

"I will earn freedom if I learn?" she said in what she knew was less than fluid Greek.

Damian nodded. "That is my promise. Varangian, take her into the courtyard for her lessons."

He watched the two Nordics glide away in their long-legged gaits. The courtyard would be perfect. Erik Heimdalsson would have the quiet needed to tutor the girl and the eyes of the whole household might be upon them at any time, so no untoward behavior would go unnoticed.

"Yes, Valdis, you may earn your freedom," Damian said under his breath as his gaze followed the graceful curve of her retreating spine. "But it may be more difficult than you think."

"Regret, like any other emotion, is a monumental waste of time."
—from the secret journal of Damian Aristarchus

CHAPTER SEVEN

"The boy's broken arm seems to have healed cleanly with no lasting ill effects," Damian's informant told him. "He still rides that stallion of his as recklessly as ever, much to his mother's sorrow."

"That doesn't trouble me, Onesimus. It only proves his spirit was not broken along with the bone," Damian said with a satisfied nod. "And what of his studies? He still has Lector Epiphanes as his mathematics and polemics tutor, yes?"

"Indeed," Onesimus said. "I had a full report from Epiphanes. Do be aware that Lector is learned enough, but the man is quite voluble after only a bowl or two of Acacian wine. According to Lector Epiphanes, the lad is as quick with his studies as he is with his riding."

"Very well," Damian said. "We'll let him stay with his current tutor for at least another year, unless Lector's drinking becomes a problem." Damian fastened his gaze on the written report spread before him on the polished ebony desk. If a flicker of emotion showed in his eyes, he didn't want Onesimus to mark it. "What of the woman?"

"The boy's mother is set upon by a number of suitors, but seems content to remain a widow. She dotes on her son so, another man would be hard pressed to slip into her life, let alone her bed, though there are those who still try."

"Who?"

"Marcus Nobelissimus, the thematic governor, for one," Onesimus said. "Your largess has made the lady a woman of property. A steady stream of income is always of interest to an ambitious politician."

"Perhaps I shall see that this Nobelissimus finds himself removed to Gaul when the time comes for his next appointment," Damian mused. "She doesn't encourage him?"

"No, the lady is the soul of propriety," Onesimus said.

Damian smiled. He remembered a time when Calysta was anything but proper. There had been one balmy night when she slipped out of her father's villa and met him in the ruins of the temple of Eros. Together they offered a fitting sacrifice to the defunct god of lust on that soft summer evening. If he let himself, he could still taste the sweet saltiness of her skin.

"She's been well then? How did she appear to you?" Damian asked, reminding himself that the image he carried of her was undoubtedly veiled by time's shroud.

"There are a few silver strands in her dark hair, but her waist is still slender as a girl's. The years have been kind to the lady," Onesimus said, wringing his hands before him in a habitual gesture of nervousness. "And though you don't ever ask, I feel I should tell you the boy is more like you with each passing year."

Damian studied his steepled fingers for a moment, unsure how to catalog what he was feeling. Pride? Certainly, but mingled with a wave of uneasiness as well. All fathers long to see their likeness stamped on the faces of their offspring, and yet beyond providing lavishly, if anonymously, for the boy, Damian had done little to be a father to him.

Because he was unable to be a husband to the lad's mother.

"If I may be so bold as to suggest, Excellency," Onesimus said, "perhaps you'd do well to reveal yourself to your family. I'm sure your lady wonders at the largess that comes each year. Without constant tending, even the most sagacious of investments dry up after a time. The lady is no fool. She must suspect you live yet."

Damian rose and gave his back to his informer, trying to school his features into passivity and knowing he failed miserably. "You forget yourself, Onesimus. I ask only for your observations, not your counsel." He waved his servant away. "I will hear no more on the subject. Rest yourself for a week and then resume your duties. Unless there are unexpected developments, I will look for your next report three months hence. You are excused."

Damian didn't turn around at the rough slap of leather on the Corinthian marble of the study floor as Onesimus took his leave. His informer's reports were always gut-wrenching, but he demanded them with each turn of the seasons, torturing himself with scraps of his family's life, knowing he could allow himself nothing more.

He crumpled the spy's report into a ball. Calysta and his son were safe. They were both healthy and well provided for. It should be enough.

It never could be.

Damian poured himself a glass of the Etruscan vintage from the decanter on his desk and swirled the amber liquid for a moment, sending its delicate perfume into the air. He sipped it slowly. The flavor was un-marred by poppy juice now, but the first time he tasted it the wine had been laced with opiate. It was wine from the same vineyard they gave to all the men who were unmade that terrible day ten years ago.

His regiment had been routed in a bloody skirmish with a particularly fierce Bulgar tribe. Sometimes in night phantoms, Damian could still hear their inhu-man war cries as they gloried over the devastating Byzantine loss.

In older times, the practice of decimation, the killing of every tenth man from among a defeated Roman unit, would have been employed as a means of convincing the remaining soldiers to fight all the harder. The Bulgar-Slayer reasoned that castration might have an even more stimulating effect and at the same time, cre-ate a number of well-trained eunuchs to move into Im-perial service.

Damian had been a tenth man.

Going home to Calysta was out of the question. Bet-ter to let her believe him dead than gelded. Damian could learn to live as a highly placed eunuch serving the emperor's pleasure. He could still provide for his family, perhaps even more bountifully than as an intact man since he'd risen to a position of great influence.

But he couldn't bear the sight of pity in his wife's liq-uid dark eyes, or see his son's contempt when he learned his father was half a man.

Perhaps he should draft another assignment for Onesimus. He considered having his spy investigate the affairs of Calysta's would-be suitor, Nobelissimus. If the man turned out to be at all decent, the honorable thing for Damian to do would be to engineer a match for his wife. It would be easy to arrange. All he need do was in-clude a stipulation for the next payment of his family's support, requiring her to remarry in order for the flow of bezants to continue. It would free Calysta of any remaining doubts about his death.

But as he took another sip of Etruscan grape, he knew it was no longer in his nature to do the honorable thing.

The delights of a thousand dreams await within,
Yet I stand rooted outside your window,
trembling like a tamarind in the breeze.
Unable to move,
Unable to breathe,
Hoping for one flutter of your curtain.

Valdis closed the book of poetry and laid it beside her on the porphyry bench. She leaned down and scratched Loki behind his ear. After a few moments, the mongrel abandoned her to stretch out in the sun. "You must admit," she said to Erik, "my accent is improving."

Erik nodded tersely as he continued to pace around the tinkling fountain in the center of the courtyard. "The eunuch was right to teach you to read the language as well as speak it. I only wonder at his choice of material."

"Don't tell me you've never enjoyed a maidensong?" she asked incredulously. No Nordic skald's repertoire was complete without one or two love stories. Even though they were forbidden in some realms, skalds braved the edicts against them and continued to weave tales of mighty passion.

"Maidensongs are fine in their place," Erik said. "But don't you ever wonder why your master requires you to always be reading of love?"

"I assume it will have something to do with whatever my 'assignment' will be," Valdis said with a toss of her hair. "It's still quite mysterious. First I'm to pretend to prescient abilities I don't possess, then I'm evidently to entertain with recitations of love poetry. Perhaps he intends to make a skald of me. I can't begin to imagine what goes on in Damian's mind."

"I can," Erik growled in Norse.

Even though her master had decreed they speak Greek only, she and Erik occasionally slipped into their mother tongue. Usually it felt as comfortable as a worn sandal to converse, however briefly, in the language in which she still dreamed. Now, something in Erik's tone gave her pause.

"What do you mean?"

"Only that I have eyes," Erik said as he stopped pacing and fisted his hands at his waist. "Aristarchus can't seem to be in a room with you without touching your hair, your cheek, hanging on every syllable that drops from your lips. That Greek ox wants you."

She laughed despite the heat she felt creeping up her neck. "How absurd. He's a eunuch. That's like imagining a blind man could fashion a mosaic."

"Mayhap not, but a blind man could still carve a statue well enough," Erik said.

She ran a fingertip along the spine of the poetry book and shook her head. "I don't understand. Your tongue is as twisted as the Byzantine's. What's that supposed to mean?"

"Just that there are ways for a man to have a woman, ways to pleasure her that your master is fully capable of and he knows it." A small muscle tensed in his jaw. "Why else would he fill your mind with love poetry?"

"You almost sound jealous," she said. "Does the bull wish to trade places with an ox?"

He scowled at her. "I'm only trying to warn you. He may be an ox, but his heart, his thoughts are bullish."

"Well, now you've tickled my thoughts," she said, enjoying his obvious discomfort. If she didn't know better, she'd think he was beginning to feel possessive of her. "Just how might our 'ox' pleasure the cow without any 'bullish' attributes?"

Erik's eyes darkened as he walked toward her. "Are you sure you wish to know?"

She held his gaze for a moment, then glanced away lest he see how his intense look unsettled her. Her heart fluttered like a snared bird against her ribs. She drew a deep breath and gathered her courage in both hands.

"Are you offering to show me?" she asked in a small voice, still unable to meet his gaze.

She heard his sharp intake of breath as he settled beside her on the bench. He moved the book away and sat with his knees spread. He leaned his elbows on his muscular thighs and laced his fingers together, the knuckles white with tension.

"I dare not," he said.

"Are you afraid of Damian?" she asked, shocked by his admission.

He snorted. "No, I don't fear your master," he said gruffly. Then he turned and looked at her again, the expression on his face unreadable. He reached a hand up slowly and pushed an errant strand of hair out of her eyes, tucking it behind her ear. A shiver of pleasure snaked down her neck as his rough finger brushed her earlobe. "But I confess myself terrified of you."

"Of me?"

"And of what I might do to you," Erik said. Despite his dire words, he leaned toward her, closing the space by finger-widths, as if drawn against his will.

Valdis let his warning settle in even as she wondered what it would be like to feel his mustache brush over her lips. "From the first time I met you, you've tried to help me. I can't believe you have it in you to do me hurt."

"Believe it."

"I will not." His mouth was so close now, all she need do was turn her head and he'd be on her in a heartbeat. Valdis tilted her face toward him, daring him to take her lips. She closed her eyes in invitation.

"Varangian!" Damian's voice made her eyes snap open. Erik was on his feet. Valdis's belly churned with disappointment. "That will be all."

Erik fisted his hand on his chest in the prescribed salute and strode from the courtyard. He paused at the archway and turned back to look at her. A half smile tugged at his mouth and he recited in Norse part of the poem she'd read to him earlier.

"*I stand rooted outside your window,*
Unable to move,
Unable to breathe,
Hoping for one flutter of your curtain."

And then he was gone, but hope leaped in her chest. His declaration held the ring of promise. She would part her curtains and look for him on her portico when the moon rose full.

Damian frowned after him, then turned his attention back to Valdis.

"You are aware that your usefulness to me is predicated on your purity," he said with coldness.

She nodded. "You need have no concern on that score. I am as I was when you acquired me, *master.*" She couldn't keep sarcasm from her tone when she named him thus. Damian appeared not to notice.

"That is certainly not the way it appeared a moment ago," Damian said, tapping his foot against the flagstones with nervous energy. "The Northman has been an acceptable language tutor, but take care that his tuition does not stray into other disciplines. You are

aware, are you not, that he is in exile from his homeland for the crime of murder?"

"I know that."

"And do you know he murdered his own brother?"

Valdis nodded. "Erik told me as much."

"And did he also tell you it was because he found his
wife in his brother's bed?"

Her jaw sagged. Erik never mentioned a wife. No
wonder he resisted kissing her. He'd been betrayed by
two people he should have been able to trust implicitly.

"There is a phenomenon unique to Northmen.
Berserkr, I believe they call it. Some type of madness
that stalks their warrior class. Erik slew his brother in
that black rage without giving him a chance to defend
himself. He very nearly murdered his wife as well."

"How can you know all this?"

"I always investigate those who are in my employ
with thoroughness," Damian said. "And his fellow
Varangian, Haukon Gottricksson is willing to spin tales
if plied with enough wine. Erik's friend was free enough
with the details. Seems he stayed Erik's hand when the
sword was at the wife's throat. If not for his intervention,
your Norse tutor would have been garroted for killing
his wayward wife as well as his brother."

Valdis felt her stomach juices churn. No wonder Erik
feared what he might do to her. He knew himself capable of killing a woman.

"I see that surprises you," Damian said. "There is
something else you may find surprising. It's time you
learned the consequences of straying from my instructions. Come."

He grasped her hand with a strength that shocked
her and dragged her from the courtyard.

"The rational being will choose safety over all else."
—from the secret journal of Damian Aristarchus

CHAPTER EIGHT

Valdis was forced to trot to keep up with Damian as he pulled her along with far less gentleness than she'd come to expect from him. He led her down the corridor bordering the northern side of the courtyard.

She'd never been in any of the rooms in that part of the villa, but she'd heard the northern section housed Damian's small army of servants in cell-like chambers. She could see no windows from the outside when she tromped around the edifice with Loki at her heels earlier that day. Having no way to look out on the world, no chance to see the rising sun or glimpse the first flicker of the stars in the heavens seemed almost as bad as imprisonment. She pitied the slaves who slept in the tiny chambers.

Damian's favor was evident from the lavish style of dress he provided for Valdis and from the opulent room she'd been given. Now she wondered if she'd taken her status of preferment for granted. She'd never seen such a fierce scowl on her master's face.

Mayhap Erik was right. Was it possible the eunuch had feelings for her?

Damian slowed his pace only when they entered the kitchen, a large utilitarian room in the northwest corner of the villa. A round woman with a merry face dipped a headless chicken into a vat of boiling water for a few moments, then lifted it out and began ripping off the sodden feathers. A group of three more women were seated in a semicircle on the floor in one corner, pounding millet into flour.

"The time for your studies with the Northman is nearing an end," Damian said.

"But why?" Valdis asked. "There is still more Erik can teach me."

"That is precisely what concerns me. Your fluency is growing by the day, but the Varangian's obvious attraction to you is a danger we can ill afford. It's time for you to make the acquaintance of your new tutor. Chloe!" He signaled to one of the millet women.

A petite slave immediately rose and sketched a graceful bow in Damian's direction. Valdis stared at her with interest. The woman was easily a head shorter than Valdis, perfectly proportioned with slender wrists and ankles. Even though her palla was linen instead of silk, she carried herself with dignity that Valdis found surprising for a kitchen slave. A long lock of raven hair escaped from under her headdress and her large dark eyes were expertly rimmed with kohl. The rest of her face was hidden beneath an opaque veil.

"What does my master require of me?" Chloe asked in a curiously hollow-sounding voice.

"This is Valdis," Damian said with a gesture in her direction. "You are relieved of your current duties effective immediately, Chloe. Your new assignment is to instruct Valdis in the arts of an odalisque."

"*Odalisque?* I do not know the meaning of that word," Valdis said. "Obviously, my language studies are incomplete."

"The meaning will become clear to you soon enough," Damian said curtly before he turned back to Chloe. "She will learn to dance, to serve at an intimate dinner, to entertain with clever conversation and you will teach her all you know of pleasuring a man."

Chloe nodded her understanding as Valdis's eyes widened. Odalisque, he'd called it. Her master obviously intended to turn her into a well-educated whore, but before she could speak Damian cut her off with a dismissive gesture.

"The first lesson you will teach is the price to be paid for impurity." Damian's face was as hard as the granite slab on which the cook chopped the denuded chicken. "Remove your veil."

Chloe's dark eyes filled with tears that trembled on her thick lashes. She reached up a slim-fingered hand and detached the stiff veil from behind her shell-shaped ear and let it hang free. Her face was a perfect oval, the smooth skin flawless. The deep berry-colored lips formed a delicate bow above her sweetly dimpled chin.

But where her nose should have been there were only two dark slits. The cartilaginous openings were hideous insults to an otherwise striking face. A single tear slid down Chloe's olive cheek.

Valdis suppressed a shudder and averted her eyes, but Damian grasped her chin and forced her to look.

"Mark this and mark it well," he ordered. "Experience is the best teacher, but a wise pupil learns from the experience of others. You are being prepared to serve in a harem, a place of the sacred womb. There can be no room for unchastity, especially if you hope to earn your freedom once your usefulness in that position is ended."

A harem. Valdis's stomach roiled and she feared she might be sick on the spot. She didn't know which was more repugnant, being forced to look at Chloe's ruined face or the idea of entering one of those mysterious gilded prisons.

"Chloe was once a favorite in a great man's harem. For this purpose she was trained from childhood." Damian skewered Valdis with an assessing glare. "I can see this shocks you, but in her village, a position in a harem is highly coveted. A safe, secure life behind the sheltering zenana walls, pampered and well fed, is more than most parents of limited means can aspire to for their daughters. If she'd conceived a son she might even have been elevated to the status of a wife."

Damian released his hold on Valdis's chin, but she found she still couldn't look away. She stared at Chloe in horrified fascination, her mind trying to make sense of the woman's truncated features. Chloe met her eyes for a moment, then cast her gaze at Valdis's hemline.

"You may cover yourself now, Chloe," Damian said in a milder tone. "Come with us to the courtyard."

Chloe reattached her veil. Valdis noticed that a piece of carved wood was cunningly incorporated into the half-mask and fitted over the slits so that with the fabric in place, Chloe's deformity was virtually undetectable. She might still be deemed a desirable woman.

Unless, of course, she spoke. Her missing nose was the reason for Chloe's unusual hollow-sounding voice.

As they walked back to the courtyard together, Valdis's mind whirled. She'd known Damian wanted to use her for some unspecified assignment. He'd treated her with such deference, she never suspected he would turn into a whore monger. Despair clawed at her belly. She wanted her freedom so badly.

She never expected the price would be so high.

When they reached the spurting fountain, Damian inclined his head toward Chloe. "I will leave you to your lessons then. She must be ready in three weeks' time. Can you do it?"

Chloe cast an appraising glance at Valdis. "She is well-formed and moves with grace despite her size. Her height is most unfortunate, but cannot be helped. No doubt you saw other qualities in her that outweigh her obvious deficiencies."

Valdis flinched at the candid assessment. She'd felt gawky around the smaller women of the house at times, but she never expected pity from a woman without a nose.

"Valdis is intelligent enough, else you would not have trained her thus far," Chloe said. "In three weeks' time, our progress will please you, my master."

Damian gave a quick nod and strode from the courtyard.

"What a pig!" Valdis said in Norse. Then she switched to Greek. "I'm sorry he forced you to remove your veil in public. It was coarse of him to order you to do so."

The covering shifted and Valdis suspected Chloe's lips lifted in a sad smile.

"He only did it for your edification. Besides, my punishment was deserved. Do not fault the master for my sins," she said. "If not for him, I would have died in the streets long since. Damian Aristarchus is a great man."

"I hardly think the term 'man' can be applied to a eunuch," Valdis said with a sniff.

Chloe's eyes flashed a warning. "Do not judge people based on what they have lost. What remains is the most important. Testicles do not define a man. Courage and heart make a man. And if you add compassion, it makes an exceptional man."

"If he's set on delivering me to a harem, he's not shown much compassion."

Chloe cocked her head at Valdis. "Where did the master find you?"

"At an auction." Valdis shifted her weight from one foot to the other.

Chloe narrowed her eyes. "And in the time since you have lived beneath his roof, has he beaten you?"

"No."

"Worked you to exhaustion?"

Valdis shook her head.

"Starved you into a more biddable frame of mind, perhaps?"

"If anything, I've gained flesh since I came to Miklagard."

"So has the master made you sleep in the stables?"

"No, he has treated me well," Valdis admitted. "But going to a harem, being some man's property—"

"You are already that."

Valdis sighed. "I have known no man. To be taken without care, without love . . ." Her voice caught in her throat. "I don't think I can bear it."

"Then you are not as strong as you look," Chloe said with bluntness. "A woman can bear a great deal more than she thinks." A shadow passed behind her large shimmering eyes. "Even the death of love."

Chloe seemed to retreat into herself for a moment, then she clapped her slim hands together and assumed a graceful pose.

"Come, Valdis. We dance," she said. "And maybe you will forget that the world is only about yourself."

*   *   *

Valdis perched on the edge of the fountain and splashed cool water on her face. What Chloe called dancing felt more like contortions to Valdis's gangling frame. She learned to writhe like a serpent and isolate parts of her body to move with sinuous slowness while holding the rest immobile. Valdis created graceful waves with her long arms, making sure to tuck her thumbs and keep her wrists supple. After all the undulations, Valdis felt as if every joint in her body were loose as an unpinned carriage wheel.

"Very good, Valdis," Chloe said. "You have made exceptional progress. I had no idea someone so large could move with such grace."

"And I had no idea someone so small could hurl insults without a qualm," Valdis returned. "In my country it is said that a fox baits a bear at his peril."

Chloe cocked her head. "You are right. I should not berate you for your deformity any more than you should pity me for mine." The little woman settled beside Valdis as if they were dear friends instead of prickly acquaintances. "Forgive me. You are the first new person to see me unveiled in a long time. The shock on your face was . . . unsettling. Living here with those who know me and care for me, I had forgotten how hideous I must be. I am sorry for taking my anger out on you."

Valdis was stung by Chloe's apology. "You aren't hideous," she said. "You said you deserved your punishment, but what could you have done to warrant such a thing?"

Chloe spread her graceful hands in a self-deprecating gesture that was purely Eastern. "As the master said, I was a favorite in a great man's harem, but I took a lover. When I was found to be guilty of impurity, my punishment had to be vicious and highly visible as a warning to others."

"I've heard that harems are closely guarded. How could you possibly have taken a lover?"

Chloe's dark brow arched with delicacy. "When one is in love, the how ceases to matter. Love finds its own way. In my case, my love was within the household walls. He was a harpist and I was deemed a fine singer. It was natural for us to spend time together practicing for each evening's entertainment." Chloe closed her eyes for a moment, as if conjuring the feel of her lover's talented fingers strumming across her body. "At first, the eunuchs were vigilant. Later they grew complacent and our longing seized every opportunity to sate itself with furtive lust."

"But you were caught?"

Chloe nodded. "The priests tell us, 'Be sure your sins will find you out.' Mine certainly did. We were taken while trying to escape the household together."

Valdis let her new friend's sadness wash over her. "So your lover no longer wanted you after they cut off your nose. . . . That's what you meant when you said a woman can bear much, even the death of love."

Chloe's eyes seemed to sink deeper in their sockets. "No. He never saw me harmed, but I was forced to watch while they took him apart joint by joint. He died in agony, cursing my name. I could not fault him for it, but no sweet memory of our lovemaking can over-shadow those ugly rants. That is the death of love."

Valdis gnawed the inside of her cheek. She decided she would not look for Erik outside her window when the moon rose full. She might dare much for him, but she couldn't bear the thought of seeing him tortured for her sake.

"Only then, after he died, did the knife-wielders turn their attention to me. I thought they would kill me. That would have been a mercy. But they chose to do the more hurtful thing. I was maimed, cut as you see me and cast still bleeding to the streets. By disfiguring me in this way, my voice was altered. I was unable to support myself as a singer. I could either beg or prostitute myself to those pox-ridden wretches whom other whores would not accommodate. A noseless woman has no cause to be choosy, you see," Chloe explained. "Or I could starve."

In the silence that stretched between them, Valdis heard only the patter of the fountain and the slight rustle of the breeze in the tip of the cypress.

"Starvation. That was the course I had chosen for myself," Chloe said. "And then the master found me, cowering in the Forum of the Ox. He remembered hearing me sing at a banquet and somehow still recognized me, though I can't imagine how. Damian Aristarchus lifted me from the streets and brought me here to work in this beautiful villa. And I serve him with a grateful heart. If I have regrets, it is that I no longer know a man's love."

Chloe gave herself a small shake. "But that is past. I have found forgiveness if not forgetfulness and if I can spare you my anguish, I am content. Be wise and learn of me, Valdis. Guard the flower of your womanhood, for it is the most precious gift you possess."

Chloe leaned back and closed her eyes, obviously enjoying the play of slanting sunlight on her forehead. "Learn this as well. Today is all we have and we gain nothing from dwelling on that which is lost. Today we are strong and the sun is shining. That alone is enough that we should dance."

She stood and clapped her thin hands. "Again."

*"Of all the creatures the Lord God made, the horse is
by far the silliest. Unless you count a man in love.
Then the horse is a poor second."*
—from the secret journal of Damian Aristarchus

CHAPTER NINE

"You've made some terrible mistakes in the past," Erik
muttered to himself as he stomped out of the small
chamber allotted to him. The spartan cell adjoined the
stables, a not-so-subtle reminder that the eunuch
thought him little better than an animal. The way Erik
was following his cock around, he wondered if
Aristarchus wasn't right. "This is, bar none, the stupidest
thing you've ever done."

He'd wrestled with himself on his narrow cot, fighting
sleep, then seeking it with urgency, ordering his body to
rest, then unable to bridle his wandering mind. He finally abandoned the struggle for a moonlight stroll.

And if he chanced to pass the chamber occupied by
a certain Nordic woman, so be it. Some things you had
to toss to fate.

Like reciting that love poem to Valdis. He winced at the
memory. His attempt at winning her favor was so lame,
if he'd been a horse, someone would end his suffering.

What was he thinking?

The moon had risen, a round shield of silver against an obsidian sky. Its bright light shone through the line of cypress trees, casting sharp shadows on his path as he circuited the large square of the villa.

The rest of the house was dark, but the flicker of a candle glowed in the room he knew was hers. He stopped for a moment, only a moment he told himself, just to see if she would look for him.

This was worse than folly. It bordered on madness. He had no business involving himself with a woman, especially this woman. Still, he had all but promised her he'd be here. He might be a murderer, but he had yet to break his word.

The door to her chamber stood open with only a gauzy curtain floating across it, a wide portal to let in the fresh night.

Or a fresh suitor?

It did seem almost an invitation. A silhouette slid past the curtained door and his heart hammered like a woodpecker on gnarled oak. The shadow stopped, then retreated deeper into the room. He forced himself to breathe as he waited to see if she would come again.

Every fiber of his being strained toward the billowing curtain, but he held himself back. He'd never entered a woman's bedchamber by stealth before and he wouldn't start now. Still, without his conscious volition, he took a step forward.

The candle in her room winked out.

Valdis tried to lie down, but the moonlight tormented her, slanting ambient silver rays through her filmy curtains and fingering across her sleeping couch. Surely he wouldn't be there, waiting for her in the dark.

Perhaps she should see if Erik really was there. No,

that could lead to disaster. She tried to conjure the image of Chloe's desecrated face, but instead she saw Erik, the heat in his ice-gray eyes, the power in his warrior's body. He could show her how a man might please a woman without disturbing her all-important flower. Curiosity was driving her to madness.

She couldn't bring him to ruin.

There was every reason in the world to stay in bed.

Her feet hit the cool marble floor and she was pulling back the curtain before she could talk herself out of it. She looked out on the neatly clipped yard beyond. The world was awash in shades of gray, deep charcoal on the cypress trees, pale ash for the marble benches and nude statuary dotting the lawn, lead-gray for the paving stones of the garden path. She stepped through the door and onto the portico, silent as a wraith, her white night shift silvered by moonlight.

She looked down the length of the villa. Damian's room was dark. No light showed in any of the other rooms. Her gaze swept once more over the garden.

She didn't see Erik.

Valdis sighed and tried to quiet the downward spiral in her belly.

It's just as well, she told herself fiercely, trying to deny her disappointment. *No good could come of—*

A flicker of movement drew her eye. A man stepped from behind the trees and stood motionless, his pale hair molten silver, his face hidden in shadow.

Valdis stepped off the slate porch and into the cool grass, the blades soft and pliant beneath her bare feet. Her breath came in short gasps, as if taking in too much might cause her to float away.

This is wrong, she reasoned.

But she couldn't stop her forward motion. Like the strange furry lemmings of her homeland who are compelled for some inexplicable reason to hurl themselves into the sea, she was drawn to this man. There was no right or wrong about it. Like the lemmings' suicidal migration, it just was.

The night had the tiptoe feel of a dream, as if she were insubstantial as the shadows around her. She finally stopped an arm's length away from him. His lips were slightly parted, as if he didn't believe what he was seeing either. An eerie sense of unreality settled over her.

"We mustn't," she whispered.

"I know," he agreed.

And then, suddenly, without knowing how, she was in his arms. His mouth was on hers, hungry and insistent, nipping at her lips and toying with her tongue. This was no kiss. It was a possession. Waves of desire washed over her. If he hadn't been holding her, her knees might have buckled and she'd have dropped on the spot.

He was hard and strong, a rock of a man, and she felt herself melt into him, her insides going soft as warm butter. His mouth was everywhere, her cheeks, her closed eyelids, her earlobes. He grasped a handful of her heavy hair and pulled her head back so his lips could savage the hollow of her throat.

She surrendered to his fierce exploration.

He brought her palm to his mouth and planted a lover's kiss in its center before moving up to sample the thin, soft skin at her wrist and the crease of her elbow.

White heat seared through her and settled in her loins. She shuddered with the intensity of the sensation.

"Valdis," he whispered.

She covered his mouth with her fingers. "We've had enough of words, you and I."

She kissed him then, with the same ferocity he showed when he'd taken her mouth. Erik might be a worthy tutor, but she would show herself an equally adept student.

But just when she felt she'd mastered the art of the kiss, his big hands came into play. He found her breasts and teased her nipples to aching tautness, tracing slow circles around them with the pad of his thumbs, dancing close without actually touching the sensitive tips. She groaned into his mouth.

A soft breeze washed over her fevered skin, setting her diaphanous night shift in motion, lifting it ever so slightly, cooling her steamy legs. His hands caught the billow and the heat of his callused palms warmed her thighs with fire that had nothing to do with the balmy night.

He lifted her in an easy motion, then lowered her to the ground. Valdis stretched out with the luscious grass tickling the backs of her knees and her night shift bunched around her waist. Erik's mouth trailed a course down her neck to the tops of her breasts.

A nameless longing engulfed her. Valdis trembled with need. She wanted, knowing not exactly what it was she desired. All she knew was that white-hot demand would grant her no peace till whatever her body craved was given to her.

Erik seemed to know what she sought. He massaged one of her breasts with his thick, blunt fingertips, then suckled the pebble-hard nipple through the thin fabric of her gown. She was floating, lifted out of herself, as if she'd burst out of her own skin.

"What are you—" she gasped.

He covered her mouth with his to silence her, swallowing her halfhearted protest. Still, the action served to remind her that getting caught in this position would be dangerous.

For both of them.

Chloe's ruined face rose in her mind. Even more ominous, her dancing tutor's words came back to haunt her.

The death of love.

If Valdis feared only for herself, this wild maelstrom of sensation would be enough to tempt her to abandon reason. But to do so might be Erik's undoing as well.

No. Valdis struggled under Erik and forced her arms between them. She pushed against his chest with all her strength, but she was no match for the big Varangian.

"No," she whispered fiercely. "Stop."

"You don't mean it," he murmured into her ear as he grasped her ankle and a shiver streaked up her legs to set her crotch quivering. He ran his hand up her leg, stopping to dally in the sensitive crease behind her knee. She couldn't summon the will to move.

He kissed her again and as his tongue coaxed her lips open, his wandering hand caused her legs to part of their own accord. His skilled fingers found and teased the curls at the apex of her thighs. Even though her mind knew what she must do, her body betrayed her. Liquid warmth met him. Her delicate folds parted easily and he slid a fingertip down the length of her moist cleft.

Her breath caught as he gently invaded her, drawing out her abundant dew. He stroked her soft secrets and circled her most sensitive spot with maddening slowness. Valdis's world spiraled down to the warmth of his breath on her neck and the intoxicating movement of his hand. When he finally grazed her point of pleasure, a jolt of exquisite anguish shot through her and she moaned.

"You see. I can feel you don't really want me to stop."

The smugness in his voice pulled her back from the

edge of surrender. Didn't he realize the danger if they were caught?

I was forced to watch as they took him apart joint by joint. . . .

"Feel this." She brought her knee up hard against his groin. Erik rolled away from her, clutching his damaged part. Valdis had wrestled with her brothers often enough when she was growing up to know a man's weakest spot. She also knew the debilitation was temporary at best, and she needed to make good on her escape before he found his strength once again. She scrambled to her feet and ran to her open doorway as if the dragon, Fafnir, flapped his leathery wings after her.

Valdis didn't dare look back. If she saw bewilderment or hurt on Erik's face, she might be tempted to return to him.

She shut her door and threw the bolt.

Valdis leaned against the portal, willing her heart to stop cavorting in her chest and the blood pounding in her groin to subside. There could be no second chances. She didn't have it in her to pull away from him again.

"No one is privy to the life of another's mind. Such is our blessing and our curse."
—from the secret journal of Damian Aristarchus

CHAPTER TEN

Loki wandered forlornly around the edge of the courtyard. When Valdis was dancing, she had no time for her little dog. Erik watched him nose the shrubbery. Tail drooping, the mongrel worked his way along until he came to Erik's boots. Then Loki plopped his bottom down and cast his sad black eyes upward, as if Erik could fix the problem.

"Don't look at me, pal," Erik said in whispered Norse. "Of the two of us, you're the only one who's sleeping in her bed. You've got no complaint coming."

With a sneeze, Loki stood and started to waddle away, then seemed to think better of it and turned back to lift his leg on Erik's boot.

"What the—? Get away from me." He shooed the animal as the reedy music began once more.

Erik watched from the shadows of the corridor while Valdis and her dancing master went through their paces in the slanting sunlight of the courtyard. The eunuch was seated like a grand pasha in a high-backed chair near the fountain. Erik stifled a snort. Aristarchus might follow the fluid movement of the women with intense concentration, but the eunuch would never suffer the jolt of desire that seared through Erik as he eyed the same dance.

He'd seen a number of fine dancers during his stay in Miklagard. Erik and his friend Hauk even enjoyed a more than passing acquaintance with some of them. They were women who exuded raw sexual energy on and off the dance floor, but Valdis surpassed anything he'd ever seen. The combination of her lithe body and long Nordic limbs with the sensual mating dance she'd been taught was a more potent intoxicant than the strongest wine. She moved with the grace of a leopard on the hunt, sinuous muscles undulating beneath her flawless skin. Erik couldn't tear his gaze from her.

She wouldn't even glance his way.

"Well done," the eunuch said when the women finally dropped to a deep curtsy, veils fluttering to earth around them. "Chloe, you have exceeded my expectations yet again, and with time to spare. What of the other elements of your tutelage?"

Chloe raised her gaze to her master, but remained in a respectful crouch. If not for Erik's attraction to Valdis, he'd have been captivated by this Greek woman's speaking dark eyes. Beneath the veil that hid the lower half of her face, she was undoubtedly a woman of deep beauty.

"She excels in all areas, though the praise goes to Valdis, not me," Chloe said in a soft, sibilant voice. "She is exceptionally quick-minded. You will find her table manners impeccable and her dinner conversation sparkling."

"And the art of love?" Damian demanded. "You have schooled her in the techniques of pleasuring a man?"

Erik winced. He'd tried to teach Valdis that himself, but found her a less than willing pupil.

"We have left that subject for last," Chloe explained. "Dance is the foundation of sybaritic arts. I want Valdis to be comfortable in her own skin before I educate her on tormenting someone else in theirs."

She needs no further instruction, Erik thought ruefully. *The woman already understands the principles of that type of torture well enough.*

He wasn't going to lurk about for more torment if he could help it. Valdis had been too busy with her new teacher to take another language lesson from him since that ill-starred night outside her chamber. In truth, she hardly needed further instruction. She was a natural mimic with a fine ear for the cadence of Greek. Despite a slight accent, Valdis was fairly conversant in her new language. She didn't need him anymore and she obviously didn't want him, either.

Erik strode with purpose into the sunlight toward Aristarchus and the two women. He sketched a fisted salute to the eunuch and steeled himself not to look at Valdis.

"I have taught Valdis Ivorsdottir all I can of your tongue. I am no longer needed here," Erik began. "But while I loll away the days in your villa, my century is being led by another. I would not see my pledge-men sent into danger without me at their head. Release me from your service and allow me to return to the city and my command."

Damian nodded with a smug smile that told Erik he was truly glad to see him go. He also enjoyed making Erik beg for the privilege. "Very well. You have lived up to your part of the bargain, Varangian. Valdis has progressed in her language skills far more than I could have hoped in such a short span. If you but stay till the sun reaches its zenith, I will compose a commendation for you to carry to your general. I will urge Quintilian not to remove you permanently from your command over this leave of absence." Damian stood and the smugness left his face. "We may not agree on much, you and I, but we both honor the same master. The emperor is fortunate to have you in his service, as I have been. You stand relieved."

"No," Valdis interrupted. "He mustn't go."

Both men looked at her sharply; then the eunuch turned a sardonic glare toward Erik.

"I see you have failed to instill in her a more biddable frame of mind," Damian said.

"In the Northlands, our women enjoy more freedom in both speech and conduct—" Erik began.

"Which is one of the reasons your people have earned the title *barbaroi,*" Damian finished for him. "A woman should be silent unless she is invited to speak."

"Yet in the North our women are renowned for their wisdom," Erik countered. "Anyone strong enough to thrive in our harsh land deserves a voice. If a Norsewoman speaks, she will be heard. Valdis must have some reason for not wanting me to go." He tried to disguise the hopefulness in his words by saying them with gruffness.

"Well, Valdis?" Damian turned back to her. "Why should I detain the centurion further?"

"There is yet something I must learn from this Northman, something he offered to teach me," she stammered.

Ja, but you didn't seem to want to learn the other night, did you? he almost blurted out.

"What could that be?" Damian asked.

Her gaze flicked first to Erik, and then back to Aristarchus. "You may not be aware of it, but in our homeland, Erik Heimdalsson is considered a master of *seid,* the very craft you wish me to emulate."

"I thought your men usually don't practice magic," Damian said with a wicked grin. "Seems I heard that those who do are deemed effeminate. If it's true, that must surely be something you'd like to keep from your pledge-men." He fixed Erik with a stare. "Are you a *seid*-man?"

From over Damian's shoulder, Valdis cast him a look of entreaty. She wanted him to stay. And she was willing to lie to keep him here. He was tempted, if only to discover what she was playing at, but his balls still ached from the bruising she gave them. Even so, he was reluctant to call her a liar to her face.

"*Seid* is not something entered into lightly. I've no time to train a novitiate in the mysteries now." He turned to go.

"But what of runes?" Valdis hurried on. "If you finished teaching me runic writing, I could use them to send a message."

Erik didn't know a rune from a goat track, but he was tripped by his first lie into agreeing with another. "You write Greek well enough. That should suffice."

"Quintilian should have told me you were an adept at runic writing, but then, perhaps he doesn't know," Damian said with eyelids lowered in frank reappraisal. "If a Greek missive is intercepted, its contents swirl around the entire city before the sun sets, but if it were written in runes . . ." Damian shrugged eloquently. "They are crude enough to be mistaken for random lines and scratches. Those who can read them, even among you Northmen, are few and far between. It would be worthwhile for Valdis to be able to send a message in such writing. You will see that she is equipped with the knowledge. Only then shall we discuss your return to your cohort." Damian signaled Chloe to follow him. "I leave you to your studies. See that I am briefed on her progress, Northman."

Erik watched the eunuch's retreating back before turning to face Valdis. He wished his heart wasn't pounding so. It hadn't rioted this much since the last time he went into battle. But he was better armed then against his foe than he was now against this woman. He folded his arms across his chest.

"Aristarchus will use any ruse to get his own way. Congratulations, Valdis. You have learned to think like a Greek," he said with gravel in his voice. "But a lie does not become your lips."

"And trying to sneak off without giving me a chance to explain doesn't become a Varangian, either," Valdis said, refusing to be shamed by her actions. She draped herself across a stone bench, arranging the gossamer folds of her palla around her as if she were unaware the sight of her in the filmy garment set his cock to rising. She gestured with a graceful wave for him to sit in the eunuch's vacant chair. "Don't you want to know why I fled from you?"

"Not particularly." He decided it would be safer to remain standing. If a man lowered his guard around this shield-maiden, he might well find his heart skewered.

Or his balls.

Her mismatched eyes glistened as she focused her attention on him. He almost thought she was near tears, but dismissed that notion as fanciful. A she-spider sheds no tears over the males she consumes. Valdis broke off her intense stare and cast her gaze on the pebbled walkway.

"I was only trying to protect you," she said in a whisper.

Erik snorted. "May the gods deliver me from your further protection."

"You don't understand." She told him of the horrible disfigurement hidden by Chloe's veil and the story of the Greek woman's dismembered lover. "If we'd been caught that night, you would have suffered terribly," Valdis explained. "I couldn't bear to see you hurt."

"So you took it upon yourself to do the hurting," he said with a wry grin. "I can take care of myself, Valdis. Perhaps you might allow that a Varangian could protect himself and his woman better than a Greek harpist."

His woman. Had he actually called her that?

He turned away from her lest she spell him with her eyes again. Erik paced around the fountain with restless energy.

"I had not thought of that." Valdis pensively fingered the folds of her palla. "You're right. Chloe's lover was no warrior."

"No one will harm you as long as I breathe. We can lay aside the threat of someone lopping off your nose just now," he said, determined to change the subject. "But the immediate problem is the one you've embroiled us in with your not-so-clever lies. You know full well I'm no rune-master. I can't teach you what I don't know."

"Ah, but I can teach you." She all but pounced upon the stylus and tablet at her side. "I already know runes."

He cocked his head at her. The woman was full of surprises. "So you did more than love-spelling when you dabbled in *seid?*"

She nodded enthusiastically. "*Seid*-men and -women want you to believe there is malignant power in the symbols, but truly, they are benign." She began to work the tip of the stylus into the soft wax tablet. "If there is magic in runic writing, it is that sounds can be captured and turned into simple slashes to be understood by another. Look, this is your name."

She pointed to each individual mark, voicing the separate sounds, then putting them together to speak his name. Then she handed him the writing implements. "Here, you try."

His natural impulse was to shy away from anything smacking of *seid*. Old prejudices die hard. A man who could not prove himself on the field of combat often turned to *seid* as a means of acquiring power. Real men were revolted by the simpering *seid* practitioners.

And fearful at the same time. A curse could not be turned by a shield or a spelling undone by the stroke of an ax. No amount of armor would protect a man from a *seid*-master's ill-wish. Magic was beyond the scope of Erik's experience. The spiritual world was a shadowy realm, inaccessible to the warrior, unless one counted the madness of *berserkr*.

He'd experienced that black foray into the world of the spirit intimately. The Rage had driven him to slay his brother without even being aware he'd done it until afterward. Even now, he had no clear recollection of the murder, only the bloody aftermath and his wife's keening sobs.

"Truly, Erik, there is no magic here," Valdis said, her eyes sending mixed messages of light and dark. The violet one was clear and guileless, but the deep brown one had darkened to onyx. Erik felt the pull toward her strengthen even as he resisted it. If the woman believed there was no magic swirling about her, she was delusional.

Against his better judgment, he took the stylus from her hand.

For the rest of the day, Valdis led him through the maze of the *futhark*, the Norse alphabet. He mastered the individual sounds and the symbols that called them forth, but with the slowness of a snail's pace. More than once he was tempted to throw the tablet down in disgust.

"Really, you are doing quite well. We must walk before we run," Valdis said as she peered over his shoulder to inspect his work. "Didn't you practice many hours before you learned to use the *gladius* of the Christians?"

Erik nodded with reluctance. The short sword favored by the Byzantines was a more subtle weapon than a Nordic ax and, at close range, just as lethal. Erik had sweated on the practice field with a wooden *gladius* for weeks before the hilt of a real one was placed in his big hand. He gripped the stylus tighter and tried again to copy the phrase Valdis had written for him.

"Have you deciphered the meaning yet?" she said with a feline smile playing about her lips.

"One thing at a time," he grumbled as he faithfully reproduced the last slash. "Let me get it written first."

Chloe joined them in the courtyard and Eric lowered the stylus, feigning reading in silence the message Valdis had carved in the soft wax.

"A thousand pardons for interrupting," Chloe said with a graceful inclination of her head.

"We are nearly finished here, anyway." If Erik hadn't known what desecration lurked behind her veil, he would have thought her a striking woman. Even if she was guilty of impurity, what kind of animal, he wondered, would disfigure a woman so horribly instead of just killing her outright? Christians were always carping on about the quality of mercy. If Chloe's scarred life were an example of that attribute, Erik thought mercy had little to commend it.

"What do you want?" he asked the Greek woman.

"It is time for Valdis to begin the last stage of her lessons with me," Chloe said.

The arts of love, Erik remembered. Harlot's tricks and cheats, feigned passion and cock-teases. Valdis was a virgin daughter of the North; even though he lusted after her himself, it made his blood boil to think of her being cheapened by such false carnal knowledge. Her passage into full womanhood should be made with a man who cared for her, who could teach her the mystic connection the act of love created between lovers. She should find the beauty and power of *inn mattki munr,* the mighty passion, with a man who loved her more than life.

After his failed marriage, Erik knew he was not the man to teach Valdis love. But he certainly wouldn't mind showing her the delights of the love couch.

Short of breaking his oath and stealing her away, there was nothing he could do to prevent Valdis from receiving a sybaritic education. Damian was her legal master and if he wanted her trained as a whore, he was within his rights.

Erik's heart tightened like a fist in his chest. He dismissed Valdis with a wave, not trusting his voice to speak.

Valdis, however, suffered from no such difficulty. "Thank you for my instruction," she said with a polite half bow. "Please read the last message with care to make sure I wrote it correctly."

Then she turned and followed the much smaller woman from the courtyard with a bewitching roll of her hips.

"Read the message," he muttered once he was able to tear his gaze from her disappearing form. He forced his concentration back on the tablet, where the slashes began to take shape as words in his mind.

If you . . .

He strained at the next set of words.

If you would make me . . .

When the meaning became clear, he nearly dropped the tablet. He worked through the symbols again to be sure he was not mistaken.

If you would make me your woman, my door stands open. Come to me at moonrise.

"A general may claim never to send one of his soldiers on a mission he would not attempt himself. I do not have that luxury."
—*from the secret journal of Damian Aristarchus*

CHAPTER ELEVEN

Chloe led Valdis into the bathhouse, a white marble building separate from the main villa. The interior was spacious and the stone floors radiated heat from the hot air funneled beneath them through the hypocaust. A deep clear pool sent tendrils of steam into the air.

"Before a woman can please a man," Chloe explained as she gathered her heavy dark hair in one hand and pinned it in a knot on top of her head, "she must know what pleases herself."

"It would please me not to be sent to the bed of a strange man," Valdis said stonily.

"Life gives us few choices, but one we always have is to choose joy, despite our circumstances," Chloe said. "If you are to be an odalisque, a woman of the sacred womb, you must have your own source of joy, for your future master may take little interest in providing it for you."

"As your source of joy was your lover?" Valdis asked, and was immediately sorry for it. A deep shadow passed behind Chloe's eyes.

"I am trying to teach you to take pleasure in all areas of life, not just your bed. Your joy must come from inside yourself," Chloe said. "You must decide to enjoy every moment of your life, for it is fleeting and most uncertain. For example, this lovely bath. Is it not a delight to the senses? Are your eyes not pleased by the order and beauty they see? The patter of water into the base of the fountain calms the spirit, does it not? Does the scent of rose-water and jasmine not tickle your nose?"

Valdis inhaled deeply and smiled despite her determination not to cooperate with Chloe. The air was heavy with the sweetness of flowers, but Valdis suddenly realized that Chloe must not be able to smell them. "But you cannot—"

"No, I cannot," she said with sadness. "But I see the petals and I remember their fragrance as one recalls the face of a loved one. As I told you before, do not judge a life by what is lost. After all, you too have lost much. Your home, your family, your freedom." Chloe ticked off the list with relentless ease.

Valdis's mouth tightened into a hard line. She didn't relish the reminder of her family's abandonment.

"And yet life can be full of joy. *If*"—Chloe paused for emphasis—"you choose for it to be."

Valdis nodded slowly. Choice gave her a measure of power in her powerless life. Perhaps that was why she'd made the choice to invite Erik to come to her. She had the power to choose to accept the pleasure he offered. She'd been reared to regard the *Havamal,* the sayings of Odin, as the fount of wisdom by which to measure her life. Yet here was wisdom that rang truer in her ears than the dry homilies of the one-eyed All-Father. Even as a slave, Valdis could choose joy and it would be real.

"Show me more," she said.

"The act of love should be one of joy," Chloe began.

"Even if it is not accompanied by true love?"

"True love is another subject altogether. We are speaking of joy now. Of course, the congress of a man and a woman is enhanced by love. Yet even without it, if the woman is skillful, a full measure of pleasure may still be found. The natural impulse of a man is quickness. They see something they want and they move to take it," Chloe said. "It is the job of the woman not to stop him, but to slow him down. A rush to the prize diminishes its value. In the deferment of desire, its coals are stoked."

"I don't understand," Valdis said.

"Let the dance be your teacher," Chloe said. "Did we begin with large movements?"

"No, slow and small."

"Yes, and so should it be with a lover," Chloe said. "Let us begin with the unveiling. Your master may wish to undress you himself. Some men do, but if he allows it, you may set the tone for your dalliance by how you reveal yourself to him. Imagine, if you will, that your master wishes you to dance for him while disrobing. How would you do it?"

Valdis's eyes widened. The idea of undressing before a strange man made her belly writhe like a ball of snakes. "I don't think I could."

"Nonsense," Chloe said. "I have heard the rumors. The master will see you freed if you comply with his wishes and complete the task he assigns. Do you not want your freedom?"

Valdis gnawed the inside of her cheek and nodded.

"Then wipe that pained expression from your face and use your imagination," Chloe said. "One way a woman can wring joy from a forced match is to imagine. Banish the real man. Picture instead the man you could love. See him clear in your mind. Hold that thought and dance for him."

Valdis squeezed her eyes shut, and immediately Erik's face came into focus. Could she love him? She couldn't say, but she had known little peace since that night in the garden when her body stirred to his. She'd relived each kiss, each touch a hundred times, till her body ached for release. When he said he was leaving, panic clawed at her belly. She was beginning to think he was the only one she could trust in this Byzantine household, the only one whose gruff, straightforward way of thinking she understood.

Besides, she also wanted to give him a chance to show her what pleasure they could share without taking her maidenhead and putting them both at risk. But love? She just didn't know. She only knew that if he came to her chamber at moonrise, she wouldn't send him away again.

But for now, she would use his image as Chloe commanded. His features were taut with the hunger she'd first seen in him at the slave market.

"Can you see him? Does he desire you?"

"Yes." Valdis swayed a little, remembering the white-hot longing that robbed her of sleep after their last tryst.

"Then reflect that desire back to him as a piece of polished brass shows you your own face. Feel his heat. Let it burn you to your inmost place," Chloe's voice urged with a rasp. "Now dance."

Chloe began to beat time on the floor with her palms, and Valdis started to move. What had started as a lesson in joy became an exercise in longing. As Valdis performed the prescribed steps, she saw how natural it was to slide a thumb beneath her palla to bare her shoulder, how the dance was designed so she could send smoldering gazes at her imaginary lover as she slowly allowed part of her dress to drift down to expose her breasts.

Erik had seemed delighted with them. She heard the echo of his growl of pleasure when he claimed her nipple.

She cupped her breasts in her hands and offered them up to her phantom man, the pink tips aching. She ran the pads of her thumbs around her nipples and they puckered with longing. In her imagination, Erik's mouth was upon them once more and she groaned with need.

She turned her back on the dream-Erik and lifted her arms above her head. Her palla dropped to her undulating hips and she arched her back, feeling the brush of her long hair against the dimples above her buttocks. She imagined his sharp intake of breath as she lifted her heavy hair to expose the curve of her spine and the delicate crevice at its base.

The tempo quickened and she spun to face her invisible lover. Her hands started at the base of her own throat and roved over her body, flickers of pleasure following the trail left by her fingers. She shoved the palla past her hips and stepped out of it, her limbs free as she moved with abandon, the core of her being aflame. His fingers, those blessed talented fingers, were teasing her seat of pleasure till it plumped like a ripe fruit, the skin near to bursting. She slid her own hands down to spread the lips of her sex. The kiss of air on that charged secret flesh drove her to the edge.

The dance became a frenzy and she whirled till she collapsed in a splayed heap. The heartbeat between her legs pounded with as much insistence as the one in her chest.

Lying on the marble floor, Valdis gasped for air as she willed herself to find a measure of calm. Kissing Erik in the moonlight had whipped up this aching fury. Bare imagining that she danced and disrobed for him unhinged her reason just as much. Her body screamed for release.

Chloe said a woman must slow a man, but the demand from her body would brook no delay. If Erik were with her in truth, she'd beg him to end this torment, to still this bewildering need. She rubbed the heel of her hand over her groin and her anguish deepened.

Chloe came over and leaned to peer down at her. Valdis startled when she entered her field of vision. In her intimate abandon, she'd forgotten her teacher was even there.

"You have a very fine imagination," she said. "It will serve you well. Dance like that for your new master and you will undoubtedly become a favorite in no time. Come and have your bath and I will tell you what I know of bringing a man to the same edge of passion. You will learn that to torment another with desire is to treble your own."

Treble the longing she felt now? Valdis doubted she could bear even a single drop more. Yet if Erik were the man leading her into the labyrinth of desire, she'd be willing to try.

"A woman who can keep hold of reason in the throes of passion is either a valiant ally. Or a fearsome foe."
—*from the secret journal of Damian Aristarchus*

CHAPTER TWELVE

He's not coming.

Valdis sighed as the moon continued its climb into the black vault of the sky. With each warbling call of the nightjar, each rustle of the jasmine-scented breeze through the cypress, Valdis fancied she heard Erik's approach. But when she padded to the open doorway to greet him all she saw was the empty moon-washed garden.

Perhaps he couldn't decipher the runes. She brushed the thought aside.

Erik was too intelligent not to grasp the concept of sound married to symbol. Besides, she hadn't even told him about the tricky part, the way each rune stood for not only a sound, but also a separate word or idea. A true rune-master could devise a devilishly clever message within a message.

Surely he was coming. Hadn't he all but called her his woman?

Chloe's teaching spun in her mind. If knowledge were power, then Valdis was formidable indeed. She knew exactly what she'd do once Erik came; how she'd entice and torment him, how to allow only so much intimacy and then withdraw so he'd pant after her all the more. Chloe had taught her how to find a man's most sensitive spots, to tease his nipples and nip at his earlobes, to stroke his ballocks till they tightened into hard knots. The Greek woman spent a large portion of the afternoon on the caresses best suited to enflame a man's member to stiff potency.

"After all," Chloe explained, "a man who rules a harem must sport a rod like a bull since he will use it every night. Yet even the most potent male is prone to occasional failure. A favorite is one who knows how to make him rise without effort on his part. And woe betide the odalisque who causes the master's rod to fall."

"But why is the woman blamed for the man's failure?" Valdis asked. "That's not fair."

"Fair or not, the fault will assuredly be assigned to her, not him. She will be banished to the far corner of the zenana, never to be called for again. If that happens, a woman is as good as dead, for she is fit for nothing but drudgery and servitude. But cheer up, my dove," Chloe said. "That fate will not claim you, not with the tricks I will teach you to harden your master's resolve."

Valdis didn't think Erik would need such coaxing. She'd felt his groin stiffen when they kissed without any further encouragement on her part. Still, she wanted to try some of her newfound knowledge on him, just to see his reaction. Maybe even the part about using her tongue. . . .

Of course, she must guard the flower of her womanhood, but the preliminaries would be tantalizing enough even without full consummation. Hadn't Erik already told her he could give her pleasure without disturbing her flower? Now she was armed with the knowledge of how to please him, as well.

After the knee to his groin, she had a bit to atone for, and she looked forward to it.

Valdis sighed and trudged back to her sleeping couch. She sank into the fine linens, telling herself to enjoy the sleek coolness on her skin. *"Seize the joy in each moment,"* Chloe had admonished her. There was wisdom in the Greek woman's teachings; if only Valdis could put them into practice.

The scrape of a booted foot on her threshold made her bolt upright. He was framed in the open doorway, moonlight dusting his hair and broad shoulders with silver. His face was hidden in shadow, but when he pushed back the gauze curtain and stepped inside, the whites of his eyes gleamed, flashing feral in the dark.

She ran to his side, her heart skipping like a kid in the meadow. *Steady,* she ordered herself. *This is only about pleasure.*

"Valdis, *dyrr.*" He moved to embrace her, but she straight-armed him and put a finger to his lips. She eased the door closed behind him, then knelt to unlatch his boots and help him out of them. The last thing she needed was for Damian to hear her Northman stomping around through the wall separating them. While she helped him toe off his boots, he ran his large hand over the crown of her head with such tenderness, she felt her insides melt at his touch.

"We must be quiet," she whispered when she straightened to look up at Erik. His eyes were dark with excitement already, but she was determined to use the new knowledge she'd gained to heighten his pleasure further. "I wish I had music, but you will just have to imagine it."

Valdis began her dance of seduction, but Erik grasped both her wrists and pulled her to his chest.

"What do you think you're doing?" he demanded in a furious whisper.

"I'm dancing for you. Doesn't it please you?"

"Just to look at you pleases me. I need no whore's tricks. If we are to do this, let it be just us—one man, one woman. I'll not share a bed with both you and your odalisque teacher. Honest and open, with no feigned passion," he said. "I'm here for you, not for some exotic sexual technique Chloe has taught you."

"But Chloe said—"

"Chloe's not the one I want to bed." Erik's breath was warm on her face. "Valdis." He caressed her name. "I've wanted you since I laid eyes on you, but not if we aren't to have anything true pass between us. Let it be real or let me walk out that door right now."

Moonlight shafted in through the windows, casting its pure radiance on his square, open features. She lifted a hand to stroke his jaw, his neatly trimmed beard a bristly pelt beneath her palm. The raw hunger in his eyes threatened to buckle her knees. He wanted her. *Her.* Not the sexual romp she'd been trained to give him.

She stood on tiptoe to bring her lips to his in the slightest brush of a kiss.

"We'll have it true," she agreed.

He was on her then, claiming her mouth, pouring the frustrated lust of the past weeks into a kiss that threatened to draw her soul from her body. Then he suddenly pulled back, as if reining in a warhorse.

"This much is true, then," he said hoarsely. "You are pledged to go to another, and only oath-breaking could change that. My honor is little enough, but it's all I have. I cannot change your destiny. I can offer you nothing but this night."

"I would not have you break your oath for me. Freedom waits for me to earn it myself." She kissed him softly, letting her body melt into his. "But if I am to go to another, let me take this night with me. Should I go through life never knowing tenderness, never knowing anything real? Love me now, Erik, even if it's only for now, and it will be enough."

He folded her into his arms and their mouths met. He held her head immobile while his tongue played a lover's game with her lips, teeth and tongue. She reciprocated, darting her tongue between his lips till he groaned into her mouth. The kisses sent a message to her womb, rippling through her with the crackle of heat lightning. She felt a growing warmth between her legs.

He clasped her hands, their fingers entwined for a moment. Then slowly, he slid his calloused palms up her bare arms and skimmed his fingertips over the thin bones that ran from her shoulders to the hollow at the base of her throat. His touch left a trail of sparks on her skin.

"You're so beautiful," he whispered between kisses. "And so soft." He released her mouth long enough to bend down and pull her night shift over her head. A slight breeze wafted in through the open window, cooling her fevered skin.

Erik stepped back a pace, intent on drinking in the sight of her. The heat in his eyes branded her as his gaze traveled over her breasts, down her ribs to the indentation of her navel, to the crisp golden triangle of curls covering her sex.

"My turn," she said, as she tugged his shirt over his head. She stared at him as well, taking in the battle-hardened lines of him, his broad, heavily muscled chest and tapering waist. He stood perfectly still and let her look. Solid, strong, proud—he was everything she knew about a man.

She wanted to know more.

When she reached to untie the drawstring at the waist of his trousers, he caught her hand. "Careful. You have a maidenhead to guard. If you want to still be as you are now by the end of this night, one of us needs to stay dressed from the waist down."

She sighed in disappointment.

"But that doesn't mean we can't take turns," he said with a grin.

She stepped into his waiting arms.

Valdis was engulfed by this man, drowning in the sharp tang of his masculine smell, her skin tingling where his fingertips trailed, her nipples hardened against his chest. All the amatory arts she'd been taught fled from her mind. Instead, she learned Erik by heart, discovering clenched muscle beneath taut skin, finding old scars on his ribs and healing them with a lover's kiss.

All the tender places his gaze had touched his hands now explored, the rough calluses at the base of his fingers setting her skin afire. He whispered her name, over and over. It played in her head like waves beating against a rocky shore. When his fingers finally claimed the cleft between her legs, he found a warm, wet welcome. Erik dropped to his knees before her.

Valdis gasped as his tongue invaded her. *Chloe failed to mention this! Odin! What is he doing to me?* He stroked, he nibbled, he took her tender spot between his lips and suckled.

She ground her teeth together to keep from crying out as she twisted her fingers in his hair. Her belly clenched as her insides knotted tighter and tighter. She was stretched thin as a piece of parchment. Then in a blinding heartbeat, the knot loosened and the cord of her being began to unravel, snapping like a whip cracked over a speeding chariot team. She would have collapsed, but Erik caught her before she fell. Her head lolled back as he carried her to her couch and stretched her out. She didn't care what he did with her. Her spirit wandered along the outstretched limbs of the World Tree Yggdrasil, trembling with joy.

When she fluttered back to herself, she found Erik standing over her, a smug grin on his handsome face. He knew full well he'd sent her halfway to Valhalla without so much as hearing a Valkyrie's song.

She lifted her arms to him in invitation. Erik didn't hesitate. He settled on her and she gloried in the weight of his body. He kissed her again, with more urgency this time, and she tasted herself on his mouth, musky and pungent.

"You are delicious." He trailed a series of baby kisses down her neck, along her jawline and finally nipped at her earlobe. "Everywhere."

"What did you do to me?" she asked, her heart still banging against her ribs.

"Liked that, did you?" he said as he stroked her belly. "Want to go again?"

In answer, she pulled his head down and kissed him hard, thrusting her tongue into his mouth. She felt his deep, self-satisfied chuckle.

"Remember that for later," he ordered. "Roll over."

Obediently, she turned onto her stomach. Erik pushed her hair out of the way and ran his warm hand down the length of her spine. His fingers teased the crevice of her buttocks and traced the curve of those mounds. Tingles of pleasure streaked over her.

Valdis surrendered to his gentle exploration, spreading her legs for his invasion. He tugged at her small hairs, teasing her cleft from this backward angle. She rose to his hand, giving him unfettered access to all her secrets. She was tinder waiting for the spark. But before he pushed her into the void once more, he rolled her back over and kissed her.

He settled his hand over her hot mound. "Now, you're in control," he said. "My hand will move again only when and how you kiss me."

She brushed her lips on his and his finger flicked her sensitive spot, light as a feather. She gasped. He lifted a brow at her.

"See how this game is played?"

She thrust her tongue between his lips and his finger plunged into her, stopping just shy of the thin barrier of her purity. She toyed with his lips and he did the same to her, setting her writhing under his hand.

Remembering Chloe's advice about delayed delight, she nipped at his mouth, teasing both of them to the edge of madness. Finally she found the way to kiss him that set his talented fingers in the rhythmic motion guaranteed to speed her to that dark place bursting with light.

After the moments of madness when her body bucked with the strength of her release, she found his groin pressed against her hip, hard and relentless. The knot he'd just loosened began to build in her again, but there was no question of allowing him to fill her aching womb. It was one thing for him to show her the delights of the love couch, but quite another for her to let him take her virginity. Still, it wasn't right for her to take all the pleasure from their loving. She pushed against his shoulders and he rolled away from her.

"Trust me, Valdis," he whispered. "I will not—"

"I know you won't," she mouthed into his ear. "But you have given me joy and I would like to return it."

"Giving to you is better than taking from anyone else." He traced slow circles around her taut nipples. "In pleasing you, I please myself."

"*Ja,* I see that." She nipped at his lower lip. "But you are not so pleased as I mean for you to be. Lie back and don't move." She grinned wickedly at him. "If you can."

He accepted her challenge with a raised brow and laced his fingers behind his head, daring her to do whatever she wished. She rose from the bed long enough to don her night shift, though the thin fabric was no barrier if he should decide not to honor his pledge to guard her maidenhead. Then she tugged off his leggings.

Valdis feasted her eyes on his long body, stretched out in the moonlight, his muscles rounded mounds, his nipples dark and phallus achingly erect. She'd seen statues of Frey and the wildly exaggerated erection in the mosaic in Damian's foyer, but Erik was the first real man she'd laid eyes on. A pearl of milky liquid formed at the tip of him.

"If all you're going to do is look, it's going to be a long night," he said dryly.

Valdis swung a leg over him and settled on his groin at the base of his erection. She could feel his ballocks beneath her, the soft bag tightening at her nearness. Starting at the base, she ran one finger over the length of him. His phallus rose to her touch.

Erik's breathing quickened. "Now what?"

In answer, she leaned forward and kissed him. Then she gathered her hair in her hand and tossed its length up over his face. Slowly, she raised back up, drawing her hair across his chest, a thousand tiny fingers caressing him.

He gasped. "Did Chloe teach you that?"

"No, I made it up on my own." A thrill ran through her belly at his pleasure. "You said no whore's tricks, remember? So you'll just have to put up with my fumbling."

"Gladly."

"No more words," she ordered. With fingers and

mouth, she explored him, acutely aware of every snatched breath and quivering muscle. When he groaned softly, she showed pity and took him in her hand. They fell into a galloping rhythm. Valdis discovered that if she leaned forward and ground her hips against him, she could also tease her exquisite point of pleasure almost beyond bearing. She raised her night shift so she could feel the hard length of him against her skin.

The pressure built inside her steadily, straining her to breaking. Then as she shattered again, Erik's ballocks tightened beneath her. He stiffened and she felt a rhythmic pulse on her belly as his seed spilled onto her.

Spent and gasping, he pulled her down to lay her head on his chest. She kissed the base of his sweat-dampened throat, tasting the saltiness of him. After a few moments, their breathing returned to normal and their hearts fell into rhythm with each other, beating as one.

Erik finally rolled her off him slowly, as if he were loath to sever the connection between them. She feared he was leaving her as he groped in the dark for his discarded tunic. Instead, he returned to her side and used his garment to gently clean his seed from the smooth skin of her belly.

"I'm sorry—" he began.

"Hush," she said with a finger to his lips. "No need for regrets between us."

His smile flashed in the darkness. Then he settled beside her, molding his large body to her contours, his hand splayed possessively over her breast.

Valdis breathed deeply, the joy of their loving still draped over her like the gauzy canopy over her sleeping couch. Her body went slack and boneless. She'd never felt such peace. She fought to keep from drifting into drowsy delirium. Falling asleep now would mean

disaster—a slow painful death for Erik and hideous disfigurement for her.

That thought alone conspired to keep her eyes open.
She listened to Erik's deep, even breathing, certain that
he slept. Other small sounds began to tickle her ear.
She heard a dog bark in the distant stables, the hunting
cry of an owl, the creak of her sleeping couch when she
shifted her weight. A tingle of alarm fingered up her
spine when she heard the twitter of a lark.

"Erik, please. You must wake," she whispered urgently.

He raised his head from her pillow and focused his
hooded gaze on her.

"I lied to you," he slurred drowsily.

"What do you mean?"

"One night will not be enough."

"It may well be all we ever have if you don't leave
right now." She gathered his clothing, retrieving his leggings, his undergarment, the stockings and the linen
strips he'd wind about his calves to hold them up. "You
dare not delay." She held out his leggings for him, but
he grasped her wrist instead.

"What if I want more?" he asked. "What if I want us to
leave together right now?"

"So now you're ready to surrender your honor for another night in my bed?" She pulled him to his feet. "I'm
flattered, but I can't count myself worth breaking your
oath over."

"'Tis no flattery. I'm serious."

"So am I. Your pledge is precious to you. If you think
I'll let you give up the one thing you hold dear, you need
to think again." She forced his tunic over his head. "We
can't talk now. Please, Erik, it will be dawn soon. If you
want to see me as noseless as Chloe, just keep dallying."

That got him moving. He tugged up his leggings and
finished dressing in surly silence. He stalked to the

doorway, carrying his hobnail boots. Erik stopped at the threshold and turned back to face her.

Valdis padded over to him. She wanted this idyll to end in the sweetness of his mouth on hers once more. Instead he parted the neckline of her nightshift and bent his head down to grasp her nipple between his lips, suckling so hard, she nearly cried out as his teeth grazed her sensitive areola.

Blood pounded in her groin. In only a few moments, she was so hot and ready for him again, all rational thought fled from her mind. She'd lie down on the cool marble floor and spread her legs if he only gave the word.

But he didn't try to take her. He stood straight and looked down at her, determination blocking all tenderness from his features.

"I don't care what you say, Valdis, this is not over. Oath or no oath, I will find a way to have you." He covered her mouth with his in a possessive kiss. "All of you."

And then he was gone, disappearing into the last watch of the night with the silence of a wraith.

"In the currency of politics, information is more precious than bezants."
—from the secret journal of Damian Aristarchus

CHAPTER THIRTEEN

Valdis was seated beside Erik on one of the marble benches near the fountain. She shifted, edging away lest she accidentally brush against him. Being near him without being able to bed him was hellish enough. Touching him would be unbearable. She focused on the wax tablet on her lap. Under the guise of receiving instruction in the mystery of runes, she continued to teach him.

She peered at him from under her lashes. He seemed intent on the slate before him, his tongue clamped firmly between his teeth in concentration as he faithfully reproduced her work. She'd taught him how to mark the runes within two roughly parallel lines so they didn't wander all over the tablet, disordered and meaningless. His slashes writhed across the wax surface encased in a serpent's body, a pattern favored by many carvers of standing runestones.

When one of Damian's servants wandered into the

courtyard, Erik leaned over and cast an appraising eye at her tablet.

"No, that's not right," he said loudly in Greek for the servant's benefit. "You've formed the last symbol backwards. Try it again."

There was nothing at all wrong with her writing, but she scraped away the offending slash and etched it again.

"Could you be any more heavy-handed?" she asked in Norse, mindful to keep her tone contrite, playing the recently chastised student.

"There was a time when you didn't complain of my hands, heavy or otherwise."

Valdis bit her lower lip. His touch left her more fuzzy-headed than six bowls of the Christians' strong wine, but she dared not let herself conjure up the memory of that soul-shattering night. Nothing would be served by dwelling on what she couldn't have.

"Please, can we try to concentrate on the runes?" she asked. "Once I am in the harem, they may be the only way I can send a message."

Erik grunted his reluctant assent and gouged another slash in the wax.

"Careful," she warned. "Now you're the one who's turned a rune on its head."

Erik glared at her as he smoothed out the soft wax to start over. Valdis wished it were that easy to start over in other things, as well.

"Your door was closed again last night," he said softly.

So he had been there, after all. Even though she'd never caught sight of him, Valdis sensed his presence when she peeked from behind her billowy curtains into the shadows of the garden. She had been acutely aware of him. Her entire being strained toward him, but she reined herself back.

And she assuredly would not open her door.

"Has so much changed for you in so short a time?" he asked.

"Erik, it's too dangerous for us to be together. You must see that."

"Only if we stay here," he said. "It would be different if I were satisfied just to be your lover. I thought I could take you in small pieces, Valdis, but I can't."

He covered her hand with his briefly, then released it. Valdis glanced around, mindful that Damian's other servants were constantly coming and going from the courtyard. He obviously had given orders that the two Nordic members of the household were to be under many watchful eyes during the day. It had always surprised Valdis that her door was unguarded at night. Perhaps Damian believed the nearness of his personal chamber and the warning of Chloe's disfigurement was enough to protect her purity.

But that wasn't what kept her door shut. Her recurring nightmare of Erik's ambush had returned, and with it her fear for him if they were caught together trebled.

"The first time we met, you begged me to steal you away. Now I'm of a mind to do it." Erik leaned toward her, as if he might sweep her into his arms at any moment. "The world is wide. Surely there's a place somewhere in Midgard where we can be together."

Little Loki scampered past, snapping his tiny jaws after a butterfly. Valdis scooped him into her arms and clutched the dog to her chest like a shield. The mongrel was barely recognizable as the same scruffy creature Valdis had befriended outside the Hippodrome. Loki had become a household favorite, fed choice tidbits from everyone's plate, bathed and trimmed and perfumed by one of the serving girls and petted and spoiled by everyone. He still hovered around Valdis as closely as any *seid*-woman's familiar by day, but he'd yet to warm up to Erik. Loki bared his little white teeth and emitted a low growl at the big Northman.

"Where would we go?" Valdis asked as she grasped the dog's muzzle to silence him. "The North is barred to us. Suppose you did break your oath to the emperor and run off with a slave girl—would the world welcome us? No, the entire Byzantine Empire would close in on us like a snare around a pair of coneys. Then where shall we run? To the Bulgars? The Pechenegs? Mayhap there's a Caliphate in the Moorish lands willing to offend their Byzantine trading partners by taking us in." She shook her head. "We cannot run."

Erik studied the paving stones between his feet. "So what passed between us was nothing to you."

It was everything, she wanted to say. But she couldn't tell him so. It would only strengthen his resolve.

"It was just as you said. You promised me one night, and I accepted it." She put the dog down and watched him sniff the ferns at the fountain's edge. "There's the end to it."

"Then you care nothing for me at all."

Valdis squeezed her eyes shut. How could she begin to catalog the feelings she had for this infuriatingly single-minded man? "Erik, you told me after you were banished that it took you many months to find a place for yourself here among the Byzantines. Your oath to the emperor has given you a chance to reclaim your lost honor. Would you throw it away for a woman again?"

She felt the anger rolling off him as she reminded him that he hadn't stopped at the murder of his own brother over a woman, his wayward wife. Valdis trembled, but he seemed to master himself, even though he'd lain the tablet aside and ground one fist into the other palm.

"Sometimes even a man's honor can be held too dear. You rate yourself too humbly. You're not just some camp girl I enjoyed tumbling. The truth is I can't bear to think of you going to another," he admitted.

Valdis shivered involuntarily. "I feel it too, bleak as if I am forced to pass through a cold, dark tunnel. But my freedom lies at the end of that passage. Don't try to dissuade me from going through it." She made the mistake of looking directly at him. "Once I'm free, who knows what might happen?"

It was the wrong thing to say. Erik wouldn't want her after she'd been with another man.

But surprisingly he seemed to take heart at her words. "Your courage shames me. *Ja,* where there's life, there's hope." He fixed Valdis with a determined stare. "Do whatever you must, though it grates my soul. Only live, Valdis. At least that way, there's a chance for us."

Finally, he understood. The frenzy of lust might feel like enough on a star-spangled night, but they must live in the world by morning. She hoped to spare his honor so that once she was free, they might find a way to be together with the blessing of society. She longed to melt into his arms, but Damian himself strode into the courtyard at that precise moment. They both stood in his presence.

"How is the training progressing?" he asked Erik.

"Valdis is so quick. Already she bests me at the magic of runes," Erik said truthfully.

"Then if she sent you a runic message, you would understand her?"

"*Ja,*" Erik said with a soul-piercing glance at her. "We understand each other."

"Good," Damian said. "I have received dispatches which tell me the time for our departure to the city draws near. Now all that remains is to determine how best to trigger a touch of the falling sickness so Valdis will come to the attention of those I intend for her to impress."

"It's not something I can conjure from thin air," she said. "The spells steal over me when I least expect them. If I knew what caused them, be assured I would avoid it."

"Knowledge is power. Knowing what causes the fits is profitable to you. Use it now when you must. Protect yourself with the same knowledge later," Damian said. "Think back to each time the spirits possessed you. What were you doing?"

Valdis sank back onto the bench. He was asking her to call up her demon and make it do her bidding. She didn't think she could summon that power.

Or possessed the will to grasp and wield it.

"At the Hippodrome, I was watching the chariot race, as you were," she said. "There was nothing out of the ordinary."

"What of the other times?" Damian demanded. "Surely there were other episodes."

She nodded. "Before the *jarl's* assembly in Birka."

"Large crowds, both times then. There's one point of commonality and a press of people is something we'll find in abundance in the city. What else?"

Valdis remembered waking on the Nordic hillside, her clothing stained from thrashing on the long grass. She had no knowledge of what had befallen her and no one nearby but a flock of geese. "I was not always in a crowd."

"Then it must be something else." Damian rubbed a hand over his face. "A sound, a sight, a smell, a visitation of the falling sickness must be heralded by something. Think."

Valdis squeezed her eyes shut and tried to retrace her

steps. She was shooing the geese down the hill toward the settlement. She stopped and looked out over the distant fjord, hoping to catch a glimpse of Ragnvald's *drakar* gliding into the harbor. It was one of those unusually bright days of high summer and she raised a hand to shield her eyes from the harsh glare of sun on the water. The incoming tide made the light ripple in rhythmic pulses. A tingle shot from the top of her head down her spine.

Light?

Was it possible so small a thing could call up the beast within her?

She'd tried to banish the horrible day of her humiliation before the *jarlhof* from her mind, but now she combed that memory as well. She'd ridden in her family's wagon, lumbering into the settlement at a walk as they approached the *jarlhof.* All the *jarl's* pledge-men, their mail gleaming, were lined up on either side of the plank road as a sign of honor and welcome to Ragnvald's bride.

Her father couldn't resist showing off the speed his team could reach on solid planking instead of the spongy ruts that served as roads leading into Birka. He chirruped to the horses and they were off at a gallop, clacking over the faster surface toward the massive *jarlhof,* where Ragnvald and his father waited for them. The pledge-men's mail glinted at Valdis in repetitive flashes as she sped along. Her sister Jana giggled in delight at their speed, but the sound seemed distant to Valdis's ear.

It was her last clear memory of the day that upended her world.

Again, light.

And at the Hippodrome, just before Loki began growling his warning, the gilt spokes of the chariot wheels spun like glittering circles in her head.

Could it be? She opened her eyes and decided to test her theory. Every one in Damian's household enjoyed the fountain in the courtyard, but while Valdis liked its cheerful patter, she rarely looked at it. Now she turned her full attention on the falling water.

The crystalline drops fell in the same pattern, one always on another's heels. That would provide her the repetition she sought.

Now for the light.

Sun sparkled on the south side of the fountain. From this angle, a small star pulsed at the summit of the water's path, glinting relentlessly. Valdis stared at the point of light, wondering if so ethereal a thing might be the gateway to the falling sickness.

The men were talking in low tones and she heard Erik exclaim that if Damian truly wanted to pass Valdis off as a *seid*-woman, there was only one way. Damian seemed to be arguing with Erik, but his voice grew indistinct and muffled. Valdis couldn't understand him. Her fingertips tingled and at her hemline, Loki growled softly and nosed her ankles. She couldn't seem to tear her gaze from the dancing light. The little dog whined.

Blackness so deep it engulfed even the light of the star wrapped itself around Valdis and she knew no more.

"Now look what you've done," Erik accused as he cradled Valdis's bucking body. Her splendidly mismatched eyes rolled in their sockets, showing only the whites.

"Let her be," Damian ordered. "I want to see what she'll do."

"No, she might injure herself." Erik held her all the tighter. "Why did you drive her to this?"

Damian rubbed his hands together, barely containing his elation. "She drove herself to it, and so quickly too. Once she recovers from a fit, the superstitious will believe every word that drops from her lips."

Valdis thrashed with more violence.

"I'd believe it myself if I didn't know the sickness for what it is," Damian whispered in awe as the spell started to pass and Valdis ceased struggling. A thin ribbon of blood trickled from the corner of her mouth where she'd bitten herself. "We'd be fools not to use so powerful a weapon placed in our hands."

"She's not a weapon," Erik said. "She's a woman."

"Valdis is merely a means to an end—the further glory of the New Rome."

Damian took time from congratulating himself on his own cleverness to cast a superior sneer at Erik. "As a military man, I am surprised you do not know the value not only of covertly gathered information, but also about the spread of false information to your enemy. Valdis is the perfect conduit for both."

As her body shuddered once more, Erik decided he could think of only one enemy worth destroying: the posturing eunuch named Damian Aristarchus.

"Always know how the dice are weighted before you make your throw."
—from the secret journal of Damian Aristarchus

CHAPTER FOURTEEN

Within days of Valdis's dance with her demon, Damian Aristarchus ordered them back to Miklagard. Much to Erik's disgust, the eunuch occupied all Valdis's waking hours. While the servants packed, Aristarchus filled her head with the nonsense she must convince some poor dupe was premonition directly from the world of spirits.

By night, her door remained closed.

Erik reluctantly admitted her wisdom in the matter. He was shamed by his willingness to endanger her with another visit to her chamber, but he'd have dared it if she so much as crooked her smallest finger his way. He thought she'd witched him before; now he was certain of it.

And to his surprise, he didn't mind one bit.

During the ride back to the great city, though the eunuch's constant presence allowed them no private speech, Erik was satisfied just to be near her, to hear her voice, and to watch the play of light on her entrancing features.

To be there in case she changed her mind and decided to chance making a run with him for parts unknown.

But then the party arrived back at the Imperial Palace and Valdis disappeared into her silken gaol. Erik was summarily dismissed. Every day since, he'd made an appearance at the royal residence, demanding speech with the chief eunuch, only to be told that Damian Aristarchus was an exceedingly busy personage, but perhaps time might be made to see him later if the Varangian cared to put his request in writing. Oh! But of course a *barbaroi* couldn't be expected to be able to write out his request. So sorry. If the Varangian officer would be pleased to return on the morrow, or better yet, some time next week . . .

There was no question of him seeing Valdis. She was locked up tighter than a vestal virgin in temple of the eunuch's chambers, waiting until Aristarchus was ready to initiate his much vaunted plan. But one evening, Erik thought he caught a glimpse of her standing on the balcony, looking out over the granite heads of the Acropolis toward the blue waters of the Bosporus.

Did she regret not running away with him?

Whether she did or not, Erik could not rest, could not even report back to his commander till he knew for certain that Aristarchus would heed him in the matter they'd quarreled over before Valdis fell into that last shuddering fit. She was still bound for a zenana. That much was certain. Erik might not be able to change her fate, but he might make the tunnel she must pass through a little less dark.

It was worth a try.

That morning he decided he was done with Byzantine delaying tactics. He shoved past the first eunuch who tried to bar his way. When the distraught official called for assistance, the *tagmata* who responded turned out to be a man Erik knew from skirmishes on the practice field.

"I have business with the chief eunuch that won't wait," he explained to his fellow soldier.

"It's all right, Benedict," the *tagmata* told the fluttering eunuch. "He means no harm. If this Varangian were up to no good, your hands would already be looking for your head. Let the man pass and see to his business."

Still, the little eunuch had insisted that Erik be disarmed. Once he handed over his battle ax and gladius, Erik was escorted through the polished marble halls and down the many stairs to Damian's lair.

He pounded on the silver-plated door, and when he heard no word granting him admittance, he shoved the portal open anyway. The chief eunuch was at his desk, as he'd been when Erik was first forced into the man's service, still absorbed by the administrative documents instead of looking up to see who had just battered down his door.

"Hello, Varangian," he said without removing his gaze from his desk. Then he cast a quick glance at Erik before returning to perusing the scroll before him. "Don't look so surprised. Do you think I wouldn't know the moment you set foot on Imperial marble that you were on your way to see me? I have eyes in places you would never think to look."

"Then you know I've tried several times. Why did you refuse me?" Erik growled.

"Because as you can see, I'm a very busy man." Damian spread his hands over the paperwork on his desk. "And you have yet to report back to your commander. If I told Quintilian you've been released from my service for over a week, he'd hang you as a deserter. I've heard that Northmen put much store in the manner

of their death. What's so important that you'd risk an ig-
noble departure from this life?"

Damian indicated that Erik should sit in the chair opposite him. While he would have preferred to stand, this
was the eunuch's home ground. The engagement must
be fought under his rules. Until Erik could find a way to
change them.

"It concerns Valdis."

"I surmised as much." Damian nodded, steepling his
hands before him. "Put your mind at ease. She is content and ready to begin her new life."

"It's the manner of that life that troubles me. You still
wish to convince someone that she is a *seid*-woman, *ja?*"

Damian lifted an eyebrow in assent.

"Then you must make sure whoever takes her into
his harem is aware that in order for a *seid*-woman to
work her magic and foretell events, there are certain
requirements."

"You insist she must remain a virgin?"

"A true adept keeps herself pure to focus all her energies on spelling. As you well know, power exacts a price,
and spiritual power is even more demanding than
worldly power. If you could find another *seid* master
here in Miklagard to confirm it, he would tell you the
same." Erik was confident no *seid*-man would be found
beyond the cozy reach of his own fire in the far north.

"And yet a male *seid* practitioner does not maintain
the same virtue?"

Erik grimaced. Damian had probably looked into his
background when he first came into his service and
knew he was not above frequenting the company of
dancers and whores on occasion. "*Seid*-men are required to make other sacrifices on the altar of the powers. Besides, are not the rules for men and women
different all over the world?"

Damian snorted at that. "You have a point."

Aristarchus might be only a half-man, but Erik suspected he wouldn't change places with a woman on a bet. Unless a Byzantine woman was a member of the royal family, she had far less personal freedom than her Nordic sisters.

"Valdis may be only shamming the power, but something of *seid* must be true in order for her to be convincing." Erik pressed his advantage. "Wherever she is placed, her prescient abilities provide more opportunities to gather information than as a concubine."

"You might be surprised what a man will tell his bed partner if he's properly . . . motivated," Damian said with drollness.

"But he'll take advice from someone whose wisdom he trusts," Erik countered. "As a respected voice of counsel, Valdis can spread the misinformation you intend with far more credibility than as a bed slave."

"Valdis has received training to be an odalisque. Since she was promised freedom, she's been willing to perform in whatever capacity deemed necessary for the good of the Empire. That seems to bother you inordinately." Damian stood and crossed over to a side table that held an amphora of wine. He splashed some of the amber liquid into a silver chalice and took a sip, failing to offer any to Erik, though a second chalice stood waiting. "Why is that, I wonder?"

Erik decided to ignore the question. He stood to go. "Since you asked me to prepare Valdis to pretend to have *seid* abilities my only concern is to make sure she is as convincing as possible, both for her safety and the success of the mission. If your frustrated fixation with the bedchamber leads you to disregard my advice, so be it. When your scheme fails, don't blame me."

Erik turned and stalked toward the door, the silence behind him crackling with suppressed fury. The silver chalice clattered to the floor. Erik pivoted to face the eunuch, whose face was flushed crimson.

"I am not some whore-mongering *barbaroi* who struts about *pretending* to serve the Emperor," Damian said through clenched teeth. "Everything I do is pointed to one purpose—the glory of the Empire. How dare you imply otherwise?"

Erik inclined his head slightly. "If I wrong you, I apologize. Our goal is one and the same. And as your ally and the emperor's servant, I urge you to heed me in this matter."

Damian narrowed his eyes at Erik, searching for evidence of guile. "Very well. I agree. Whatever makes Valdis more authentic as a *seid*-woman furthers our cause. When I part with her, I will admonish her future master that she must remain pure to retain her powers."

Erik struggled to keep from showing the triumph he felt.

"But Valdis is an exceedingly comely woman," Damian said. "If her next master is minded to sacrifice her prescient abilities for her other attributes, I cannot gainsay him."

"Who are you planning to sell her to?" Erik asked.

Damian bared his teeth in a grimace that couldn't be mistaken for a smile. "That is none of your concern. Leave me now. Urgent matters require my attention. I have no further time to devote to your demands."

Erik strode toward the door with a lighter heart.

"Varangian." Damian's command stopped him. "Make certain to report to Quintilian by sundown, or I will know of it and will take steps to see you hung for dereliction of duty."

Erik pushed open the heavy argentine door. *Urgent matters require his attention, do they?* With any luck at all, sundown would give Erik plenty of time to learn where Valdis was bound.

Erik exchanged a handful of *nomismas* for a beggar's rough hooded cloak and took his station on the steps of the Hagia Sophia. From that vantage point, he could mark all who entered or exited the Imperial grounds. Once Valdis and her escort were underway, it was a small matter to blend into the press of people behind them. The plain cloak effectively rendered him of no account, but it was difficult to disguise his impressive height. Erik stooped his shoulders and bent his knees as he shuffled after Valdis and the chief eunuch.

Near the opulent public baths, Aristarchus met an acquaintance, a grossly fat, smooth-faced eunuch dressed in precious silks. The inordinate length of time Damian spent talking with animated gestures to the other eunuch convinced Erik this was no chance meeting. He settled in a doorway to keep watch.

Valdis stood, seemingly aloof, while the two men conversed. The little dog was still with her, its collar studded with more sparkling jewels than a whore might earn in a lifetime of leg spreading. Loki strained at the end of his tether, then suddenly stopped, sniffed the air and turned back to his mistress, whining in distress.

Valdis collapsed to the pavement in a convulsing heap.

"By Odin's lost eye," Erik swore softly. "The damned dog does seem to know when it's about to happen."

A crowd gathered, curious gawkers circling about the woman writhing on the ground. Erik could no longer see Valdis through all the bystanders. He fought the urge to push through the press of bodies and start knocking heads about for their thoughtless nosiness.

Then he heard her voice, weak at first, then growing stronger with each syllable. She prophesied a windfall of good fortune for someone whose name Erik didn't recognize.

Habib Ibn Mahomet.

Erik stood. He had what he needed. He saw the fat eunuch dangling a purse before Damian's face. Aristarchus waved it away and took Valdis's arm with every sign of solicitousness, leading her back toward the palace. The other man followed a few steps before giving up, but Erik heard him call out.

"If this prophecy turns out to be true, you may name your price and my master will pay."

Canny, Erik thought. Even though Damian was chomping at the bit to place Valdis in this Mahomet's household, he had arranged matters so his mark would pay handsomely for the privilege of having a spy at his side.

Erik strode toward his commander's office. Once he rounded a corner, he tossed the cloak to a scruffy-looking street child. He had no further need of disguise.

Two can play this game, Aristarchus. And I always play to win.

"Never offer up the truth when a well-crafted lie will serve."
—*from the secret journal of Damian Aristarchus*

CHAPTER FIFTEEN

The general in command of the Varangian Guard did not occupy a silver-plated, sweet-scented office like the chief eunuch. Quintilian Maximus was a soldier first and an administrator a distant second. But that didn't mean he had no head for intrigue. A man didn't rise to a position of authority within the Empire without knowing how to navigate the serpentine river of plots and counterplots.

At least that's what Erik was counting on.

He stepped into Quintilian's spartan quarters and fisted a smart salute.

"Ah, Heimdalsson," the general said. "Back from your tour of duty with the third sex, I see. About time too. That gang of ruffians of yours misses you. They nearly ran your replacement into retirement, and he's not a day over thirty. I assume you're ready to resume your duties."

Erik allowed himself a quick smile. "With a will, sir. If

ever I darken another perfumed chamber that doesn't
have a woman in it, it will be too soon."

The general guffawed. "They are an odd bunch, those
ball-less wonders, without doubt. But the Empire
wouldn't make it through a day without them. Their be-
jeweled fingers stir everyone's pot." He made a dismissive gesture. "But of all the half-men I've known,
Aristarchus is the least like a eunuch of any of them.
Still carries himself like a man, that one. I respect that."

Erik nodded his grudging agreement. "But as you say,
into everyone's business."

The general's eyes narrowed in speculation. "And
just whose business is the chief eunuch most interested in now?"

"A silk trader of all people. No one you need trouble
yourself about," Erik said, hoping Quintilian would rise
to the bait. "Now if you've no further need of me—"

"Stay a moment," his commander said. "The merchant's name. Who is he?"

Erik frowned, as if straining to call up the name.
"Habib Ibn Maho . . ."—he let the name dangle unfin-
ished for a few heartbeats—"Mahomet, I think. *Ja*, that's
it. Habib Ibn Mahomet."

Quintilian drummed his thick fingers on the desktop.
"I know of him. A leading player in guild politics. What
does the chief eunuch want with a silk merchant?"

Erik shrugged. "I doubt he's concerned about new
hangings for his apartments. After all, Aristarchus has
gone to quite a bit of trouble to insert a new informant
into the man's household."

"Has he indeed? Something big must be afoot."

"You may be right," Erik agreed, shaking his head in
disgust. "But what can we do? The armed services never
get the proper respect due us. Men of action frequently

take a poor second to others when it comes to intrigue. The chief eunuch sits like a spider in the center of a web of a thousand strands, just waiting for one of them to vibrate. It's a pity that a perfumed courtier like Damian Aristarchus will earn the gratitude of the emperor when whatever Mahomet is involved in comes to light."

The general cleared his throat with a growl. "I'm not going to let a bunch of fat aunties steal the march on the Guard. Not without a fight. You had no indication what Aristarchus suspects?"

"He's closemouthed as a corpse when it suits him."

"Then we'll have to dig up the information on our own." Quintilian leaned back and folded his arms across his beefy chest. "But time is against us. It's no easy task to buy a reliable set of ears and eyes in some places. If it's taken Aristarchus months to arrange a plan, how could we expect to accomplish it in less?"

Erik hoped the general wouldn't mark his excitement. He gave his beard a thoughtful stroke, as if trying to think up a course of action. "I suppose you could tell Mahomet that you've caught wind of an assassination plot against him. If, as you say, he's a leading man in the silk guild, such a threat has the ring of truth. Isn't it often said that men of power attract enemies like a dung pile does flies?"

Quintilian grunted his agreement with the earthy comparison. "This Mahomet can probably think of at least a handful of traders he's cheated over the years who would shed no tears over his untimely demise. Good plan. Puts him off balance. I like it. Then I could offer to place a member of the Varangian Guard in his household to oversee matters of security till we've run the plot against him to earth."

"An excellent idea, General, but you might insist

rather than offer," Erik suggested. "Couch the mandate as a mark of Imperial favor and Mahomet would be unable to refuse."

The general nodded. "An excellent plan. And I have just the man for the job."

Erik held his breath.

"You'll have to put off getting back to your cohort for a while longer, I'm afraid. A month, maybe less if you do your job quickly."

"Me? I'm no spy."

"No, you're not, which makes you perfect for this. Mahomet will never suspect there's a worm in this apple even after he takes a bite." The general dipped his stylus in the ink pot on his desk and started scratching out Erik's orders. "With your ear for languages, you'll be picking up some Arabic, I shouldn't wonder. I'll expect weekly reports, oftener if something urgent arises. Whatever you do, don't let Aristarchus realize you're there on my account."

"I doubt he'll think that." Damian would know full well Erik was there for Valdis.

"I believe your time with Aristarchus was well spent. Congratulations, Heimdalsson," the general said as he sifted sand over the parchment to set the ink on his missive. "You've learned to think like a Roman."

Erik tucked the scroll into the pouch at his waist and saluted the general. Thinking like a Roman? It wasn't a compliment he sought, but the weapon of guile fit as neatly to his hand as the handle of his ax these days. Deception wasn't a blade he felt comfortable using, but if it put him within sight of Valdis, it was a sword he was willing to sling.

Damian burst through his apartment doors rubbing his hands together with barely disguised glee. "The deed is done, Valdis," he said. "You are one step closer to freedom."

Her belly fluttered at this news. She'd been sold as Damian planned. Since the day she'd had her last public spell, she'd known this was coming. Now that it was upon her, all she could think was that she was about to enter a harem, a silk-lined prison from which few women ever emerge.

"You've agreed on a price?"

Damian smiled. "Even more than I hoped. I won't even have to dip into the emperor's treasury to pay my agents for their work in making sure your prophecy came true. Mahomet will be paying for his own windfall, so to speak."

Valdis had been instructed to predict an obscene profit for the silk merchant. Damian held up all the *dhows* bearing the luxurious fabric in specious customs inspections. All except the ones consigned to Mahomet. For a few days, the Arab trader enjoyed an effective monopoly on the cloth of choice and was able to charge exorbitant prices for his wares. Several other members of the silk guild were beggared, but Damian counted that an acceptable loss when so much was at stake.

"And what of Erik's suggestion?"

"That you remain a virgin to ensure you retain your powers? Yes, yes, he's agreed to all that even though it makes little sense to him." Damian bustled around the room brimming with nervous energy. "After all, in Habib Ibn Mahomet's homeland, as here, a woman lives to give birth to a son. The fact that you will not even have a chance to demonstrate your fertility will make you an object of pity among the other women of the zenana."

Valdis cared little for that so long as she could save herself from bedding a stranger.

There'd been no time to bid Erik farewell when he parted company with her master's entourage; no time to arrange for her to find him if she finally managed to win her freedom.

No, not *if. When,* she told herself with sternness. Nothing would interfere with that goal.

"Hurry, Valdis. You can stare into space later. You've got some packing to do." Damian directed Lentulus to gather Valdis's wardrobe into a large chest. He loaded the pots of paint and her silver comb into a smaller chest himself. "Publius is sending a sedan chair for you and he expects you to present yourself ready to go by sunset."

Valdis forced herself to rise and mechanically go about the business of packing her belongings. She realized with a start that as Damian's slave, she'd amassed an amazing cache of goods—beautiful pallas made of the sheerest silk, soft kid-soled sandals with gilt leather straps, and an amazing assortment of jewelry. She refused a nosering and Damian didn't force her, but she delighted in the tinkling earrings that dropped from her lobes, the gold bangles on her wrists and ankles and multiple rings on her fingers and toes.

It was all part of the illusion. If Valdis was to be taken for a woman of power and importance, she must dress the part. Even little Loki had been fitted out with an extravagant collar crusted with gems. She'd trained herself to stare at the flashing lights emanating from the dog's neck to bring about a spell when Damian signaled for one. So far, it had worked each time she tried.

Damian was right. Knowledge was power. She knew the trigger that caused her fits. One of them, anyway. Repetitive flashes of bright light. She hoped never to discover more, because this one was easy to avoid. Loki still seemed able to sense the onset of a seizure. He always growled and tugged at her hemline before she slipped into the abyss of the sickness.

She picked up the little dog and hugged him till he squirmed. "I will be able to take him, won't I?"

"Of course," Damian said. "I told Publius the dog was your familiar and Loki will be allowed to stay with you in the zenana. I hope you realize what a concession that was. It was almost harder than the virginity clause, because a dog is considered a dirty animal."

"Loki is cleaner than most people." Valdis dropped a quick kiss on the little dog's muzzle and set him down. "Thank you. I will be grateful for his company in a strange place."

"You won't be completely alone," Damian said. "I will still visit you. I convinced Publius that I must administer a special infusion of herbs to you each day in order for you to be able to control your powers. Since I will maintain contact with you, I suppose there was no need for you to learn to read and write Greek."

"And yet I'm glad I did," Valdis said as she picked up the leather-bound volume of poetry. She flipped the thin sheets of vellum till her eye fell on the poem Erik had recited to her.

The delights of a thousand dreams await within,
Yet I stand rooted outside your window,
trembling like a tamarind in the breeze.
Unable to move,
Unable to breathe,
Hoping for one flutter of your curtain.

Would he ever wait for her again? She put the book down.

"Take that with you, if it pleases you," Damian said.

"You mean it?" Valdis snatched the book up again. Of

all the treasures her master had heaped upon her, this book was the most precious. Costly to produce, difficult to obtain, owning a book was such a mark of wealth, even some illiterates who had amassed enough disposable income made a great show of purchasing one. "You would truly give this to me?"

Damian cast her a self-deprecating grimace. "What use do I have for love poetry? Read it to your new master, if you would like to please him. Surely Chloe has taught you that being alluring while being unobtainable is the most powerful aphrodisiac employed by womankind."

Valdis nodded. Even the stylized hand movements of the dance Chloe had taught her mimicked alternating invitation and refusal. "Come here—go away" was a persistent theme, a method of seduction all harem favorites mastered. Even though a master might take his women by force on occasion, a man of refinement such as Habib Ibn Mahomet would surely prefer at least the pretense of courtship and overcoming maidenly defenses by his own amatory skills.

"Now that I think on it, literacy in a woman is something Mahomet has yet to encounter," Damian said. "It will set you apart and place you in his confidence. Make use of it."

Valdis nodded. She would do what Damian asked. It was her only path to freedom. The only chance to be with Erik in honor instead of living as fugitives. She finished packing with efficiency.

"The sedan chair has arrived," Lentulus announced as he peered out the window.

Damian escorted her to the Imperial gates.

"I'm surprised you would see me off yourself," Valdis said as the gilded gates closed behind her for the final time.

"It is vital that Publius's servants be impressed with your importance from the outset. Begin as you mean to continue, Valdis. Let no one show you disrespect. Guard your stature in the harem as fiercely as a lioness," Damian advised in a whisper; then as he handed her into the waiting chair, he raised his voice. "I will visit you on the morrow to deliver your medicinal herbs, Valdis Ivorsdottir. Your powers have been of inestimable value to me. Go with your gods."

Damian's benediction gave her no comfort. She was entering a strange man's home under a pretext of lies with the intent to spy. Valdis doubted any of her gods would approve of the charade she was about to begin, with the possible exception of Loki, the shape-shifting trickster. And didn't the sagas teach that he will be the one responsible for the onset of *Ragnarok*, the battle at the end of the world that heralds the Doom of the Gods?

As Valdis jostled along in the sedan chair, her stomach curdled. If only the most unreliable god in the Nordic pantheon would lend his blessing to her deception, it boded ill for the entire venture. Either she must seek a different mode of life . . . or a different god.

"The falconer never knows if his training worked, till the moment he first lets the bird fly free."
—*from the secret journal of Damian Aristarchus*

CHAPTER SIXTEEN

Valdis had ridden in a sedan chair only once before, right after Damian purchased her off the auction dais, her feet still bleeding from the beating they'd taken with the bastinado and her soul in a state of profound shock. That day the bizarre city careened past her jumbled senses in swirls of color and sound that made little sense to her dazed mind. The calm man who'd bought her spoke soothingly, if unintelligibly, to her. Only his steadying presence kept her from screaming at the madness around her.

But this time Damian was not with her. She was alone in the cushioned, curtained chair, save for the small black dog on her lap, a slave borne along by four other slaves. She kept herself veiled as Damian had instructed, but she couldn't resist the opportunity to peep out of the enclosure to see where she was headed.

They trotted through the bustling market, where vendors touted their wares in strident superlatives. Exotic spices tickled Valdis's nose. Her bearers took her by way of colonnaded forums and splashing fountains, then turned off the *Mese,* the main thoroughfare, into a residential district. There was no code in the city requiring homes of a certain degree of luxury to be situated near each other. A hovel and a mansion might coexist uneasily on the same narrow street. But as her bearers started an uphill climb, Valdis noted that hovels were few in this district.

She saw a long alley curving between the white marble buildings and for just a moment, considered leaping from the chaise and making a run for it. If her feet hadn't been damaged on her last ride through Miklagard, it's what she would have done without a moment's hesitation.

Now she was wiser. Though she understood the language and had a better chance at flight than she would have had when she first stepped off the dock, Valdis knew more of the dangers, as well. Miklagard was not all showy palaces and gilt statues. It was also pox-ridden brothels and rotting tenements and opium-addicted cutpurses and thugs. The city was a large carnivorous beast that regularly ate its own young.

But she would not be one of its victims. Even though she lost her freedom, she was gaining the safety of a harem, a coveted place of preferment for many women, Chloe had told her. It still seemed a type of prison to Valdis. She looked up at the open sky. Would the first peeping stars seem different this evening once the bars of the harem swung shut behind her?

She didn't have long to puzzle over it, for suddenly they reached their destination. The chair turned under a sheltered portico and through a set of wide double doors that seemed to open for them by magic. The porter closed them behind Valdis with a resounding thud.

The silken gaol had iron bars after all.

"There you are. Finally." Damian had told her the fat eunuch who ruled Habib Ibn Mahomet's harem was called Publius. Damian regarded him as something of a fool, but he assured Valdis that Publius had a reputation for treating his charges as if he were the hen and they his chicks. He puffed up to the sedan chair and proffered his meaty hand. "Come Valdis, let's have a look at you."

He waddled around her once, making appraising noises. "Not bad," he muttered under his breath. "I've worked with far less. Let's see if we can't remove some of the road dirt before you're presented, shall we?"

He clapped his hands together and a veritable swarm of servants appeared to gather up Valdis's luggage and haul it after them.

Valdis followed the eunuch's lumbering pace with mincing steps as Chloe had instructed her. The Imperial Palace was opulent at every turn, but Mahomet's house exuded its own brand of excess. The house was a large three-story affair organized around a central courtyard garden where hibiscus bloomed around a deep pool. Vines from the roof garden tumbled down a trellis in one corner. Any unpleasant stench from the city would be smothered by the fragrance of flowers within this great house.

"You'll be on the third floor with the rest of the women," Publius said as he began the grueling process of mounting the curving stairs.

The rest of the women. Valdis drew herself up to her full height. "I'm sure the chief eunuch informed you of the requirement my power places on me."

Publius nodded and swiped the perspiration that gathered on the back of his bull-like neck. "You'll only be housed within the zenana for your protection. Rest assured, after your recent prophecy came true, your prescient abilities are uppermost in our master's mind. Nothing will be done to disturb your powers." He frowned down at Loki. "Are you certain the dog is absolutely necessary?"

Valdis picked him up and held him close. "Before each visitation from the realm of spirits, Loki announces their coming. I need his warning to prepare myself to receive their messages."

When a fit was about to claim his mistress, Loki hadn't failed to warn of its onset. After consulting with an Egyptian physician, Damian explained to her that some animals do seem to be able to sense the advent of a seizure. The doctor hypothesized that some minute change in the human's natural odor must be the reason, but Damian rejected this notion as pure fantasy. Whatever the reason, when Loki sounded his alarm, Valdis knew to lie down to avoid injuring herself in the throes of the fit.

"The dog's presence is vital," Valdis asserted. "He assists me in my congress with the spirits."

"Very well, you may keep it in your private apartments," Publius said, making the sign against evil with one hand, as if Loki were a demon instead of a small scruffy stray. "Just be sure to keep it out of the master's sight. He despises all animals except his horse."

Armed with that cryptic insight into the character of the man who now presumed to be her master, Valdis climbed the stairs behind Publius. The eunuch was panting by the time they reached the top floor.

"This is the zenana common room." He waved a flabby arm toward the spacious open area dotted with couches and ottomans. Lustrous silk draped the walls and festooned the columns. Nearly two dozen feminine faces gazed at her in open appraisal. "These are master's wives and concubines. There are too many to introduce you to right now, but they will make your acquaintance hereafter, you may be certain. You may unveil yourself here, if you wish. In accordance with our custom, you will cover your face when you are in other portions of the house."

Might as well satisfy their curiosity, Valdis thought as she reached up to lift the sheer fabric from the lower half of her face.

"How very ordinary," she heard one of the older women say. "And tall as a man. Habib Ibn Mahomet is no Roman to favor catamites and beardless young men. What's gotten into your head, Publius, to bring this ... this giantess into our midst?"

"Take no offense," Publius murmured under his breath. "Haidah is the master's oldest wife and has been out of favor for so long, no one can even remember the last time she was requested." Then he raised his voice. "Sheath your claws, Haidah. This is Valdis, the seeress you've heard so much about. She is not a member of the zenana, per se, but will be staying with you for propriety's sake as long as she bides under the master's protection."

Once it became clear that Valdis was a threat to no one, the women's expressions changed to a wide assortment of emotions ranging from disinterest to curiosity to open friendliness. But Valdis had no opportunity for conversation. Publius was already leading her away down a long balustraded corridor that was open on one side to the courtyard.

When he reached the corner, he ushered her into her own small suite of rooms. There was a sitting room with brocade cushions strewn about, a bedroom with hangings to rival the empress's own and a small adjoining bath. Even if she'd married Ragnvald back in Birka she'd never have had rooms so decadently splendid.

Still, the sense of imprisonment made her feel as if the walls were crowding in on her.

"I trust this meets with your approval," Publius said. "The master ordered that you have the best quarters the zenana offers, save for the one given to the mother of his heir, of course."

"The rooms are lovely," she answered truthfully as she wandered over to gaze out the small window that presented a view of the Hagia Sophia in the distance. The aperture was designed mostly to allow for the admittance of fresh air and was only large enough to allow her head to pass through. All the other windows opened only onto the central courtyard. Her world had become very small indeed. Then she had an inspiration. "In the Northlands, *seid*-women seek knowledge wherever it may be found. I'm sure Damian told you that in my quest for new wisdom, I am investigating the mysteries of the Christian's three-headed god. I shall require a visit to the great church yonder once a week."

Publius frowned. "The women of the zenana are followers of the Prophet."

"Ah, but as you pointed out, I am not quite one of the others, am I?" She sensed indecision in him and quickly pressed her advantage. "I'm sure your master would want me to continue to be receptive to the spiritual realm. Where better to seek such things than at the Hagia Sophia, Church of Holy Wisdom?"

"The priests there take vows of celibacy and pose no threat," he reasoned. "I suppose it could be arranged. With proper supervision, of course."

Valdis breathed an inner sigh of relief. Knowing she'd escape these walls at least once a week made her confinement feel more bearable. Until she could win her freedom with honor and fly away from this gilded cell.

"Come now." Publius pulled out a chair for her to sit before a large polished silver disc. "Let us see if we can make your appearance less jarring, shall we? Your skin is fine enough, milk-white and unmarred by blemishes, and your hair cannot fail to please due to its novelty." He pinched her arm. "What a pity Aristarchus was unable to put much flesh on your bones."

"I was not purchased for my looks," she said as she rubbed her arm.

"Assuredly not," he said without compunction. "But there's no reason not to try to improve them, especially since you'll be presented to the master this evening. He usually makes up his mind about how much time he'll spend with a girl upon the first meeting."

"I care not—"

He raised a hand to forestall her protest. "You must care. Of course, the time he'll give to you will be different from the others, but you may as well learn from the first that time spent with the master is the currency of the zenana. It determines everything, from the quality of the clothing on your back to the experience level and number of servants you are allotted. No matter how startlingly accurate your predictions, he won't want a seeress who's hard on his eyes. So sit back and let me do a little magic of my own."

Publius rifled through Valdis's cache of paint pots and rimmed her large eyes with kohl. Then, to her surprise, he darkened her pale eyebrows and even extended them with feathery strokes, so they nearly met over the bridge of her nose.

"There," he said, resting his hands on his protruding belly. "That's better. Now, can you do anything besides prognosticate?"

Valdis frowned at him, hearing implied criticism in

his question. Then she realized he meant to ask what other feminine skills she might possess. She blessed Chloe for her tutelage.

"I have been trained in the arts of an odalisque, waiting at table and leading an engaging conversation." She ticked off her accomplishments on her long slim fingers, purposely leaving off the instruction Chloe had given her in pleasuring a man. "And I can dance."

"Can you?" He seemed surprised. "A demonstration, please."

Valdis assumed the pose Chloe had taught her and closed her eyes, imagining the reedy instrument they'd danced to in Damian's mountain villa. When she opened them, she began to move, slow and sinuous, in the prescribed steps of the dance.

After a few well-executed turns, Publius stopped her with a clap of his fat hands.

"Enough. That will do," he said. "Yes, indeed, the master will be pleased. Come, Valdis. It is time. Veil yourself."

The scent of night-blooming narcissus was heavy in the air as she followed Publius back along the open corridor and through the zenana common room. All the women, their beauty enhanced by expert use of cosmetics, their competing perfumes warring in the air, were dressed in their finery as they waited to see which of them would be called to attend the master's needs, sexual or otherwise.

Only one woman kept to a corner, as if she wished to avoid the sharp piggy eyes of their keeper. But Valdis noticed her, and when the girl looked back at her there was a spark of recognition on her heart-shaped face.

It was the Frankish girl who'd lost her twin on the slave caïque to Miklagard. The girl opened her mouth to call a greeting, then seemed to think better of it and turned away.

After Valdis met her new master, she'd seek out her old shipmate. In this strange place, they could both use a friend.

"I wonder if a flute-maker resents turning over his fine creation to be played by another. And as often as not, played badly."
—from the secret journal of Damian Aristarchus

CHAPTER SEVENTEEN

"Now, in order to truly impress the master, this is how you must proceed." Publius stopped outside the entrance to the dining hall, where given the sounds of music and male conversation, Valdis guessed there was a small banquet in progress. "I will go in and announce you. When the music begins again, you will enter the master's presence with the dance."

Valdis nodded. The prescribed movements would relax her and make this meeting easier. She smiled at Publius. He really seemed to be trying to smooth matters for her. So far, he'd shown no sign of being the fool Damian asserted he was.

Publius turned to go, then stopped short. "Oh! The master has dinner guests tonight."

"I guessed as much from the noise," Valdis said.

"Even though there will be many eyes upon you, be careful only to direct your fondest gaze at the master," Publius warned. "Habib Ibn Mahomet will not tolerate a woman with wayward eyes, not even if she is a sooth-sayer extraordinaire."

"Very well. How will I know which one is the master?" Valdis asked. "I have never seen him before."

"You are a seeress," Publius said, drawing his darkened brows together. "The master expects you to know him by your art. He was very particular on that point. You may look at each of the men in the room for a moment, then once you have located the master, you are to dance as if he is the only man in the room. Surely it will be no trouble at all for you to divine his identity with but a look, and what a triumph for me when you do."

"How is that a triumph for you?" She felt the blood drain from her head and forced herself to draw a deep breath.

"It was I who suggested you be given the opportunity to publicly display your abilities before his guests and the master devised this small demonstration, with my prompting. No need to thank me now. You may show your appreciation later."

"But you don't understand," Valdis said in a panic. "That's not how *seid* craft works. It's not as if I can summon up a message from the spirit world. It comes when it will or not at all."

"If that's the case, don't despair. The master will always welcome another comely maiden into his embrace. But if you wish to retain the virginity that feeds your power, well, hope that the spirits speak with you now." Publius cocked his head to listen. "Oh! There's a lull in the music. A perfect time for me to announce you. Now, dance beautifully, Valdis and all will be well. See to it you do not disgrace me."

The eunuch left her speechless in the hallway. Damian was right. Publius was indeed a fool, but there were clearly no soft edges on her new master. Habib Ibn Mahomet wasn't fully convinced by the fortuitous profits she'd predicted for him. He meant to test her.

If failure only meant she'd be sent back to Damian as a fraud, she'd take her chances with the chief eunuch's displeasure. But the thought that Mahomet might decide to keep her to use as his odalisque rather than admit he'd been taken in by a cunning plot made Valdis's belly churn with distaste. How in all the nine worlds could she be expected to do this?

A pair of flutes played, accompanied by a shimmer of percussion and a steady sensual beat. Valdis drew a deep breath to steady herself. Ready or not, the music beckoned her to make her entrance. Somehow, she must try to identify Mahomet or be exposed as a sham before she even began her secret life as Damian's informer.

She entered the room without looking around, her gaze affixed to the polished floor a step or two ahead of her own light tread. When she reached the spot she judged to be the center, she lifted her arm to provide an additional veil for her face and let the sinuous music translate itself into the undulations of her body. She turned a slow circle, rising on the ball of her left foot, her arms extended palms up as though she held a full platter balanced on each hand. As she pivoted, she took in the seven men seated cross-legged on cushions about the room. The conversation died as her dance captured their attention.

A turbaned fellow was seated dead center along the eastern wall. The plumper cushion beneath him raised him a hand's width higher than his companions. Surely Habib Ibn Mahomet wouldn't seat himself in a place of honor and then set the puzzle of his identity before her. Or would he expect her to discount the obvious and therefore, hide in the most obvious spot?

Her head spun at the labyrinthine trail her thoughts must travel.

At that man's elbow, there was servant—a lean, hawkish man with a raptor's glint in his dark eyes. A tingle of recognition fingered over her spine, but she couldn't place him. Perhaps his had been one of the many faces gawking at her on the slave dais when she first arrived in Miklagard. She need waste no time on a servant, but it bothered her that she couldn't remember where she'd seen him.

She allowed her gaze to move to the man's right as she started a grapevine pattern with her feet. While alternating her steps forward and back, her long arms first issued a stylized invitation and then held up a palm in rejection.

One of the guests was a Nubian who flashed his blindingly white teeth at her. She resisted the urge to smile back at the man, because he was clearly not her new master. She knew Habib Ibn Mahomet was a son of the Prophet from Cordoba. She could safely eliminate the Nubian from consideration as well as the beardless young man with pale skin at his side.

The third fellow on the southern side of the room was a Greek with clipped bangs curled across his forehead. Unless Mahomet was a true master of disguise, she could forgo putting this man on the list of potential candidates.

Valdis executed a graceful turn to grapevine her way back along the northern side, but she nearly stumbled when she got a clear look at the man seated at the end of the row of diners.

It was Erik.

Bold as brass, he lifted a goblet of pomegranate juice and pledged her over the red-stained rim.

Valdis jerked her gaze from him. *What is he doing*

here? She forced herself to concentrate on the steps, to point her toes whenever a foot left the floor, to tuck her thumbs to present her hands in the most flattering light, as Chloe had taught her. Valdis fought to draw a breath and sneaked another glance just to be sure she hadn't imagined him.

Erik raised one pale eyebrow at her.

She often wished to dance for Erik, but not like this, not when her path to freedom hung in the balance. He met her gaze squarely, then flicked his eyes toward the raised cushions. On Erik's left, nearer the seat of honor, were two men, either of whom might be Habib Ibn Mahomet. They were both brown-skinned, as Valdis imagined her new master would be. They wore garish, striped silk trousers in the baggy Arabic style. Winking gems encrusted their fingers, proclaiming their wealth.

Was Erik trying to tell her one of them was her new master?

The one nearest Erik had a scraggly scarlet beard and narrow eyes. Valdis suppressed a shudder and glanced at the next man. He was portly as a eunuch, but the naked desire on his face made her dismiss that notion immediately. If this man were her new master, whether she possessed *seid* powers or not, she doubted anything would trump his lust.

She turned on her toes and began drawing circles with her hips, large slow ones at first, then spiraling down to small and fast. Valdis closed her eyes, weighing her options. The pompous fellow on the tall cushion, the scarlet-bearded gent, or the lecher. What a miserable choice. She forced her lips into an enigmatic smile, as Chloe had advised, even though her face felt brittle enough to crack like Frankish glass.

What had Erik tried to tell her with his darting glance? She peeped from between her lashes at the man on the cushion, and as she continued to spin, she caught the flash of a ring. But it wasn't on the turbaned man's hand. It was on the hand of the servant at his side. The piece was a heavy one, spreading from the base of the servant's forefinger to the first knuckle. She'd swear it was a signet ring, a ring of power and prestige, the seal of a man's will and symbol of his authority. It was similar to the one Damian never removed from his hand.

Her eyes flew open wide. She looked the servant full in the face. Heavy dark brows frowned above deep-set eyes and an elegantly crooked nose was set above an unsmiling mouth. Even though his dark beard was shot with silver, it was a proud, fierce, dangerously attractive face. With a shock, she remembered where she'd seen it before.

Through Erik's strange ocular device at the Hippodrome. Wasn't this servant one of the two men Damian asked her to describe as she observed them in their opulent box? But the man wasn't dressed as a servant that day. He was the confidant of the emperor's nephew.

So this was Habib Ibn Mahomet.

She smiled in earnest now and never let her gaze stray from the man she supposed to be her new master. As she began the dizzying twirls that ended her dance, she used his face as her touch point to retain her balance and keep from becoming disoriented by the final whirling moments of the dance.

Faster and faster, she spun until the music climbed to a fever pitch. On the final note, Valdis collapsed into a graceful bow, one leg tucked beneath her, the other extended as she bent down to touch her forehead to her knee. She let her veil flutter to the ground around her as her toe pointed to the servant she suspected was really Mahomet.

The men pounded the floor with their palms in appreciation, but Valdis didn't move. She tried to settle her pounding heart. If she were wrong, she'd just confused her new master with a servant, an unmistakable insult.

Habib Ibn Mahomet did not have a reputation for forgiving slights.

When she lifted her head, the servant had not moved a muscle.

Valdis gritted her teeth and determined to brazen it out. She rose to her full height and looked him squarely in the eye. "Have I the pleasure of addressing Habib Ibn Mahomet?"

The man's cheek ticked and a grudging smile tugged at the corners of this thin-lipped mouth. "You have," he said as he gave the man sitting on the raised cushion a swift kick. "Back to the kitchens with you, Ibrahim. You failed to present a convincing decoy."

The man on the cushion scrambled to his knees and pressed his forehead to the floor. "A thousand pardons, my master. Your poor servant is unequal to the mighty task of impersonating so great a man as yourself. Please don't send me from the light of your presence, lest the sun grow dark in my eyes."

"Very well," Mahomet said. "You may remain as my valet and butler, but see that you look well to your duties."

The servant raised himself to his feet, quickly stripping off the fine silk outer tunic he'd donned for the deception. He held the garment for Habib to slip into.

"Fool!" Mahomet backhanded the groveling servant's cheek and Valdis flinched in sympathy. A slap was the most demeaning insult one could offer in the Northlands. "Have that cleaned before I wear it again. Better yet, burn it."

Satisfied he'd chastised his valet enough, Mahomet settled onto the cushion and turned his attention back to Valdis. He studied her frankly for several moments before speaking. "You are too tall for a woman."

"Where I come from, the men grow like mighty trees," she said with poetic license. "Such towering men must come from tall women."

He weighed this reasoning for a moment. " 'Tis a failing easily remedied. Sit beside me, Valdis Ivorsdottir," Habib Ibn Mahomet said, the harsh syllables of her name clearly grating his tongue. He motioned to a spot on the thick carpet that edged the room. She settled next to his cushion, the difference in their seating guaranteeing her head was a good bit lower than his. "It's a good thing you dance well; otherwise, I'd have to shorten you by cutting off your feet."

He laughed, but Valdis wasn't convinced he was joking. His ruthlessness was not confined to the marketplace. Damian had warned her of his temper. So far, Habib Ibn Mahomet lived up to his reputation as a dangerous man.

"So, by your dark arts you divined my true identity?"

In the interest of peace, Valdis could have agreed with him, but then he might expect even more outlandish displays of prescience. The truth, leavened with a bit of flattery, would serve her better now.

"Alas, my power to see into the mists of the unknowable is not one I can conjure at will," she said. "I deduced you were master here by simple observation. A servant's garb could not obliterate your aura of authority."

"Then it seems those unusual eyes of yours see quite well enough without the benefit of additional Sight." He dropped his voice so only she could hear him as the reedy music resumed. "Observe then, my seeress, and tell me what you divine in each of my dinner companions."

Valdis glanced down the row of diners and began

with a safe guess. "The Nubian is a trading partner of yours, is he not?"

Mahomet nodded and raised his goblet to drink.

"He is as he appears—a man in whom there is no guile," Valdis said, deciding to reward the man for his open smile. "He will drive a hard bargain, but he will not cheat you."

Habib grunted his agreement.

Valdis studied the man beside the Nubian. "The young man next to him has traveled far to reach the great city," Valdis finally said.

"How can you know that?"

"The tops of his sandals are freshly gilded, but the soles are thin and worn. Judging by his clothing, I would say he is a son of wealth, possibly Frankish," she added when she noticed the unique embroidery at the man's cuffs. She'd seen similar ornamentation on the Frankish twin's clothing.

"Remarkable," Mahomet said. "He is indeed a Frank. He claims to be a glass dealer wanting to establish a trading link between his house and mine, but I don't trust him. What is his true business in my home?"

"It would require a visitation of the spirit world for me to know that, master," she said with a deferential nod. It was strange that in all the time she was under Damian's roof, he never made her feel a slave as this man did. She knew she must tread carefully or Mahomet would do her harm. The steely glint in his dark eyes warned of black rages, and she'd already seen him debase his valet before dinner guests. After his comment about cutting off her feet, she'd decided it would be unwise to stretch to her full height in his presence again. He was a man without limits. Who knew what he might do to a woman who displeased him?

"Seek such a visitation then and be quick about it," he grumbled.

"Alas, the spirit world summons me, not the other way around, but," she hastened to add, "I will attempt to discover this Frank's motives for you."

Surely Damian had someone he could order to spy upon the fellow and find out if his interest in Mahomet was truly just trade. She'd ask Aristarchus tomorrow when he brought her "medicinal herbs."

Her promise seemed to pacify Mahomet, and she saw his razor-sharp gaze cut to the Greek at the end of the row.

"The Greek is not a man of great stature, but he has the ear of one, else he would not be dining with you." Before he could ask how she knew this, she explained, "If he himself were a man of importance, he would be seated near you."

Mahomet nodded sagely. "And the others?"

Valdis glanced at the remaining guests and then leaned toward Mahomet to speak. "The fat fellow's gods are his belly and his purse. Fatten either and he is your friend . . . until he finds someone who offers him more."

"And what can you tell me of Achmed Ibn Abdullah?" Mahomet inclined his head toward the man with the scarlet beard. The gentleman in question acknowledged the gesture with a pinched smile.

Valdis decided to let her personal distaste for this man taint her characterization of him. If she wronged him, she would never know, but every strand of intuition she possessed quivered violently whenever she looked at Achmed Ibn Abdullah.

"That one has the look of a dog-fox," Valdis said. "It is said that Loki, our trickster godling, takes the form of a fox when he wishes to outwit someone. This man may profess to love you, but look to your back."

"This I have suspected for some time. You merely confirm my thoughts on the matter." Mahomet took a sip from his iced goblet. "And the Varangian, a countryman of yours, I gather? I would know his true purpose. What do you see in him?"

The man I could love till I am but dust on the waves, almost leapt to her lips. She allowed herself a quick glance at Erik. How had he managed to attach himself to Mahomet's household so quickly?

Once again, only the truth would serve. She suspected Habib Ibn Mahomet had not advanced so far in business and politics without being able to scent a lie.

"The Varangian is here to protect someone." She didn't add that the someone was herself.

"You have hit the mark squarely," Mahomet said. "Perhaps you have the ability to call upon your familiar spirits more often than you realize. Such acute perception is power in itself. I definitely have use for someone with your talents." He popped a ripe olive into his mouth and chewed it slowly, as if ruminating on Valdis's revelations. "Publius has pleased me greatly by acquiring you. I will instruct him to accord you all honor available to a woman of the zenana. Welcome to my humble household. You may retire now."

Summarily dismissed, Valdis rose in a fluid motion.

"Valdis of the North, you would do well to remember this," Mahomet warned. "I reward with a lavish hand all who please me. And with an equally lavish hand, I punish those who do not."

"I will remember, master," she said with a bow. She walked from the room, conscious of the many pairs of male eyes intent on every swish of silk.

She didn't dare a parting glance at Erik, but felt the

heat of his gaze anyway. Even though they breathed the same air, he was as unreachable as if he were back in the Northlands.

How would she bear knowing he was within the same marble walls?

"Distraction is the most frequent cause of failure."
—from the secret journal of Damian Aristarchus

CHAPTER EIGHTEEN

"Ask whatever you will of me and I will happily comply." Publius positively preened over Valdis's successful debut with his master. "What will you have?"

She wanted her freedom, but knew his effusiveness would only extend so far. Publius had been a slave since he was gelded, which Damian told her was fairly early in his life. He probably wouldn't even understand her desire to own herself.

"Come, my dear, don't be shy. Would you like some special delicacy? An iced drink perhaps?"

Valdis recognized this as an enormous mark of favor. Ice was decadently expensive, shipped overland from the mountains in straw-packed crates in a race against time. But to a daughter of the North, ice was only a reminder of the bitterness of winter.

"Just bring me what the other women are having," Valdis said. Special treatment would breed resentment among the inhabitants of the zenana and she might need all the friends she could cultivate behind these gilded bars.

She was surprised when Habib Ibn Mahomet sent her away after her success without offering her even a mouthful of his sumptuous banquet. Publius explained that occasionally the master dined alone with one of his wives or concubines, but the women of the zenana never ate before other male guests.

"A woman unveiled and placing items in her mouth, of all unseemly things!" Publius was horrified when she mentioned it. "Such a sight might so enflame a man's passions that he could not be held responsible for his actions even if he insulted his host by ravishing the brazen woman on the spot."

Perhaps her tutelage in the carnal arts wasn't as complete as she imagined. If seeing a woman eat was all it took to render a man incapable of self-control, Valdis thought the men who visited Mahomet's household too easily roused.

Publius left her, promising to see to her supper with his own hands. He wasn't gone more than a few heartbeats when Valdis heard a timid rap on her door.

It was the Frankish girl.

"Oh, it is you!" she said in heavily accented Greek. "I thought so, but feared my mind was playing tricks on me again. Do you remember me? We were sold together. Our captors wouldn't let us speak much when they brought us to this horrid city, but you were ever kind to me and . . . my sister."

"Come in," Valdis said, before anyone could mark that she and the Frank appeared to know each other. "I'm called Valdis Ivorsdottir."

"Of course, first things first. I am Landina. There is no need to give you my full title. Such things are of no import in this house." The Frank made nervous fluttering motions with her hands as she spoke, as if she feared her words might go astray and she must be ready to catch them. "My sister and I always spoke of you as the Norse princess since we did not know your name."

Her heart-shaped face puckered into an expression of such sadness, Valdis felt tears prick at her own eyes in empathy.

"Valdis," Landina said, letting the name settle on her tongue. "How did you come to this terrible place?"

Valdis couldn't very well tell the Frank she'd been carefully placed in this zenana by a Byzantine spymaster, so she deflected the question with one of her own. "What makes it so terrible?"

A guarded look came into Landina's emerald eyes. "You have not been here long enough or you would not ask."

"So far, I have been treated with respect. My room is sumptuous, far grander than anything I might have aspired to in my own country." Damian had warned her to trust no one. If the girl had been sent to spy for signs of discontent, Valdis would give her nothing to report. "You are well-clothed and look like you've gained flesh since I last saw you, so they must feed you well." Valdis took the girl's hand and led her into her sitting room. "What has happened to you here to render you so unhappy?"

"You have not yet been called to serve the monster who calls himself our master. At least not in his bedchamber," Landina said with bitterness. "He has what that fat lout, Publius, calls 'particular tastes.' With each of the women in his harem, Habib Ibn Mahomet—may he writhe in the hottest flames of Hell—indulges in a different perversion."

Landina slipped her tunic off one delicate shoulder and turned to bare her back to Valdis. The girl's pale skin was crisscrossed with tiny welts and barely healed narrow scars.

"As you can see, he uses me to assuage his need to inflict pain." Landina covered herself again and Valdis noticed for the first time the network of tiny lines that had gathered at the corners of the girl's eyes and mouth. Habib Ibn Mahomet may have been careful to whip the girl only where the scars would not show, but the bitterness of her degradation left a mark of its own.

"I suppose I should count myself lucky," Landina went on. "Poor Fatima had all her teeth yanked out, lest she accidentally graze his member with a tooth. Have you any idea why Publius acquired you?"

Valdis explained the carefully rehearsed recital of her supposed powers. Landina looked suitably impressed and Valdis didn't doubt the tale would grow with each telling as it circulated in the zenana.

"Then you are of all women most fortunate," Landina said. "My only hope is in my memories, and those have become so real to me, I fear for my mind sometimes. Do you know, I actually thought I saw Bernard in the courtyard earlier today?"

"Who is he?"

"The young man I was betrothed to in my own country." Landina wandered toward the couch. She wore a long tunic over baggy pantalets gathered at the ankle. A gauzy slitted skirt covered the pantalets, yet allowed them to peep out with each step the girl took. Landina draped herself on a couch and spread the silk skirts to cover her delicate ankles as she tucked up her tiny feet. "If I had not been abducted by those Moorish pirates, I would be married, probably a mother happily made, by now."

"What did your young man look like?"

"He was tall—oh, not as your people count tallness—

but among we Franks he stood out well enough. His eyes were amber brown, the windows to a good soul, I always thought. His hair was a ruddy hue, like a maple leaf in autumn."

She described the pale fellow dining next to the Nubian down to the eyelash. "And you thought you saw him today?"

"Yes, when I chanced to peep out the window of the common room this afternoon, shortly before you came. A man who resembled Bernard dismounted and walked across the courtyard. He moved just as I remember him, confident and swift." Landina's mouth tightened into a thin line. "You see now why I had to come to your room. Twice today, I thought myself visited by a ghost from my past and I had to see if it truly was you or if my mind was leaving me."

"There is nothing wrong with your mind," Valdis said. "Sometimes we all see what we most wish to see, whether it is there or not." Valdis decided not to tell her Bernard was actually here till she was certain of it. The Frank at Mahomet's table might be just a trader as he'd claimed.

But if Bernard was in Mahomet's house, the danger to Landina increased tenfold. If their master beat her merely for pleasure, what would he do if he found her with a lover?

"Whether it is seemly or not, Publius, I must take Loki out from time to time," Valdis argued. "He is well-trained, but I'm sure you don't wish to clean up after a dog in this lovely room."

"But—"

"You may accompany me if you wish, though I hardly think seeing to a dog's toilet is appropriate for one of your stature."

"Certainly not," Publius said with distaste. He puffed his flabby chest out like a pigeon. "One of the pages can take the beast out."

"Loki is accustomed to me, and as you know, this little dog and I are linked by my special powers, which have so endeared you to your master." Valdis stooped down and attached a slender leash to Loki's collar. "I must go with him into the courtyard whenever possible. Be assured, I will remain veiled and will conduct myself with the utmost decorum."

Publius frowned.

"It would be a terrible shame if my powers of divination were to diminish because I had not spent enough time with my familiar," Valdis said. "Besides, it is dark enough now—who will even know Loki and I have visited the garden?"

Publius said nothing, obviously wavering. He waddled to the large open window and peered into the empty courtyard.

"You did tell me to ask for whatever I wish," she said, pressing her advantage.

"It's not as though you are one of the master's concubines, I suppose. Very well, go. But go veiled and go quietly." He grasped her arm with a grip that was surprisingly strong for one with such a soft-looking countenance. "But if you cause me a moment's concern I will see you whipped, Valdis. Don't think I won't."

"I will return before you know I am gone." She slipped a dark cloak over her light palla and adjusted her veil to cover the lower half of her face.

Valdis padded swiftly along the open corridor. The women of the zenana had retired for the night, except for the chosen one. From the master's chambers on the second level, she heard the sounds of a woman wailing and pleading in what struck Valdis's ears as feigned passion. If the woman indulged in harlot's tricks, Valdis couldn't fault her for it. The women of the zenana did what they must to survive.

As Valdis crept down the steps to the lowest level, her soft-soled slippers made no noise on the polished marble, but Loki's claws clicked a pattering rhythm as they descended. She made a mental note to trim them lest she lose this privilege. Being allowed to leave the third floor on her own was a breath of freedom, a small taste of what she so earnestly desired.

She found a sheltered alcove near the deep pool and settled on a stone bench to watch Loki investigate the flowerbed in the moonlight. The air was heavy with the scent of lotus blossoms and Valdis breathed deeply, taking pleasure in the moment, as Chloe had advised.

The thought of pleasure inevitably led to Erik and she wondered if he were merely a dinner guest or if the big Northman was still within these walls. And if he were here, which of the rooms in Mahomet's stately house had been allotted to him?

Suddenly, the shrubbery near her cursed. Loki scurried away from it to huddle by her ankles.

Erik pushed through the hedge to stand before her. "That damn dog finally succeeded in pissing on my boots."

Valdis covered her mouth to stifle her giggle.

"It's not funny."

"No," she agreed, choking on a laugh. "It's not."

"Single-minded little bugger." She heard his low chuckle. She joined him. After the stress of her first day in Mahomet's house, she needed to laugh.

He put a finger to his lips, then took her into his arms. Slowly he unhooked her veil from behind her ear. He traced her lower lip with his fingertips, sending shivers of anticipation over her. He pressed fevered kisses up

the side of her neck and finally claimed her mouth as
his possession. Pleasure washed over her. Her whole
being thrummed with life. If they died for it, she
wouldn't have broken off this kiss for all the nine worlds.

"I'm sorry, Valdis," Erik whispered when he finally released her lips. "I shouldn't endanger you this way, but I
can't help myself."

"Me neither," she mouthed into his ear. "But what are
you doing here? How did you manage to insinuate yourself into this household?"

"The same as you. By guile," Erik said. "But if that
hadn't worked, I'd have swum in from the river Lycus to
this pool through the underground conduit."

"The river is a good distance from here. You'd drown."

"I'm a strong swimmer, Valdis. Back in the North, I
could hold my breath longer than any other man in
Hordaland." A grin creased his face, a perfect match for
this boyish braggadocio. Then the grin dissolved into
dead seriousness. "There's nothing I wouldn't dare to be
near you."

Loki whimpered softly and Erik released her. Usually,
the little dog growled at Erik, but after urinating on his
boots, Loki wasn't about to push his luck. He'd let Erik
into the alcove with his mistress without a sound. Now
the dog was looking in the direction of the main gate.
Valdis froze.

In the dark alcove, she and Erik were all but invisible,
but they had a clear view of the rest of the courtyard.
The Greek Valdis had seen at Mahomet's dinner was being helped onto the back of a small donkey. The man
was weaving, obviously the worse for something far
stronger than pomegranate juice.

"My imperial frien . . . friend will be grateful," he
said, his words slurring. The massive gates creaked
open to allow him to depart. A link boy with a torch to

light his way across the city stood waiting to lead his donkey home.

"And your friend will be even more grateful if you keep your teeth together," a gruff voice said.

Valdis didn't recognize the speaker, but Erik did.

"Barak, head of security for Mahomet," Erik whispered. "Till I came."

As the *clip-clop* of the donkey's hooves faded, Barak signaled one of his underlings. "Follow that Greek fool and see that he does not reach his home this night. Kill the link boy too. Better yet, run ahead of him and lie in wait at his home. It will appear he interrupted a robbery. We want no true tales spread to Leo. Don't return until it is done."

"Why the boy?"

"You do not question me. Just do as I say. Now go."

Valdis gasped a breath. She'd known she was going into a dangerous situation when she entered this household, but the casual bloodthirstiness in Barak's order was still a shock.

"Wait here, till I draw them away." Erik pulled her close and whispered into her ear. "Which room is yours?"

She pointed to her corner apartment, where sturdy vines rose from the courtyard to the roof garden.

He smiled. "I think that trellis will hold me."

"We shouldn't meet again like this," she said, still shaken by Barak's murderous order.

"Leave a runic message here on this bench, then. I must know how it is with you."

"I will," she promised. "Oh! Find out what you can about the Frank who dined with you tonight."

"Why?"

"There is someone in the zenana who wants to know. His name will do for a start."

"That I can already give you. Bernard of Cologne. He is a trader of glassware seeking an alliance with Mahomet."

"That's not all he's seeking," Valdis said. "His betrothed is an odalisque in Mahomet's harem."

"Then he and I have much in common," Erik said with a grin. "I shall have to see what I can do to help him."

Barak turned and seemed to look right at them. Valdis knew the darkness hid her from his sight, but his eyes blazed feral in the night like a wolf's. He cocked his head as if straining for a sound, something that would betray her.

Fortunately Loki crouched by her ankles and would not move. The dog must have sensed her trepidation.

Then Barak turned away and cast his gaze along the roof of the villa.

"Wait till all is clear," Erik said, pressing a kiss into her open palm. "I'll distract the guard for a bit, then I'll find a secret way out of this house."

"Where are you going?"

"To stop a murder."

He moved away with amazing stealth for a man of his size. He was silent as a cat when he wished to be. If Valdis hadn't known it was Erik in the garden, she'd have thought it was merely the soughing of the night breeze that rustled the greenery.

"Ho, Barak," Erik said loudly from the far end of the courtyard. "Near the second watch and you still haven't found your bed?"

Valdis couldn't make out the grumbling reply, but the man took several steps toward Erik.

"Since neither of us is sleepy, now's as good a time as any for you to show me the provisions for security you have made," she heard Erik suggest. "We both want the same thing, after all. Continued safety for your master."

Couched in that language, it was a request Barak

couldn't refuse, and he wandered off with Erik to inspect the perimeter safeguards.

Valdis scooped Loki in her arms and made a dash for the stairway. She crept up to the third floor, her heart hammering against her ribs. She and Erik were walking a knife's edge with disaster looming on either side.

And she saw no way to stop.

"Who we are when no one sees is who we really are."
—*from the secret journal of Damian Aristarchus*

CHAPTER NINETEEN

Erik disentangled himself from Barak with very little effort. The man really wanted nothing to do with a Varangian interloper. But finding a way out of Habib Ibn Mahomet's house other than through the large front gate proved a more difficult problem. He finally managed to wiggle out the chute in the kitchen, the one used to deliver charcoal for the braziers that would chase away the winter chill.

He had a pretty good idea where the Greek was heading and he doubted it was to his own home. Erik had met the man once before on a hunting outing with the emperor for which Erik's cohort provided security. The man's name was Marcus Trophimus, chief advisor to the emperor's young niece, Zoe. The girl was another hopeful heiress in the making, one the Empire recognized as "purple-born." Trophimus was obviously looking for supporters for Zoe's claim once the unthinkable happened and Basil the Bulgar-Slayer was no more.

Marcus Trophimus would not go directly to his own

home, but to Zoe's sumptuous quarters in the Palatine district. Erik's first impression of the man was that Trophimus was a capable bureaucrat, if devious in typical Byzantine fashion. He hoped the Greek wasn't as drunk as he'd seemed.

Erik was relieved to find the link boy and the donkey waiting outside the would-be empress's palace.

"You there, boy," Erik called softly as he approached.

The child startled and lifted the torch as high as his thin arm could reach. "Please don't take the donkey, sir. It belongs to my fare and he'll beat me if it's gone when he returns."

In the amber torchlight, Erik could see the child was gaunt to the point of starvation and much older than Erik first judged him based on his diminutive height.

Poor food makes a poor boy, Erik thought. But at least this child was still alive, and if Erik had anything to say about it, would remain so for at least another night. Miklagard teemed with these discarded little souls, abandoned by their families or orphaned. They were tossed into the streets to fight for scraps or sell their young bodies for a thin silver coin. The most enterprising of them served as link boys, lighting the way for well-born night travelers across the dark city. Erik admired the lad's pluckiness.

"I don't want your donkey." He took a bezant from his pouch and flipped it in the air. The boy's eyes gleamed as he tracked the coin's flight. Erik caught it and then held it out to him. "I want to give this bezant to the boy who can deliver a message and convince the man you led here to heed it."

"I can do that." The boy fairly danced with excitement.

Erik suspected a whole bezant would feed this urchin and twelve of his ragged friends for a month.

"What's the message, General?"

Erik resisted the appeal of this blatant flattery. "Tell Marcus Trophimus not to look to the follower of the Prophet for support. Death waits at Trophimus's home this night. He must lodge in the Xenon of Theophilus if he wishes to see morning. Go with him, boy, for Death has marked you as well."

The child's eyes grew round as an owl's.

"Can you remember that?" Erik asked.

When the boy repeated the message word for word, Erik tossed him the coin and turned to go. "Show him the coin and he'll take you seriously."

"But who shall I tell him gave me the message?"

"Tell him it was one of the emperor's pledge-men. A Varangian." On a whim, Erik added, "Haukon Gottricks-son."

It would do Hauk no harm since when Erik last heard his friend was fighting the Saracens in faraway Antioch. And Hauk's name would muddy the waters if by chance the boy was grilled by inquisitors later.

"Don't fail me, lad." Erik turned and disappeared into the blackness of the city's narrow alleys.

The moon dropped behind the largest of Miklagard's seven hills so only pinpricks of stars lit his way. Erik followed the map he carried in his head of the twisted byways until he came to the street where Marcus Trophimus's home sprawled in grandeur, dwarfing his neighbors on both sides.

Erik crouched in the shadows, trying to locate the would-be assassin. Anger raced in his veins. If it had only been Trophimus, Erik might have let the Greek courtier take his chances. After all, the question of who would sit on the Byzantine throne after the Bulgar-Slayer was none of his business.

But what kind of scum lies in wait to kill a child?

As his gaze made a second circuit of the area, it

struck him that he too was an assassin this night. The only difference between him and the man he intended to kill was motive. One wanted to take two lives. One wanted to protect them.

Erik had already accepted the label of "murderer." His brother's death grated his soul every day, even though he still had no clear recollection of the actual deed. The *berserkr* rage often left a warrior with holes in his memory. He supposed that was a mercy.

Battle deaths were the easiest to dismiss. In a melee, the only law was kill or be killed. Though *murderer* was branded on his heart, Erik had yet to kill someone by stealth. But tonight, if he issued a defiance and a fight ensued, the noise might rouse the neighbors or the servants of the household. Even if he killed the man, how could he explain what he'd done without compromising his covert position in Mahomet's household? And if the assassin proved a worthy opponent and Erik was sent to Valhalla, what would become of Valdis?

No, he couldn't think on her. If a man pondered what he might lose, he'd never chance a sea voyage, never raise a sword even in defense of right. He must concentrate on the business at hand.

A rustle from the vine-covered pergola in the side yard of Trophimus's estate drew Erik's attention. A flash of metal gleamed. He'd located his foe.

He moved with care, approaching from behind without a sound. He was not a murderer, he reasoned, but an executioner. If a lawspeaker were here, would this man not be condemned?

The man stood in the shadows of the pergola, waiting to kill a boy and a man whom he believed were in no state to defend themselves. And if he didn't kill them this night, he'd get them the next. His quarry only had to be unlucky once. Surely the assassin deserved no mercy, no quarter. He certainly would offer none.

Erik was close enough to hear the man's breathing, to smell his stale sweat. Close enough to slip his gladius through the grape vines and pierce the man's ribs before he even knew Erik was there. One thrust and it would be done.

Erik started to draw his blade.

And found he couldn't do it. His arm was too heavy to lift to kill by stealth.

No, he decided. Even if he died for it, he would take the risk. In his time of exile, he'd rebuilt his tattered honor into a covering his soul could live with. How could he shred that fragile integrity now with a calculated murder?

He purposely stepped on a dry vine. The crackling sound brought the man in the arbor to full alert. Erik wished suddenly for his battle ax. Its smooth handle always felt more comfortable in his big hand than a Roman short sword, but he'd taken to carrying the gladius when he was in the city.

No point it stewing over it now. It was past the time for worrying over his choice of weapons. He was already committed to this course and he must see it to its end.

The man moved from his hiding place into the open. His blade was already drawn. Even in the dim starlight, the sinuously curved blade glinted a warning.

Erik moved forward, his gladius flashing quickly from his scabbard, but the other man met it with his blade. The sharp edges grated as the men tested each other's strength. Erik was surprised by the resistance in the assassin's sword arm and had to leap backward when the man swiped at his midsection with a second blade.

Erik sidestepped, looking for an advantage. His opponent countered each move, his dark eyes slitted in concentration. At least the man hadn't cried out, as Erik feared he might. It was in the assassin's interest to kill him quietly so as not to warn away his true quarry.

Erik swallowed the battle cry that rose in his throat. This dance with death would be unaccompanied by a *berserkr*'s feral howl.

Blood pounded in Erik's ears, drowning out the small sounds of the night, the insect chorus, the whine of a dog in the next block. Erik was acutely aware of each breath, of the way each hair on his body stood at full attention as he waited for his opponent to attack. He marveled at the way his muscles and bones obeyed the dictates of his will, moving with the grace of a tried warrior.

And he knew those same muscles and bones might be no more than a heap of cooling meat in a few heartbeats.

The assassin brought his curved sword forward in a glittering arc.

Erik braced himself for the blistering attack.

"It is unwise to become attached to those one must use. I have never allowed myself such folly. Until now."
—from the secret journal of Damian Aristarchus

CHAPTER TWENTY

Valdis woke with a start, thrashing wildly. Her violent movement sent Loki into a yipping fit as he tumbled off the end of her bed. She jumped up and scooped the little dog into her arms.

"*Shh!* You must hush," she scolded. "If you make too much noise, they may take you away from me and I couldn't bear to lose you too."

She settled back into the linens, patting and soothing Loki, satisfied the dog was only startled, not injured by the short drop to the floor. She breathed deeply, willing her heart rate to slow.

Sleep had eluded her for hours after Erik left to stop the assassination last night. Then when she finally drifted off, the evil dream returned. It had been weeks since the vision had haunted her last, but it was the same dream. Erik was stealing down the same shadowy corridor and Valdis was forced to helplessly watch as he was struck down. His assailant's face was still obscured, but the blood trickling from Erik's hairline was clear enough to set her into a frenzy. She didn't for a moment believe she possessed any of the prescience Damian attributed to her, but this recurring dream was so vivid, it made her wonder if someone from the realm of spirits were trying to warn her.

There was one difference in the dream she couldn't quite put her finger on, but it troubled her more than anything else about the apparition. If only she could see the face of the one who struck Erik down.

Her belly clenched with fear. Why was she given this horrific peek into the future, if that's what it was, without the information that would help her avoid the outcome? Somehow, she must make sure her dream never came true.

She needed to see Erik right now.

She rose from her bed and pushed open the shuttered window. The pale gray sky was tinted rose with the breaking dawn. She looked down into the courtyard. A few servants busied about. Valdis inhaled deeply. The aroma of baking bread wafted up from the kitchen. Down in the garden, a serving girl clipped flowers for use in the master's sumptuous rooms.

Near the pool in the garden, there was a unique invention called a water clock. Damian had shown her the one in the Imperial Palace, explaining the intricacies of measuring the passage of time. As if people needed more than their own heartbeat to remind them that life leaked away swiftly enough without wasting time measuring its flight. Despite the fleeting nature of time, she knew it would hang heavily for her till she saw Erik again.

The sense of menace from her dream still hovered in the air. Panic clawed at her chest. If she couldn't see Erik, she could at least carve a runic message for him. An urgent one, demanding he come to her so she could warn him. It was a risk, but the evil dream convinced her not to wait.

She had no stylus and wax tablet, so she'd have to improvise. A vase of roses perfumed her room. She pulled out one and began stripping the leaves and thorns from its stem. The rose stem was woody enough for her to slash runes on its curved surface with her eating knife. She'd just finished her cryptic message when her door burst open and Damian Aristarchus entered. Valdis dropped the rose behind her chair and hoped the eunuch's sharp eyes would miss it.

"You've come early." She stood in deference to her former master. "I didn't expect you so soon."

"I bring the medicinal herbs so that your powers may be kept in check until you need them," Damian said for Publius's benefit. The fat eunuch lumbered in behind him, not bothering to cover his mouth when it opened in a cavernous yawn.

"I tried to explain to the worthy chief eunuch that we private folk do not keep Imperial hours, but he would not be put off," Publius explained with a scowl. "Pray do not overtire Valdis. She needs rest today in order to be fresh this evening. The master wishes her to dine with him." He looked expectantly at Valdis. "You may express your pleasure."

"I thank the master for this honor," Valdis said with a sinking sensation in her belly. Dining with the master meant being alone with him. Unveiled. And if Publius was correct, some men found the sight of a woman eating unbearably erotic. Her flesh felt as if a thousand ants marched across it. "But surely I am unworthy of his notice."

Publius chuckled. "Modest as well as accomplished. That is sure to please him. Not having second thoughts about selling her, are you, Damian?" Publius loosed an-

other yawn and scratched his ponderous stomach.
"Well, I leave you to your herbs and potions. You know
the way out."

Publius waddled to the door and closed it behind
him, content to return to his sleeping couch satisfied
that, as a fellow eunuch, Damian was as incapable of
injuring his charges' virtue as Publius was himself.

"Here. Drink this. Truly, I believe it will help you. It's
an infusion of mint said to be efficacious for treatment
of the falling sickness," Damian said. As soon as the
latch caught, he slipped over to listen for Publius's retreating footsteps before going on. "Good work. You've
gained Mahomet's ear in short order."

"Yes, but what do I fill it with? You and I both know I
don't have the gifts he thinks I do. So far, I've been extremely lucky." Valdis took a sip of the brew he'd
brought and found it sweetened with honey and much
tastier than she expected. "I can't count on my luck
continuing."

"You'll do what women always do. Listen more than
you speak. Then tell him what he wants to hear when
you do open your lips." Damian paced the room. "Now,
sit down and give me a full accounting of what happened last night to bring you to Mahomet's attention so
quickly."

Valdis related the tale of her presentation—her
dance and the way Mahomet asked her to size up his
dinner companions. She left nothing out of her report,
save for Erik's presence in the Arab's house. She knew it
would displease Damian and possibly endanger Erik.

"Very astute of you to be forthcoming with him about
the nature and scope of your supposed powers,"
Damian said. "Who was dining with Mahomet?"

"Traders and competitors for the most part, but the
emperor's niece, Zoe, sent her emissary last night. He

was not well-received." Valdis told about his inferior placement at the Arab's table. "In fact, I was in garden with Loki and overheard Mahomet's chief of security give the order for his assassination."

"Did he? I'll look into it. As I thought, Mahomet's support leans elsewhere," Damian said, tenting his hands, fingertips tapping against each other. His dark eyes flashed with genuine concern. "You weren't seen?"

She shook her head.

"Good work, but be careful. I haven't schooled you as much as I should about taking precautions. This is no game." His lips pressed into a tight line. "Your greatest safety lies in currying favor with your new master. Perhaps you can make use of one of the *seid* craft practices the Varangian taught you. Mahomet might find that entertaining enough to pose some telling questions."

"I suppose I could toss the knucklebones," she said uncertainly. It still bothered her to dabble in things of power. If she'd not meddled with magic in the North, perhaps she'd never have been afflicted with her horrible spells. "But I'm not sure how to interpret the fall of the bones."

"It doesn't matter. Such a display will be novel enough to capture Mahomet's imagination. Every noble in this city is caught up in some superstition or other." Damian rubbed his hands together. "Get him talking about his plans. Agree with him. Tell him the portents ensure that he will succeed. An overconfident adversary is most easily overcome."

He stopped by the window and glanced into the garden. Damian looked at Valdis and then back again into the courtyard, a frown marring his features.

"What is he doing here?"

"Who?" Valdis asked with hope.

"Erik Heimdalsson," Damian said. "I'm sure I'm not mistaken. That is the Varangian down there, isn't it?"

Valdis joined him at the open window. Sure enough, Erik was kneeling by the pool, splashing water on his face. After the vividness of her evil dream, relief at seeing him well and whole washed over her with such force she was sure Damian must sense it. When Erik stood, she held her breath lest he look up at her window. But he just walked away. Valdis thought she detected a slight limp as he strode to the stables on the far side of the courtyard.

"You knew he was here," Damian accused, slanting his eyes at her.

"What makes you say that?" she asked, neatly sidestepping the issue. "There are many people in this household. I can't begin to know them all in one night. Why, I've met only one of the dozens of women in the zenana. How can I be expected to know everyone who is lodged in this huge house?"

Damian frowned. "You are my eyes and ears here. I do expect you to know everything and everyone, when they come and when they go. And I don't want this mission jeopardized by a distraction. Stay away from the Varangian," he warned. "Keep your mind on your business."

"Of course," she said as Erik disappeared from view. "Earning my freedom is all I care about. As for the Varangian, the zenana is as safe a place as you could wish for me. Do you think Mahomet allows just anyone in his harem?"

"Don't do anything stupid, Valdis. Chloe thought she could play fast and loose with the law of the sacred womb and you saw what happened to her." Damian scowled as if his disapproval alone should be enough to keep Erik at bay.

"I will remember. Chloe was very clear on the point of guarding my purity." Valdis attempted to change the subject. "Is there anything you specifically want me to tell Mahomet when I cast the bones?"

"You might mention the name Leo." Damian drummed his fingers on the windowsill and pursed his lips as if unsure how much to say.

"What should I predict for him?"

"He's the emperor's nephew. I suspect Mahomet of colluding with Leo Porphyrogenito to hurry his uncle from the throne. Predict a successful outcome for a venture someone named Leo is considering and mark well your master's reaction," Damian said. "Oracles are by nature vague. You need not be more specific than that."

"Very well," Valdis said. "And then what?"

"Discover what the Arab's plan is," Damian said. "Remember, the sooner you discover the nature of their plot and we concoct a way to combat it, the sooner you earn your freedom."

Once Damian left, Valdis veiled herself and took Loki to the garden, where she could leave the runic message for Erik. It occurred to Valdis as she climbed the stairs back to her rooms that Damian was no longer in a position to guarantee her freedom since he was not her master. Unless, even without proof of treason, he'd intended from the very first to do away with her current master.

And if that were the case, she had to wonder which of the two men who'd claimed to own her was the more dangerous. Mahomet or Damian?

Publius oversaw her toilet in preparation for her evening with the master. He made Valdis don a costume similar to the other women of the zenana, a long narrow tunic over a sheer skirt and baggy trousers with slits up the sides. She was perfumed and pomaded and bedecked with jewels, even on her toes. The palms of her hands and soles of her feet were stained with henna.

Finally Valdis was escorted, not to the master's formal dining room where she'd met him the night before, but to his private chambers. A shiver of apprehension tickled her spine.

"Greetings, my Oracle," Habib Ibn Mahomet said. "I trust you have been made comfortable in your new home."

She inclined her head in a graceful bow. "Yes, I am quite comfortable. I thank you." Valdis sheltered behind distant courtesy. "My rooms are lovely."

"As are you," he said, patting the cushion beside him. "Sit." He clapped his hands and all the servants placed their trays of food before their master and scurried away, like roaches fleeing sudden torchlight. "You may remove your veil. We will eat together and grow better acquainted."

Valdis had never felt less like eating, but she managed to slip small bites between her lips, hoping not to enflame her master's passions. Between nervous bites, she asked questions, encouraging Mahomet to talk about himself so she might learn something of value to report to Damian. Habib was not shy about his exploits and regaled her with tales of his youth in Cordoba, hunting with trained cheetahs in Africa and business dealings in the great cities bordering Middle Earth's Inland Sea.

"But I did not bid you here to speak of myself," he finally said after doing just that through five courses. "It is time for me to learn what my hard-earned coin has bought me in you, Valdis of the North. You have said that your power comes when it wills, yes?"

"That is true."

"Then what good is it? If I own the finest steeds in the Hippodrome and have no driver to control them, what do they profit me?" He leaned on his elbow, considering her carefully with his dark gaze. "You really are most enchanting. Of course, your eyes are a bit disconcerting, but I will admit the light and dark of them is alluring in its own way. And your skin—it is like milk." He ran a blunt finger from her shoulder to the crook of her elbow. "Is it so all over?"

Valdis swallowed hard. "Yes, master. Pale and pasty from head to toe."

"Let us see." He sat up straight and clapped his hands. "Remove your clothing."

"But surely Publius explained to you that—"

"Ah, yes, if I wish to preserve your powers I must also preserve your virginity. He did tell me," Mahomet said. "Now, removing your clothing in my presence will do no damage to your purity and it will help me make a decision."

"What decision?"

"Whether or not preserving your powers is worth my sacrifice," he said. "You see, my Northern blossom, there is nothing I enjoy more than introducing an innocent to the pleasures of the flesh. They present so many . . . possibilities." His pleasant smile faded and his features hardened. "Disrobe. Now."

Valdis stood, trying to control her tremble. If she refused, she knew more than a beating on her feet with a bastinado awaited her. Habib Ibn Mahomet wouldn't just order her torture—he'd deliver her punishment himself. Remembering that Mahomet enjoyed inflicting pain on Landina, Valdis suspected he might be roused by her fear. She removed her headgear and let her hair fall to her waist.

"This is truly a bad idea." She fumbled with the tiny buttons running down the front of her tunic. "You do not yet understand the scope of my abilities."

"Ah! That is precisely what I am trying to ascertain. Do

not speak again unless I bid you," he commanded. "If you require assistance, I will ring for Publius."

The only other person she would welcome seeing at that moment was Erik, with his battle ax drawn. But since that would endanger them both, she pushed him from her mind. The thought of another pair of eyes witnessing her discomfort stiffened her spine.

"No need to summon Publius." She shook her head and continued with the buttons. "I can manage." When she unfastened the last one, she shrugged the tunic off her shoulders and let it fall to the ground.

"Pull your hair back," he said. "It is lovely, but it is obstructing my view."

She pushed her long locks behind her shoulders, baring her breasts to him.

Mahomet stared at them wordlessly for several heartbeats. He ran his tongue over her lips. "Come. Kneel and present yourself to me."

Fortunately, Chloe had prepared her for this formality. Valdis cupped her breasts with her hands and knelt before Habib Ibn Mahomet. She arched her back, as was customary for an odalisque, thrusting the pink tips toward him.

"My breasts, my breath, my very life, all are yours, my master," Valdis whispered the prescribed words as she squeezed her eyes shut. This was worse than her recurring nightmare. This was a dream from which she could not wake.

"My other women are brown or berry-colored here. You are pink. I would not have imagined them so," he said as he drew small circles around her nipples. He pinched one till she drew back in pain. "Stand."

Valdis raised herself to her feet, hoping to have failed this test. To her dismay, he grasped the waist of her filmy skirt and yanked it to her ankles. Then with infinite slowness he untied the drawstring holding up her baggy trousers. He hooked a finger on each side of her waist and drew the garment down by finger-widths. She lifted first one foot, then the other as he pulled them off. Save for the jangling jewelry shackled to her ankles, wrists and neck, she was naked as a babe before him.

"So it is true," he said in awe as he tugged at her blond pubic hairs. "They are golden, just like the hairs on your head. We pluck our women here, you see. They are bare as a young child when they come to me and I would have it so. But this, like spun gold . . ." He pulled several strands through his fingers. "I forbid you to pluck even one."

"I will happily obey," she said, the thought of yanking out those small hairs reminding her of her new master's devotion to pain-giving. She stepped back a pace. "But before you make any decisions, I must tell you more of my other powers so you have complete knowledge of my abilities."

"Complete knowledge of you is exactly my aim." He ran his jeweled fingers down the length of her thigh.

She knelt, letting her hair fall forward to provide a partial covering again, and picked up the small leather pouch she had tied to the waist of her trousers. "I may not be able to control when my visions come upon me, but with these bones, I can divine the answers to many questions. How often have you wished for a window on tomorrow?"

"What man does not wish for such a thing?" He frowned, intrigued despite himself. "How does it work?"

"In good time, my master," she replied. "But first, let me dress. My purity may yet be intact, but being in your presence thus will dilute my understanding of the bones. I would present you with inaccurate interpretations."

"Bah! Get on with it, then," he said. "And if you please

me not with this parlor trick, I have in my mind several other ways you will be of use to me."

"My dear, you were a triumph tonight," Publius said as he escorted Valdis back to her rooms. "I've never seen the master more delighted by an odalisque, though for your sake, I am sorry he sent you away and called on two others to minister to his corporeal needs. What kind of magic did you work on him?"

"One of the oldest kinds," Valdis said, still breathless from her unexpected success. "It's called *seid.*"

"You saw the events of tomorrow as though they were yesterday." Publius shook his head in amazement. "Damian said you were gifted, but I had no idea."

The eunuch practically bowed to her as he made his hasty exit. Valdis was unprepared for the way her predictions tipped the balance in all her relationships. She felt slightly light-headed still, remembering how effortless it had seemed.

At first, when she was unable to control her trembling, she feared Mahomet would sense terror for what it was, not as the manifestation of power she claimed. Then she gathered the bones in her hand. From the first throw, all that she'd gleaned from the old *seid*-woman in Birka came back to her with stark clarity. She saw patterns in the bones, meanings that she didn't have to fabricate. Her master was fascinated.

Perhaps she had more *seid* abilities than she thought.

There was only one time when she substituted Damian's prediction for the one she saw in the bones. Mentioning the imperial nephew directly by name seemed too obvious. When she described the bones alignment signifying the lion rising on the wings of an eagle, she thought Mahomet might jump out of his skin. The symbolism was potent. Leo, the emperor's nephew, was obviously the lion and the Byzantine eagle was the ubiquitous symbol of Imperial power.

If Mahomet hadn't been thinking of backing Leo before, Valdis was sure her performance tonight convinced him it was in his best interests.

As she settled into her bed she wondered if that was Damian's real objective all along. What if the chief eunuch wasn't uncovering a plot as much as he was hatching one?

Valdis shook her head. What a fanciful notion! Damian lived and breathed for the good of the Bulgar-Slayer.

Didn't he?

> *"When one is forced to depend on subordinates, even the best laid plans can go awry."*
> —*from the secret journal of Damian Aristarchus*

CHAPTER TWENTY-ONE

The lion reared on its hind legs, leaping after the eagle, who swooped barely out of reach. On one pass the eagle grasped the regal mane and yanked out a chunk with its sharp talons. The lion's cruel claws sent tail feathers fluttering to the ground like oversized snowflakes in a late spring storm. The eagle dove back down and this time the great cat plucked the raptor from the sky. They rolled together in a blur of golden fur and beating wings, beak and tooth, talon and claw.

From the North a mighty roar drowned out the cacophony of screech and growl. The otherworldly sound made the lion and the eagle stop fighting. A Nordic dragon bore down upon them, its leathery wings outstretched. The lion and eagle stood shoulder to shoulder to face the dragon. Flames erupted from the lion's mouth, incinerating the dragon in a fiery blast. The dragon sank into a boiling sea.

"No!" Valdis cried out as she woke. This night phantom with its flash of blood-reds, scent of sulfur and screams of the dying beast was even more disturbing than her evil recurring dream.

Worse, now that she was awake, a real hand clamped over her mouth. She struggled and tried to bite down on the fleshy part of his palm at the base of his thumb. Loki woke and started growling at the intruder.

"Be quiet. Valdis, it's only me." Erik's voice rumbled into her ear as he released his hold on her. "And for both our sakes, shut that damn dog up before he brings the house guard down on us."

"Loki, shh!" she ordered. Then, because she was still in the grip of the nightmare, she reached up to feel the man's face, just to make sure it really was Erik. His beard met her palm. "Oh, it is you!"

"Were you expecting someone else?" He settled onto the side of her bed with a grin. "How many runic messages did you leave in the garden, woman?"

She sat up and wrapped her arms around him, reveling in his scent, his warmth, the steady thump of his heart. His lips found hers and she gave herself up to him, surrendering her mouth to his exploration. Then she thrust her tongue and nipped at his lips in love play. In the darkness, he enveloped her, climbing atop her and pinning her against the linens. She welcomed the weight of his body.

"I came as soon as I could. The guard was annoyingly vigilant tonight." He suckled her earlobe, sending tendrils of pleasure sweeping over her. He slid off her and snuggled her close to his side.

His fingers dipped into the hollow between her breasts, touching and teasing. Her breath came in gasps. "How did you sneak past the eunuchs stationed at the top of the stairs?"

"Stairs are for weaklings. I used the vine and trellis outside your window. It is as sturdy as it looks." He untied the drawstring at her neckline and parted her night shift to bare her breasts. His face lit with desire. Her nipples hardened under his gaze, aching for his touch. As if in answer to her unspoken plea, he lowered his head and nuzzled her with his nose and lips, his beard and warm breath tickling her.

Languid warmth stole over her limbs. She sank into the heat of bliss. A low drumbeat started in her womb, throbbing for him.

"So you read the message without any trouble?"

"*Ja.* I had a good teacher," he said before shifting attention to her other breast. "I thought night would never come so I could answer your summons. It doesn't take much to lure me to your bed, Valdis."

Suddenly she remembered why he was there. She had to warn him. She grasped his hair and pulled his head up. "I didn't invite you to my bed to dally. I need to talk to you."

"Talking is vastly overrated." He circled her nipple with the tip of his tongue.

A jolt of desire streaked from her breast to her womb. "But I have to warn you," she said, torn between the need to tell him of her fears and the need for him to continue pleasuring her.

"Warn me of what?" His hand stole under the bedclothes and found her bare knee. The callused palm sent messages of delight up her thigh. Her legs parted slightly of their own accord.

"You're in terrible danger," she whispered as his mouth trailed down to her navel.

"I am now," Erik said with a smile in his voice. "If they catch me in your chamber, I'm a dead man. But I don't care. All I want is you and if you send me away now, I swear Valdis, I'll be the first man in Miklagard to die of love."

With tremendous effort, she straight-armed him and wiggled away. "Erik, I'm serious."

"What makes you think I'm not?"

"Men speak easily of love when they think it will gain them a bedding." She climbed out of the tangled linens and stood to put some distance between them. "Then by morning's light all talk of love is forgotten. Besides, there are more important issues at stake right now."

"More important than love?"

"Even more important than love. I'm talking about your life. Damian knows you're here and he's—"

"Do you think I fear that ball-less wonder?"

"No, but you should."

"The day I fear a eunuch is the day I fall on my own sword."

"But I've had such an evil dream—two of them really, and you're in mortal peril in both." The echo of the dragon's dying scream was still fresh in her ears.

He snorted. "Don't tell me you believe the nonsense Damian is touting about you—that you can see the future. Valdis, it's just a Byzantine scheme." He stood and closed the distance between them. He raised a hand to her cheek, then let his fingers trail down her neck to brush her breast. "We're wasting precious time with all this talk of danger."

"It's no waste. You presume too much," she said crossly, moving away from him and finding the wall at her back. Her nipples still tingled from his touch. "I didn't call you here because my bed is cold."

"I see that. I guess it's your heart that's cold." He folded his arms across his chest. "You offer me a stolen night of pleasure here and there and then only how and when it suits *you*." His voice was graveled with irritation. "Don't worry. I had no intention of disturbing your precious flower."

"And I had no intention of offering it. How can you think bedding me will make things better when your life is in danger?" Valdis covered her face with her hands. Erik was angry with her. She couldn't convince him of her premonition and, despite her claim that she didn't want him in her bed, the throbbing ache between her legs damned her as a liar. "We are surrounded by enemies. Everything I do here is a deception and there's no one I can trust."

"You can trust me." All the anger was gone from his voice and she saw genuine concern in his eyes. "I trust you."

"Then why can't you see I'm afraid for you?" A sob escaped with her question and her shoulders shook.

His arms came around her, pulling her close. She let him take her, too tired to continue the fight. He held her steady against his chest, his big hand stroking her hair.

"I'm sorry, Valdis" he said. "I guess I deserved that. When I found your message, I thought . . . well, it doesn't matter now. Then when I heard you were supping with the Arab, my eyes went red with *berserkr* haze. It felt just like when I found my wife with my brother. Something inside me was dying, knowing you were with another man. I wanted to break into his apartments and kill him. The only thing that stopped me was knowing that I'd endanger you."

Valdis stopped shaking as he dropped a soft kiss on her temple.

"And then when your lamp came on early and I realized he'd sent you back to your room instead of keeping you with him. . . ." He clutched her tighter. "I hoped he decided he didn't want you. No, I won't ask. Make whatever sacrifice you must to survive. Promise me."

"I'll do what I must." Valdis nodded. So Erik was

smarting from memories of his wife's faithlessness. She should have realized this situation would be painfully similar for him. "But Mahomet wants to preserve my abilities, so he sent me away and called for another to serve him. Two others."

"Then I'm glad your master is such a fool." Erik tipped her head back and kissed her deeply.

"No, that's just the trouble. He's not a fool. He's a vicious and powerful man." She hugged him tighter. "And I know you don't put any stock in such things, but my dreams keep getting worse. I summoned you to warn you. You are in peril here. I know it." In breathless whispers, she recounted her nightmares to him. "Please find some way to leave this city before it's too late."

"It's already too late."

"What do you mean?"

"The first moment I saw you, it was too late. You witched me with those eyes of yours." He pressed his lips to her closed eyelids.

She trembled at the sweetness of his kiss.

His voice was a rumbling purr in her ear. "You ask me to leave the city? I couldn't even leave this house because it would mean leaving you. You're in my blood, woman." He tucked her hand inside his tunic so she could feel the great muscle galloping in his chest. "All I am is yours."

"That sounds almost like a vow," she whispered in awe.

"It is," he said. "Even though you belong to another and cannot answer my vow, I pledge myself to you, Valdis. Upon my honor, though there are those who would say that is too small a thing to swear upon."

She put a finger to his lips to silence him. "You are the most honorable man I know."

"Then it is my great good fortune that you know so

few men," he said with a crooked smile. Then the smile faded into a look of dead seriousness. "Upon my honor, I swear I am yours until I breathe no more."

"Erik." She ran a hand over his head. "Oh, my love." She bit her lip for a moment. "My body is owned by another, so I cannot match your pledge with one of my own. Yet I would give you that which is mine to give."

She took his hand and placed his palm over her breastbone so he could feel her heart as well. "There is a part of me that Habib Ibn Mahomet cannot own, cannot touch. Even if there comes a time when he takes my body, he will never have so much as a pinch of my soul." She looked up into his dear face. In the dimness, his pale eyes were dark with desire. "My family turned me out when they saw what lurked within me. You have seen my worst and did not turn away. How could I not love you for the rest of my days?"

"I accept your pledge in fair exchange," Erik said. "But there will come a day when you own yourself again, Valdis. And on that day, I will claim you entire as you have claimed me."

He kissed her again, softly, as if she might break. When he released her, she shook her head. She'd made a decision. She had to act before she lost her nerve.

"No, I don't think that will do." She bent over and grasped her hem. In a single motion, she pulled her night shift up and over her head, baring herself before him. She stepped back into his arms. "I would have you claim me entire tonight."

"Don't tempt me." She felt his muscles tense and knew he was barely holding himself back.

"It's no temptation, Erik. It's a solemn offer." She placed a soft kiss on his neck and stepped back a pace. Just as she had done earlier before Mahomet, she cupped her breasts and arched her back. "My soul, my heart, my maidenhead, these are all things which still belong to me. But now I give them into your keeping."

"Mahomet does not have a forgiving nature. If you're found to be impure—"

She covered his mouth with her fingertips. The danger in her dreams made her adamant. She must love this man tonight or die inside by finger-widths through all her days to come. "Then I will deal with that, when and if the time comes. Our lives trickle away like the drips of the water clock. I cannot bear the thought that I might never know the joy of having you. Please, Erik. Let us have this night."

"I know I should resist, but you put too much on a simple man."

He reached out to touch her offered breasts, cradling them with gentleness. The pad of his thumbs thrummed over her nipples, setting her blood racing. Valdis could see his resolve crumble even as his eyes blazed with feral light.

"Damn tomorrow," he said with savagery. "Let the world end tonight."

He scooped her into his arms and carried her back to her sleeping couch. They fell into the linens together in a tangle of arms and legs. His mouth was everywhere, branding her skin with his heat. Her fingers flew, trying to help him out of his clothing, unwilling to separate for any longer than necessary to pull the stubborn leather and wool out of their way.

Where he was hard, she was soft. Where he was rough, she was smooth. The ecstasy of his skin on hers was almost more than she could bear. His fingers traced all her curves, all her hidden crevices, followed by his blessed mouth.

Valdis had never felt so tinglingly alive. Every fiber of her being ached, but it was a welcome ache as she strained against him.

"My turn," she whispered as she pushed him onto his back. She sat up and ran her fingertips over his chest, along the curve of his ribs and his flat belly. His maleness was swollen with need and he groaned when she stroked him. She explored his bag of seed and was surprised to find it soft at first. Then under her hand, it too tightened. The mystery of a man was becoming clear to her. Then she gazed down his well-muscled legs and frowned. A strip of linen was wrapped around one thigh. She untied the bandage to reveal a fresh, angry-looking gash.

"What happened to you?"

"Nothing to worry about," he said. "I just had a brief disagreement with that killer of children. He managed one lucky stroke, but I managed the last one."

He pulled her astraddle him and urged her down so he could nip and suckle her breasts once more. All conscious thought, even concern over his injury, fled from Valdis's mind. His hand slid down over her belly and invaded the softness throbbing between her legs. A jolt of pleasure coursed through her when his fingers grazed her most sensitive spot.

Then, suddenly, Valdis realized it was no longer his hand seeking entrance to her secret chamber of delights. The tip of Erik's thick manhood was poised at her center. She ached for him.

"There is no going back," he whispered, tension straining his words. "Are you sure, *dyr?*"

"Yes. Now," she begged. Her empty womb contracted once with need. "Now is all there is."

By finger-widths, he eased into her. He stopped when his tip reached her thin barrier. She bit the inside of her cheek to keep from crying out for him to hurry. He thrust once and she was torn forever. There was a brief pain as he filled her, a quick stab that dissipated in the joy of joining her body to his. They lay still, locked in the wonder of this new being they'd just created, this single soul they'd become. Then she kissed him and they rolled together, surging into each other with the force of the tide plunging into a deep fjord. The feel of him, thick and hard, sliding in and out of her slick wetness blotted out the rest of the world. She took him in greedily, urging him to go deeper, to impale her with his love. She watched his face, their gazes locked as the ancient rhythm of life bore them both away.

Valdis was wound tight. She felt the tension build in Erik's body in tandem, but just as she neared release, he began to pull away.

"No, wait," she pleaded.

"I can't hold off any longer."

"Then don't, but whatever you do, if you've any love for me at all, don't leave me."

His body shuddered and he plunged deep. She felt his seed surge into her hot and steady, and her body welcomed him with pulses of joy. She lost control of her limbs and bucked with the contractions. His mouth covered hers when she would have cried out at the wonder of their joining.

Her body went slack as the last of her release faded. Joy spread from her being in gentle waves.

When Valdis woke from one of her spells, she always felt limp as a broken reed. She experienced some of that same lethargy now, but with an important difference.

Now she was not alone. Erik was with her. He was firmly in her body and her heart. And she knew just as surely that she was in his. No matter if they must separate. No matter if death came for them. He would be with her for the rest of her days.

And in this splendid moment, it didn't matter to Valdis one whit how few those days might be.

*"When a tool has lost its usefulness, a master crafts-
man has no choice but to discard it, lest his work
suffer for the tool's inadequacy."*
—from the secret journal of Damian Aristarchus

CHAPTER TWENTY-TWO

It was still dark when Erik rose from Valdis's bed and
shrugged into his discarded clothes. Even though he'd
brushed it off as unimportant, the wound in his thigh
caused his leg to stiffen. Getting back down the vine
without being noticed might be more of a trick than
shinnying up it.

Valdis slept with the deep relaxation of one whose
every knot has been loosed. If he'd not been a warrior
trained to wake himself to relieve another watch, he'd
have slept just as deeply. In the dimness, he was barely
able to make out her form. He stood over her for a moment as his eyes adjusted to the darkness. She swam
into his vision a little at a time, the oval of her face, her
calm brows, her full lips parted softly in sleep. He knew
he should just go, should leave her thus entwined with
her pillow and her dreams, but he couldn't resist taking
her mouth one last time.

"Mmm," she murmured as she draped her arms

around his neck. "What a lovely way to wake. Come back to bed."

"I can't. It must be near the end of the third watch," he whispered, inhaling her musky scent. His cock rose merrily, heedless of the time. "I must be gone, love."

She sighed and cupped his jaw in her palm. "You'll come to me again?"

"No, Valdis. I shouldn't have endangered you this time," he said with reluctance. "How can we tempt fate again?"

"You must come." She held him close. "Promise me, Erik. Say you will come to me at every chance."

Every bit of reason told him to refuse, but his head could not overrule his heart.

"If I can, I will come to you," he whispered into her neck. "But now I must go. Close your eyes or I won't be able to leave."

He was relieved and surprised when she obeyed him. From the shadows of the window, his gaze swept the sleeping compound, satisfying himself that the next watch had not yet started his rounds. Then he climbed out the opening and down the sturdy vines, moving with stealth.

Overhead, he heard Loki give one yip before Valdis silenced him.

Damn dog.

Erik froze halfway to the ground, in case anyone should rouse at the sharp sound. In the distance, he heard a cock crow. It was far later, or rather far earlier, than he'd thought. From the kitchen on the opposite side of the courtyard, Erik heard the clatter of broken crockery followed by a muffled curse. The household was beginning to stir.

So far the gods had aided him in his clandestine

quest. Wasn't it said that Freya, the Lady of Asgard, smiled upon lovers and their secret trysts? Perhaps he could lean just a little longer on her help. Abandoning stealth, he clambered down as quickly as he could. When he reached the ground, he crouched, waiting to see if any had marked his progress. Except for the amber light of an oil lamp burning in the kitchen and the rattle of pots, he saw and heard nothing that betrayed another's presence.

Erik straightened and walked toward his own room near the stables, keeping to the shadows as much as possible as the sky paled to gray. When he reached his spartan quarters and closed the door behind him, he allowed himself a sigh of relief.

Until he discovered his horn-handled dagger was missing.

He retraced his steps through the courtyard, hoping it had slipped from its sheath after his climb down. He nearly ran headlong into the watchman and brazened it out by bullying the man and deriding him for being so late on his rounds.

Of the dagger, he saw no trace. He concluded that he had left the incriminating object in Valdis's bedchamber. In his frenzy to rid himself of his clothes, it must have come out of the sheath unnoticed and was now lying on her floor or, please gods, had been kicked under her sleeping couch.

Perhaps the goddess Freya wasn't so approving of his night of stolen joy, after all.

"Pray don't wait on me, friend," Damian said as Publius opened the door for him. "My business with Valdis shouldn't keep you from breaking your fast."

"Quite right," Publius said with a harrumphing cough. He turned away without bothering to enter the chamber to check on his most recent charge. "See yourself out then."

Damian was surprised to find Valdis still abed. The air in the room seemed different, muskier than usual. He set the herbal potion on the bedside table.

"Rise and shine," he said. "Publius tells me you supped privately with your new master last night. He was unusually closemouthed about it. I would hear the whole tale and don't stint the details."

Valdis struggled to sit up, her hair a tangled mess and her lips swollen with spent passion. Her mismatched eyes were decidedly bleary. Had she been crying?

Damian noted a small bloodstain on her linens as she swung her long legs over the side of the bed. She slept in the nude, which was unlike her. He allowed himself a quick look at her full breasts before averting his gaze. Obviously, she'd lacked the will to dress properly for bed after leaving her new master's side.

"So, Mahomet was unable to restrain himself," he said crisply, as if commenting on the weather. He knew women frequently were devastated over the loss of purity and he wished he could've spared Valdis this. Privately, he'd given her claim that she must remain a virgin to retain her prescient abilities only half a chance at success. If only she'd been less striking . . .

Damian noticed that her night shift lay in a crumpled heap on the floor. Before she left his home, Damian had made sure she was supplied with plenty of dried lavender to scatter amid her clothing. If she wasn't wearing the garment, it should have been neatly folded in the chest at the foot of her sleeping couch. Valdis scooped up the night shift and quickly slipped it over her head. She accepted the mint-scented chalice from his hand without meeting his eyes.

"It's a pity, but don't trouble yourself overmuch. We

both knew this was likely to happen," Damian continued. If he made light of it, perhaps she'd view it that way as well. "If you become a favorite, Mahomet will confide in you readily enough. You won't be able to feed him erroneous information as easily, but if you have his ear, you'll still be useful."

Valdis put a hand to her forehead. "What are you talking about?"

"Coyness does not become you," he said. "At least, not with me. Let us speak plainly then. If you were still bleeding when he sent you away, enough for you to leave a stain on these linens as well, Mahomet was probably brutal with you. I regret that it happened thus, but there's little to be gained by dwelling on it. Do you require a physician?"

She bit her lip.

"I'll take that as a no," Damian said, determined to keep matters businesslike. He was nearly overcome with the desire to take her into his arms to offer her comfort. "Tell me what you discussed with Mahomet. Now that your master has deflowered you, how do you intend to proceed?"

"Mahomet did not—" she started, then stopped, her eyes frozen on a spot on the polished floor.

Damian followed her gaze. A horn-handled knife lay near the open window. Damian recognized the weapon immediately.

The Varangian.

He crossed the room and all but pounced on the knife. Valdis was on his heels.

"Damian, please, you don't understand."

"Oh, I understand a good deal more than you think," he said with vehemence. "How could you be so undisciplined? So gullible? Do you realize what you've done?"

Fury rose in him that he suspected had nothing to do with the risk to the mission.

"I'll do what I can to save you, though it may not be possible," Damian said. "Mahomet will eviscerate the man."

Valdis blanched pale as a corpse. "No, please. It's not his fault."

Damian tossed a murderous look at her.

"This is all my doing. I asked Erik to come to me. I had an evil dream and I had to warn him," she said. "Then things just happened."

"Don't tell me you believe your own lie about having the Sight?" he accused. "Valdis, how could you do this? After all my instruction, after meeting Chloe and seeing what will happen to a woman who's found to be impure, how?"

"I love him," she said simply. "I couldn't bear not to let him love me."

"Love? What kind of love consigns another to the torture Mahomet will surely order?"

Her face crumpled in misery. "I don't know. I didn't think."

"If you survive this night's work, you'll have time to think," he said. "For the rest of your life, you'll be able to think about the fact that your own actions brought about the very unpleasant death that awaits your Northman."

Damian turned to go. If he told Mahomet what happened, made a clean breast of things, perhaps he could offer to buy Valdis back and still ingratiate himself into the silk merchant's household long enough to complete the plan.

"No, wait." Valdis threw herself to the floor and hugged his knees, impeding his progress. "Please, Damian. No one else knows of this. Why must you destroy everything?"

"I am not the destroyer," he said, resisting looking down into her pleading eyes. "You brought this on yourself."

"Damian, please don't," she cried. "I've done everything you asked. Mahomet trusts me and believes in my powers. We can turn him whichever way you wish. If only you guard this secret, I'll . . . I'll do anything."

Since his gelding, Damian experienced random erections. He never trusted them to last long enough for him to give a woman pleasure and he feared trying, even with a well-paid whore. It was the only thing that kept him from going back to his wife Calysta and his son. For a blinding moment, Damian had a vision of Valdis, naked and willing, spreading her legs for him so he could test the limits castration put on his sexual abilities. If there were a chance he could return to Calysta as something resembling a whole man, he'd leave the Imperial service in a heartbeat and disappear back into the Macedonian mountains to watch his son grow to manhood and redeem the lost years with the woman who'd become a memory.

"Please," the woman at his feet repeated. "I've learned where Mahomet's allegiance lies."

He looked down into her strained face, her eyes brimming with unshed tears, her full lips trembling. Valdis feared him. Perhaps that turn of events was no bad thing. It might protect her from future folly.

"And where does *your* allegiance lie?" he asked.

"With you, Damian," she said quickly. "Absolutely with you."

He knew her declaration for a lie, and an artless one, at that. If the big Northman so much as waggled his finger in her direction, Valdis would come running, no matter the cost. Well, there were ways to deal with the Varangian that Valdis never need know about.

"Very well," he conceded, hiding the damning knife in the folds of his garment. "I will keep your dirty little secret, but should your master learn of your unchaste behavior in another way, I cannot help you. And you must promise me there will be no repeat performances."

"I promise."

"Now, tell me what you have learned of the worthy merchant's politics?"

While Valdis related the events of the previous evening, in the back of his mind, Damian was already formulating a plan to remove the Varangian from Mahomet's household.

Permanently.

"The best plan never lets the right hand know what the left is doing."
—*from the secret journal of Damian Aristarchus*

CHAPTER TWENTY-THREE

Two mornings later, Erik lay on his sagging straw-filled mattress, his fingers laced behind his head. As he listened to the muttered curses of the boy tasked with mucking out the stables next to his tiny cell, Erik congratulated himself on not making a repeat visit to Valdis's chamber.

When he first came to Miklagard, a Greek *tagmata* with whom he served told him the stories of their heroes. Erik's favorite was a man named Odysseus, a great wanderer who lashed himself to the mast in order to hear the seductive song of the Sirens, but not be able to run his ship aground in a disastrous attempt to answer them. Odysseus knew the danger posed by the Sirens, but he tormented himself with their alluring voices anyway. Odysseus took a foolish but calculated risk.

Erik decided he was even more a fool than the Greek hero. He had no mast. All that kept Erik from the siren song of Valdis's nearness was his own will. Though he'd always prided himself on possessing resolve as hard as iron, he felt it melt each time a shadow passed behind her curtain.

That stolen night was the worst kind of folly. Far from slaking his thirst for her, their tryst only sharpened his desire. Now, instead of imagined delights, he had fresh memories, a myriad of tiny images, sounds and smells to torment him—the unbearable softness of the skin of her inner thigh, the small groan she tried so hard to suppress as he pleasured her, the scent of her arousal . . .

He was lost and he knew it.

She'd sent him another runic message: "Knife found." He wondered if Valdis were trying to warn him that they had been discovered and he should flee to save himself. If that was her aim, she'd be sorely disappointed. He wouldn't leave of his own volition, even if they intended to flay him alive.

Then when another day and night passed without incident, and without catching so much as a glimpse of her, Erik decided Valdis had found the knife herself and was safekeeping it.

The chief eunuch came and went with irritating frequency. Damian Aristarchus came bearing his herbs as if he were a physician instead of a secret puppet master. Erik had watched through narrowed eyes as the eunuch ascended the curving stairs to the upper story of the house.

He longed to change places with Aristarchus for those few moments.

No, whatever it cost him, he would not endanger Valdis again. As long as they bided in the silk merchant's sprawling household, he wouldn't go to her. He set all his energies toward discovering Mahomet's political bent, so he could help Valdis satisfy Aristarchus and gain her freedom faster.

Since he'd given up her ownership, Erik wasn't sure

how the chief eunuch would secure her manumission, but however he might dislike Damian, he sensed the eunuch was a man of his word. No one could rise so high in the emperor's service without some redeeming qualities.

A discreet scratch on his door brought Erik upright in a heartbeat. He forced himself to walk instead of bound to the portal. Living in Habib Ibn Mahomet's house made him jumpy. The frowning outer walls enclosed the space like a miser brooding over his hoard of coin. Far from giving him a sense of safety, the walls seemed to contract on him.

Erik's enemies were already within the gates.

The scritching noise came again, this time accompanied by a cough. If it was someone intent on mayhem, he reasoned, they'd have battered down the door instead of scratching for admittance. Still, he wished for the familiar worn hilt of his horn knife in his hand.

A eunuch clad in white linen waited for him. "The master commands your presence," the servant said tersely.

Erik dressed carefully, making sure his beard was freshly trimmed and his breastplate gleaming before mounting the stairs to Habib Ibn Mahomet's receiving room. A rat of panic gnawed at his belly. He recognized the annoyingly Christian emotion known as guilt. He'd cuckolded the man he'd come to nominally protect. Erik must be careful not to let Mahomet see his discomfort, lest he endanger Valdis.

It might be nothing, he told himself. *Mahomet may just want a report on my changes in the household security.*

If that was the case, Erik had no cause for concern. He'd beefed up the guard at the house's tall gate and set a strict schedule for patrolling the roof garden. He even pointed out the kitchen charcoal chute as a possible point of entry and ordered a lock put on it. If someone had observed him wiggling in and out of it the night he killed Barak's would-be assassin, he could always claim he was testing the perimeter of the great house for unlikely methods of entry.

He was totally unprepared to see his friend, Haukon, standing at ease, conversing in his stilted Greek with Habib Ibn Mahomet.

"Erik, you sandbagger," Hauk's voice boomed in his more comfortable mother tongue. "Is this the duty that kept you from joining us in Antioch? You should have been there. We filled the corbeys' trencher with fresh meat and made the desert run red. The Saracens will think twice before testing that Imperial outpost again."

Erik clasped forearms with Hauk. "We must raise a horn and you can tell me all about it. What are you doing here?" The words spilled out of his mouth before he felt the shrewd dark eyes of Mahomet on them. He switched to Greek. "Haukon is my countryman and friend."

"It is clear you know each other very well," Habib Ibn Mahomet said. "Perhaps it comes as no surprise to you that your worthy companion has been sent to replace you, though I myself confess to puzzlement over it. I have no complaints with your service, centurion."

"What's this?" Erik was sure Mahomet's words were genuine. The silk merchant had more inventive ways of ridding himself of people who'd displeased him. If the Arab knew of his tryst with Valdis, Erik had no doubt he'd die horribly.

Being ordered from her made him feel like a horse had just kicked him in the gut. He knew he should be relieved. At least he'd not endanger Valdis again. This was safer than Odysseus's mast.

"Why am I being replaced?"

"I'm only obeying orders," Hauk said with a slight lift of one eyebrow. He knew more than he was admitting. "You're to report to the general at once for reassignment."

"Acquaint our new security advisor with the changes you have implemented and then you may go," Mahomet said to Erik. "Please convey my thanks to the esteemed General Quintillian for his interest in the well-being of my humble household."

Mahomet put his fingertips first to his lips and then to his forehead, sketching the graceful Arabic gesture of farewell.

Erik escorted Haukon out of Mahomet's presence before he dared speak again. He walked the perimeter of the courtyard making small talk about security while his mind raced ahead. When he led Hauk past the stable, the air redolent with hay and warm horseflesh, to the room his friend would now occupy, he finally asked the question that burned on his tongue.

"What made the general order me to stand down?"

"Not what. Who. All I know is the chief eunuch was leaving the general's quarters as I was called in." Hauk tested the sagging bed and grimaced. Then he pulled a small packet from inside his tunic. "Damian Aristarchus bid me deliver this to your hand and yours alone."

Erik unwrapped the oilskin. His horn-handled knife, freshly sharpened, lay in the protective wrapping.

"Say, that looks like yours," Hauk said. "Where did you lose it?"

Erik slumped into the room's only chair and dragged a hand over his face. "In the wrong bedchamber, my friend."

Hauk clicked his tongue against his teeth and chuckled. "Then the eunuch has done you a service by returning it discreetly."

"No." Erik shook his head. "It's a warning."

"But you were in his service. You know how to speak with those court types even if you must hold your nose to do it." Hauk always complained the courtiers of Byzantium wore more perfume than high-priced whores. "What happened?"

Since Hauk was gone from the city when Erik first returned from his time in the mountain villa with Valdis and the chief eunuch, there was much to tell. Erik described how he'd tried to hold Valdis at a distance but failed.

"I love her, Hauk," he said simply, marveling at the truth of the words and angry at himself for never having said them to her.

"Then it is well that you are leaving this house," Hauk said sagely. "So far, you have been lucky. When does the Court of Asgard allow joy to reign among men for long? It is never wise to tempt the gods."

Erik's shoulders slumped. He knew his friend was right, but when it came to actually leaving Valdis in this house where she might become nothing more than another man's plaything, his eyes burned with suppressed fire.

"I can't even tell her good-bye," he said morosely.

"Carve a rune stick," Hauk suggested, shaking his head. "It's clear you've lost your head as well as your heart. I never thought to see the day you dabbled in *seid* craft."

"It's a small matter," Erik said, picking up the knife to begin his final runic message to the woman he loved. "I'd dare more than the spirits' curse for Valdis."

"The women in the harem are never allowed outside the walls?" Hauk asked, stroking his chin thoughtfully.

"Not since I've been here," Erik said. "But Valdis has asked to visit the big church of *Kristr,* near the Palatine."

His face lit up. He knew what he would carve now. "I'll tell her to try to come two days hence. That should give her time to wheedle permission from Mahomet."

His face hardened into a frown at the thought of Valdis spending time with her master. And having to beg him.

"Cheer up," Hauk said. "At least you'll be assigned an interesting duty."

"What have you heard?" Erik asked with dread. The Byzantine Empire stretched from one end of the inland sea to the other. He might be ordered anywhere.

"You're to be given command of a ship."

Erik's worst fears were realized. A sea voyage took months, years maybe. How could he leave Valdis behind? "What ship?"

"Don't act too excited. It's not what you think," Hauk said with sarcasm. "The fleet captured a pirate dhow a month back. The emperor wants a spectacle. The Greek commander is going to recreate his naval battle in the Harbor of Theodosius so the court and the populace can look on. It's all a sham, of course, every oar stroke arranged to make the Byzantine *drommonds* seem the most invincible craft in the world."

Erik scoffed. He knew a sleek Norse *drakar* could sail circles around the wallowing Greek vessel. Only the infernal weapon known as Greek Fire had kept a flotilla of dragonships from overpowering the Byzantine navy years ago.

"So now I'm to pilot one of those sea cows?"

"No," Hauk said. "You get to play pirate. You're to captain the dhow. Oh, you won't be allowed to win, of course. From what I hear, they have every turn and bowshot planned out with precision worthy of a band of eunuchs counting out tax revenues. They want no blood. This is to be a set piece, but they wanted someone to pilot the dhow with enough seamanship to give the battle a semblance of reality."

Erik nodded grimly. As he set his face to his carving, he realized Damian Aristarchus had maneuvered him into recreating another Greek tale as well. He would be Odysseus, strapped to the mast.

On a ship destined to sink.

"Holy writ would tell us 'Faithful are the wounds of a friend.' I beg to differ. Sometimes the wounds of a friend are fatal."
—from the secret journal of Damian Aristarchus

CHAPTER TWENTY-FOUR

"This is most irregular," Publius said for the twentieth time as he jostled in his sedan chair. The poor slaves manning the poles fought not to collapse under his monumental weight. "Women of the zenana hardly ever leave the protection of the master's house."

"But we are not leaving the protection of the master. That's why we have you with us," Valdis said in an attempt to placate him. In the swaying chair next to Publius, she and Landina were swathed from head to toe in modest burkas to shield them from curious eyes. "And it is not without precedent. Did you not attend Rania, the head wife, when she accompanied the master to the games in the Hippodrome only last week? Thanks to your diligent care, she returned home in safety with all proprieties observed."

Mahomet and his retinue were the guests of the emperor's nephew Leo in his curtained and guarded box for another running of the chariots. Valdis had been able to finesse the information from the eunuch and used it to her advantage. She satisfied Damian that she was busy gathering intelligence for him instead of mourning Erik's removal from the house. The less Damian knew of her true feelings the better.

Then when she pleased Mahomet with a favorable prediction, she used the head wife's successful outing to plead for her and Landina to be allowed to make a brief pilgrimage across the city to the Hagia Sophia. Landina was a follower of *Kristr,* Valdis explained, and wished to pray for a son in a manner that might meet with her God's approval. This request could not fail to meet with Habib Ibn Mahomet's favor. What man could possess too many sons?

"And you, my seeress," Mahomet had asked. "What might you be seeking among the Christians?"

"Enlightenment," she answered smoothly. "*Seid* craft bids me open myself to wisdom. Does not the name Hagia Sophia, Church of Holy Wisdom, suggest it may offer me new insight? I seek wisdom where ever it may be found that I may better serve my master."

In the end it was decided the two women would go together under Publius's watchful eye. The eight bearers of their sedan chairs could be stationed at the many doors of the great church to make sure Valdis and Landina did not slip away from them. None of the faithful Muslims wished to sully themselves by actually setting foot inside the building dedicated to the worship of another deity besides Allah the Merciful.

As they neared the basilica, Valdis too was trepidacious. The structure was designed to intimidate. Its scale was huge, a series of half-domes flanked by four spires stabbing the gray sky and crowned with a monstrous full dome. The church was a veritable beehive of activity with small knots of worshippers coming and going from the many doors.

If he was even here, how would she ever find Erik amid this throng? His last runestick had been cryptic.

Thor's day, Hagia Sophia north gallery.

Even though Erik left the house of Mahomet, Valdis regularly found a carved piece of wood near the stone bench in the courtyard. Erik had arranged for the new Varangian who'd taken his place to act as a messenger.

Beside her, her friend Landina fidgeted with excitement. She hoped to see her beloved Bernard here as well. The meeting was risky, but if Erik managed to locate him at the Xenon, where many foreign visitors to the city lodged, Landina was sure Bernard would dare to come.

"Remember," Publius admonished them, "you are not to dawdle. Make whatever obeisance the Christian god requires and return as quickly as possible. The sky is threatening." He held out his palm, testing for a drop of rain. "I've half a mind to turn around right now."

"No, no," Valdis said. If everything went well this first time, she'd be able to make this pilgrimage a regular occurrence. If she could only see Erik, even for a few moments, she'd be strengthened to continue on the path that led to her freedom. "We will be quick. I promise."

The two women scurried through the basilica's tall bronze doors. Once inside, Valdis pulled back the hood of her burka. The walls were covered with mosaics peopled with solemn-eyed figures to whom a smile would be a mystery.

"In this alcove, they have a splinter of the True Cross," Landina explained as she led Valdis to a glittering gold reliquary. When the Frank saw it, she dropped to her knees before the strange artifact.

Valdis was confused by her friend's veneration for such a tiny object, and a humble one at that. The miniscule sliver of wood was entirely ordinary looking and further obscured by its extravagant setting.

"Why is this so important to you?" Valdis asked.

"It is a piece of the very Cross on which Christ died."

Valdis shook her head. Followers of *Kristr* were fixated on his death. In the North, it was the adventures and victories of the gods that were celebrated. The Tale of Ragnarok, the Doom of the Gods, was too somber for most settings and rarely received a favorable hearing.

Valdis and her friend crept forward, drawn into the building's open central space. The sacred place was so huge, Valdis's breath caught in her throat. If the relics and mosaics left her confused, the sanctuary rendered her incapable of speech.

The ceiling soared upward and far above them; a mosaic of the *Kristr* spanned the great dome, hovering over the milling worshippers. Valdis was surprised to see the Christian's god depicted as a man, albeit a very large one, and not the three-headed being she expected. Staring up at the astonishing dome, Valdis felt the same sense of smallness she experienced as a girl when she gazed into the endless Northern night sky.

Incense rose from the altar, sending the odor of sanctity over the gathering. An unseen choir was singing, the ethereal plainsong devoid of earthly passion. In comparison to the full-throated singing of the Northlands, these southern voices were bloodless. When the song stopped, the worshippers trickled out of the sanctuary.

"Landina." A man pushed through the crowd toward them. Valdis recognized the pale Frank she'd seen at Mahomet's table the first night she entered the Arab's house. He was undoubtedly Landina's Bernard.

Even though they were in a public place, her friend threw her arms around the man and hugged him fiercely. Bernard wrapped his cloak around her and drew her toward the more private curtained arcade.

"Remember, we haven't long," Valdis whispered after them, unwilling to break the deep stillness that settled over the nearly deserted sanctuary. Landina flashed a smile of unabashed joy over her shoulder, silently thanking Valdis.

Valdis couldn't blame her friend for deserting her. Landina had no chance of earning her freedom as Valdis did. This fleeting opportunity to spend time with her beloved was all the Frankish girl was ever likely to have.

The north gallery, Erik's rune had said. Valdis took her bearings using the faint light slanting through the circle of windows at the base of the dome to orient herself. She looked up at the open balcony above the arcades lining the sanctuary. Perhaps Erik waited for her in those shadows.

She mounted the ochre-colored marble steps to the second level and walked along the aisle, conscious of the soft swish of her kid slippers on the polished floor. She paced the length of the gallery without encountering a soul. She was almost ready to turn back and try the south side when she heard someone humming softly.

The tune was a Norse drinking song, one with decidedly randy lyrics. She followed the sound and found Erik on his knees in the second row of seats. Valdis saw the glint of his knife. He was carving something on the back of the pew in front of him.

Valdis watched him a moment, burning on her memory the tiny details that would give her comfort when she contemplated Erik on her sleeping couch. She noticed the way his hair hung over one eye and how he grimaced in concentration. The tenderness in her chest threatened to burst out of her.

He must have felt her intense gaze, for he raised his eyes to meet hers. A smile stretched across his face and he was on his feet and catching her in his arms in only a few heartbeats. He kissed her, not caring that a priest or acolyte might stumble upon them at any moment.

"Valdis," he murmured into her hair. "I waited for you last Thor's day. I was afraid you wouldn't be able to come yet again, so I was trying to leave you a message."

She ran her fingertip over the runes and saw that he'd carved the first two letters of his name.

"Publius is waiting outside. We haven't much time."

"Then we'd better not waste it," he said with a wolfish grin. Erik sat down and pulled her onto his lap. "I've been dying to hold you again."

"I want you too." She buried her nose in his hair and kissed his neck, tasting the saltiness of his skin. "But we must be wise." She wiggled off his lap and sat beside him, conscious of the heat of his thigh against hers. "I know it seems there's no one about, but they say the walls have ears in this city. No doubt they have eyes as well."

"You're right," he said as he brought her hand to his lips, flicking his tongue along her knuckles. The moist touch was unbearably erotic. The fact that it was such an intimate, forbidden gesture in this public place made the jolt of desire coursing through her all the more fierce. "I wish you weren't stronger than me."

He had no idea how weak she really was. She entwined her fingers with his. How would she ever have the strength to let him go again? "Is all well with you? Tell me everything."

Erik told her of his assignment as captain of the Arab dhow in the coming spectacular. "My crewmen are all good sailors, Northmen to a man, handpicked by Quintilian. Even though the dhow handles like a pig, we've drilled for some time now and everyone knows their business. I've made a modification or two that will make the ship answer quicker to the steering oar, but she's still no *drakar*."

Valdis frowned in puzzlement. The Byzantine passion for reenactments made little sense to her mind. Had they no storytellers who could bring the event to life with well chosen words? A good skald was worth ten reenactments, for a Nordic bard sent the total experience to the minds of his listeners, inviting them to relive the tale for themselves, to walk in the hero's boots, suffer his defeats and glory in his victories as if they were the listeners' own. Spectaculars reduced the audience to mere watchers, not participants.

"If you're destined to lose, what's the point?"

"The dhow was lost during the real battle because her captain had no imagination." Erik grinned. "I've studied the reports and figured out the error made by the pirates the last time. They may think the battle planned out, but they're going to be surprised. If we're going to do this thing, why not make it an exercise that will benefit the imperial navy in case they come up against a better sailor next time?"

"Won't that be dangerous?" Valdis said. "Your commander may disapprove."

"I've discussed it with General Quintilian. There's an unspoken rivalry between the naval forces and the infantry. The general likes the idea of blackening the admiral's eye if I manage to win," Erik said with a modest shrug. "And if I lose, at least the glory of the Empire's navy will have been earned, not handed to them by a scripted battle."

"Be careful." Valdis planted a quick kiss on his cheek.

"It's just a game, *dyrr*," he said and lifted their clasped hands. "But this isn't. What we have, you and I, it's the only real thing in my life. I never thought to find it, certainly not since I was exiled. It's *inn mattki munr*."

The mighty passion. Valdis drew a sharp breath. Many couples in the North married, had children together and stumbled through their entire lives without finding the mighty passion with their mates. Despite the obstacles facing them, Valdis knew she and Erik were the lucky ones.

Erik cupped her cheeks in his big hands. "I love you Valdis, and nothing will ever change it."

She looked up at his raw-boned face. His image shimmered behind a veil of unshed tears. "I love you too."

He took her lips softly, almost chastely. Valdis felt his love wash over her, fresh and cleansing as a mountain stream. It swept away the last of her bitterness over her family's rejection. Despite her strange malady, this man loved her, needed her. Erik's declaration filled every bit of her. She had no room for past hurts, no space in her heart to nurse old wounds. Her heart was whole again and she offered it to Erik without reservation.

Finally she pulled away. "I must go. If I hope to come again, I must please Publius this time by being brief."

"Mahomet thinks you see the future. Tell your master there may be a surprise in the reenactment. The entire city will be lining the quay to watch. Perhaps he'll let you come," he said, his face almost boyish with hope. "If he does and you come here again on Thor's Day, you might see me twice next week."

"I will pray for it," she promised, unable to resist one last kiss. Then she pulled away and nearly ran from him, lest she lose her resolve. As she descended the marble steps, she decided she might pray to the Christian God. It wouldn't do to insult the deity of the great city, and the Court of Asgard had certainly been ignoring her plight.

Valdis glanced up again at the gallery. Erik was standing now, looking down at her, his face so full of love it was a wonder the entire sanctuary didn't glow with the strength of it.

"All will be well," she repeated to herself. She would complete her task for Damian and win her freedom. Erik would be waiting. Valdis hadn't felt this hopeful about her future since before that disastrous spell at the *jarlhof* that caused her to be sold into slavery.

Valdis retraced her steps, looking for Landina. Publius would be upset if they were much longer at their "devotions." She revisited the reliquary and passed the sober mosaics. Worshippers gathered in small groups, milling about as they waited for the next canonical hour to signal the beginning of another service. Valdis began asking bystanders if they'd noticed a woman in a burka just like hers. No one could recall seeing her.

The Frankish girl was nowhere to be found.

With rising panic, Valdis searched each curtained alcove of the arcade. In the last one, there was a crumpled garment shoved under the marble bench.

It was Landina's burka.

"No matter how detailed the plan, it is impossible to see all ends."
—*from the secret journal of Damian Aristarchus*

CHAPTER TWENTY-FIVE

"Where is she?" Publius demanded, his jowls quivering with rage.

"I don't know," Valdis said truthfully. She was half delighted that her friend managed to escape with her lover and half afraid over the awkward position in which Landina left her. Bernard must have brought some type of disguise into the church with him for Landina to slip on. Then he somehow spirited her past the bearers who would be looking for an odalisque in a burka. "I have no idea where she is."

Far, far away, Valdis hoped.

"How can you purport to be a seeress and not know what she was planning?" Publius turned an alarming shade of purple. "You have eyes at least. You must have seen something."

Erik's words came back to save her. *Tell your master there will be a surprise at the reenactment.*

"My Sight is turned always to the betterment of the master," Valdis lied. "I saw nothing of Landina's disappearance because the spirits chose to reveal a vision to me while I was inside the church. Mahomet will wish to hear what I have received from the powers."

Publius's face contorted into a mask of fury. He barked orders to the nearest of the bearers, who set off at a run to collect his fellows. The eunuch wrung his pudgy hands and muttered imprecations under his breath. When the bearers were assembled, Publius had formulated his plan.

"There are many places to hide in the great city, but thanks to our excellent defensive walls, only a few places by which to leave. You, Claudius to the Blanchernai." He pointed to one skinny fellow. "Demos take the Xylokerkos Gate. Argos the Pege. Get yourself to the Polyandrian, Lucan. Theos, take Lysander there with you and scour the Harbor of Theodosius. The rest of you cover the Golden Horn and pray that the tide is out or she is still seeking passage on a ship there. Well, don't stand there gaping. What are you waiting for?"

"But what of the sedan chairs?" Demos asked.

"Forget them. Leave them. Why are you still here? Go!" Publius screamed. "If your delay allows Landina to escape, I will see her weight is taken out of your miserable hides!"

A few passersby turned their heads at his outburst, then hurried on about their own business. Beating a slave was a common occurrence. Threatening one didn't merit a second glance.

"Your pardon, but . . . ," Demos spoke again with obvious reluctance. "The woman has already slipped by us once, Excellency, because we were watching for two women in bourkas. We don't know what the odalisque looks like beneath her veil."

Publius hissed like a kettle near to boiling. "She has

dark brown hair and blue eyes. Her skin is almost as fair as this one."

The eunuch skewered Valdis with a frown. In her haste to rejoin him, she'd forgotten to cover her face.

"Pull on your hood," he ordered. "Have you no decency?" Publius turned back to the bearers, holding out a hand to indicate Landina's height. "The Frankish girl you seek is this tall. She speaks with an abominable Frankish accent. When you find her, you have permission to strip her. You will know it is her by the scarring on her back." Publius cast a slant-eyed gaze at Valdis. "Landina is too timid to have done this on her own. She will no doubt be traveling with someone. You are still looking for two people. A man is with her, most likely."

Valdis could almost see the thoughts tumbling around in his brainpan. Had he remembered Bernard, the Frankish merchant who dined with Mahomet the first night Valdis entered the Arab's house?

"When you reach the gates and the harbors, tell the captain of the guard that Publius Mendalaeus will pay ten gold bezants to the man who helps you apprehend the girl and her companion. Do not leave your stations until she is found or you receive word from me that she is dead," Publius said, his alto voice ragged with rage. "Away with you now."

The slaves scurried off, making for their assigned positions. Valdis suspected they were grateful to escape the eunuch's irate presence. When Publius turned his attention back to Valdis, his eyes narrowed to slits.

"If I find you knew of the wretched girl's plans, I will make you suffer the pangs of the damned," he promised before waddling away. "Come. We must walk home now."

"We could hire a carriage," Valdis suggested, seeing how difficult it was for Publius to move his bulk along the broad Mese. Vigorous exercise would only worsen his mood.

Publius rounded on her. "Are you really in such a hurry to greet the master with this news?"

As Valdis trudged after Publius, rain started to fall. They'd both be soaked to the skin by the time they reached the master's house. Still, it was a good thing Mahomet's grand abode was situated far from the Hagia Sophia on one of Miklagard's seven hills. It would take that long for Valdis to come up with a plausible tale.

Landina's escape put Valdis in a tenuous position. Mahomet would surely demand to know, as Publius had, why she hadn't foreseen the girl's plan. Or at least why Valdis and Landina had parted company long enough for the Frank to make good on her escape. Mahomet's wrath would be terrible.

And yet, when Valdis thought of the Frankish girl, she could only pray her attempt would prove successful.

"Sprout eagle's wings, my friend," she murmured under her breath. "May they bear you home."

"Explain yourself," Mahomet demanded after he summoned Valdis to his chambers. Publius cringed in the corner, a fresh red weal rising on his quivering cheek. Mahomet held a thin lash in his hand, a drop of blood trembling on the tip. "I want an account of everything that happened in the infidel's house of worship. Leave nothing out."

Valdis drew a deep breath to calm her shivering spirit. "Landina and I—"

Mahomet cracked the whip at her, missing her by an eyelash. "Use that odalisque's name again and I shall not stay my hand a second time."

Valdis dipped her head in deference, but steeled herself not to tremble. "We entered the church together. As you know, I am no follower of *Kristr*. I seek the spirit realm where ever it may be found. There is a Presence there."

That much at least was true. Valdis decided to deviate from the truth as little as possible. It might save her from being tripped up under rigorous questioning.

"The one who was with me showed me a relic she called the Splinter of the True Cross. She knelt to pay homage to the object," Valdis said as she straightened her spine.

"As a pagan, you surely did not."

"No, but after that, the spirits who speak to me chose to reveal a vision of the future." This too was true, for wasn't Erik her future?

"Let us pretend for a moment that I believe you." Mahomet scowled at her, his thick brows meeting over his knife-sharp nose. "What did you see, my oracle?"

"I looked through the mist and there I saw a great sea battle, and yet not a battle," Valdis began. The more she could spin out her narrative, the more likely she'd convince him of her vision. "The emperor's eagle crested the waves, yet the waves were not so high as to suggest the *drommond* was on the open sea. Then I saw another craft, one not belonging to the Empire. It was low and sleek, like the ship which bore me from my homeland here to the Empress city. An Arab dhow."

Mahomet glared at Publius, who looked as if he might melt into a lardy puddle at any moment. Valdis caught a whiff of urine, the stench of fear emanating from the eunuch.

"Publius has been filling your head with news of the upcoming spectacle," Mahomet said. "So far, you tell me nothing."

Publius seemed to realize the threat to his own skin might be mitigated by Valdis's successful vision. "No, my master," he hesitantly spoke up. "I have said nothing to the seeress about the spectacle. Neither to her nor to any of the women of the zenana. Why should they desire to know anything which happens beyond these walls when the light of your presence radiates so strongly upon us here that even the sun is pale by comparison?"

Mahomet waved away the eunuch's fulsome praise, but Valdis's saw his moustache twitch with satisfaction. Publius's cringing and groveling fed the silk merchant's vanity. Mahomet turned back to Valdis.

"How fared this battle that was not a battle?"

"At first, the *drommond* and the dhow moved like a pair of dancers on the waves, circling and dipping. It was as if the turns were prearranged," she said, pressing her momentary advantage. "But then something happened which the eagle did not expect."

"What?" He all but pounced on her.

"The dhow diverted from its plan, confounding the *drommond*," she extemporized. Vagueness was essential to an oracle. "And as I was watching, a thick cloud covered both vessels and they were hidden from my sight."

One corner of his mouth curved like a scythe. "A cloud? Would you say it was like smoke, perhaps?"

"Perhaps," she conceded, pleased to have pulled him into her tale. "And then my mind was drawn back from my wanderings with the spirits, back to the Hagia Sophia. I found myself where my vision began. But alas, all that remained of my companion"—Valdis was careful not to call Landina by name—"was her discarded burka."

"You saw nothing else?"

"No, master, I did not see when she rose up or when—"

"No, no, forget her. Tell me more of the vision. You

saw no more of the battle?" He narrowed his eyes at her. "There was no other vessel?"

"There may have been another hidden in the mist," she said uncertainly. Like all fortune tellers, she hoped to hit upon what would most please her audience. She couldn't say that Erik's crew would best the Greek ship. Given the unequal nature of the contest, the finest *drommond* in the Byzantine fleet against a much smaller craft, the most Erik hoped to accomplish was to embarrass an overconfident admiral. "The outcome is shrouded, but this much is certain. The course of the prearranged battle will not go as planned. There will be an unpleasant surprise for the Emperor's force."

"Unpleasant, yes." Mahomet sank into his favorite chair, tugged his beard in thought and raised a brow at her. "I believe your vision. There will be a surprise for the emperor. You will accompany me, my Northern blossom, to the Harbor of Theodosius to view this spectacle."

Valdis fought to contain her joy. She doubted she'd be allowed to return to the Hagia Sophia any time soon after this disaster, but at least she'd be able to watch Erik pilot the dhow in circles around the Greek ships.

"But if the eagle does not disappear into the mists as you said, then I will know your prescient abilities are of no consequence," Mahomet said, motioning her to come closer. Valdis forced herself to walk calmly toward him. When she came within reach, he snaked out a hand and grasped a handful of her long hair, pulling her to her knees.

Valdis gritted her teeth, determined not to cry out. Mahomet cocked his head at her, regarding her with amused interest.

"Publius told me you have an unusually high tolerance for pain. You wouldn't cry out when your feet were

whipped with the bastinado. With the Frankish girl
gone, my garden of delights is minus one flower. If your
vision proves false, I shall enjoy plumbing the limits of
your resistance to exquisite agony."

"In the fog of battle, it is important to know the location of both your allies and your enemies."
—*from the secret journal of Damian Aristarchus*

CHAPTER TWENTY-SIX

"I don't like it," Haukon said as he helped Erik don his breastplate and back armor. "Why can't these Byzantines be satisfied with a dancing girl and a horn of ale? That's all the entertainment a man really needs."

Erik laughed in agreement with his friend.

"Don't the Greeks have skalds to tickle their ears?" Hauk wondered. "A sea battle is many things, but entertaining is not one of them. This smells wrong."

"You sound like an old woman. The emperor wants a spectacle. I intend to give him one. It's as simple as that."

"Just be sure you don't give him more than you bargain for," Hauk said morosely. "I tell you, couriers have been flying to and from Mahomet's house since last week. I followed one and guess where he ended up?"

"At the estate of Leo Porphyrogenito," Erik said as he fastened bronze greaves to his shins. Even though the plan didn't call for hand to hand fighting, it was necessary that the participants look ready for anything.

"Porphyro—what?"

"Porphyrogenito. Don't frown. It only means 'purple-born.' Leo is one of the few nobles fortunate enough to have been birthed in the royal marble chamber," Erik explained. "He had no say in the matter, but the circumstances of this birth certainly gave the man deluded ideas of his own worth."

"But how did you know Mahomet has been in contact with the emperor's nephew?"

"I kept my eyes open while I was in the Arab's household. It's obvious that Mahomet hopes to be a king-maker when the time comes for the Bulgar-Slayer to die, and he's thrown his lot with Leo. It's all politics with these Byzantines. You know that." Eric slung his battle ax over his shoulder, enjoying the familiar weight against his back. Even though the battle was staged, the weapons were real enough. He hoped he wouldn't lose any men today in this farce. "The Greeks don't take a piss without first wondering which faction will be incensed and which will be pleased with it."

"Just make sure you're not standing under the wrong balcony when they decide to release their water," Hauk said, crossing his beefy arms over his chest.

Erik cocked his head at his comrade. "That's not exactly an ill-wish, but it's still no way to send a friend into battle, even a sham one."

"You're right," Hauk said. "I wish I was going with you to watch your back."

Erik clapped a hand on Hauk's shoulder. "So do I, but you're doing something even more important for me. You're watching my heart. See that Valdis comes to no harm today."

"Depend upon it." Haukon nodded. "Luck in battle."

"Strength and honor," Erik said repeating the time-worn response. For the first time in years, the words felt right.

His honor was intact again. He'd kept faith with his pledge to the emperor and he'd not stooped to opportunistic murder of Mahomet's assassin when it might have been the safer path. He never regretted killing that slayer of innocents in fair combat, but remorse over his brother's death still dogged him. Erik suspected there was no expunging that guilt, no matter how honorably he lived.

Strange how whenever he thought of his brother of late, Erik didn't see Olaf in bed with his wife anymore. He saw his brother as he was when they were boys—hunting together in the forests, stealing honey cakes when their mother wasn't looking, standing back to back, taking on all comers when someone insulted one of them.

Olaf, his brother. His partner in a thousand youthful adventures. The traitor in his marriage bed.

Victim of Erik's *berserkr* rage.

Erik shook off the morbid reverie. No good would come from mulling over the past. Especially when today held such promise.

He would tweak the admiral's nose, win fame for his crew and hopefully distinguish himself well enough to earn a boon from the emperor. It was not unheard of. Basil II routinely rewarded those who entertained him well in the Hippodrome, granting the most grasping request with Imperial lavishness.

Why not one who gave good sport on the waters of the harbor?

Erik would ask for Valdis, the seeress belonging to Habib Ibn Mahomet, to have her as his wife. The emperor had more gold and silver than any man in all the nine worlds. He could give life to the most outlandish wish. Erik's desire was a simple one by Byzantine standards.

For now though, he banished all thoughts of Valdis

from his mind. A warrior couldn't afford a moment's distraction.

With hopeful determination, Erik stepped out of the tent near the harbor and gazed out on the cerulean water. On the open sea, a man might show his true mettle. After all the artifice, all the political intrigue in the great city, finally, he was engaged in something he understood. On the far side of the harbor, he saw the tall mast of the *drommond,* the ship his much smaller dhow would square off against.

But he knew it wasn't a contest between ships. This was a combat of captains, a test of wills, a clash of strategies.

And Erik knew some tricks that would startle the stodgy Greek admiral to the toes of his gilt sandals. He leapt over the low gunwale and took his place at the steering oar.

"All right, men," he bellowed to his crew. "Let's show these sons of noseless mothers what seamanship really is!"

In the original battle, the pirate dhow had fled from the Greek ship, and so it was planned in this exercise. Erik adhered to orders as he steered his vessel away from the ponderous adversary. With relentless precision, the Byzantine ship with its eagle standard emblazoned on every surface pursued the smaller craft. The rhythmic pounding of the drums to signal oar strokes steadily increased.

When the dhow was captured before, the pirate crew wore itself out trying to outrow the better equipped Greeks. Erik would not make the same mistake.

"To the mast," Erik shouted. "Now!"

With a sharp salute, a crewman wiggled up the main mast and loosed one of the modifications Erik had made to his craft. It was a new sail—a large square of tightly woven wool. The dhow might not be a sleek drag-onship, but Erik was determined she should be as well-dressed as one. The extra cloth caught the wind and the dhow pulled away from the *drommond* with ease.

Cries of dismay from the Greek ship carried over the water. Now the *drommond*'s crew would expend more energy trying to catch him than he would with his eva-sion tactics.

"Archers, prepare to loose," he heard the *drommond*'s commander bellow, frustration making his voice ragged.

Erik turned his eyes skyward. A black arc of arrows soared into the brilliant blue. They disappeared in the sun and he could no longer track their path.

"Up shields," he ordered. To a man, his crew huddled beneath their circular discs of hardened leather. Like an incoming swarm of hornets, the volley of arrows buzzed toward them. All around him, the harbingers of fletched death slapped into the wooden ship, quivering upright along the gunwale like the hackles on a dog's back. Once the hail of arrows ended, Erik and his crew threw back their heads and roared their defiant survival to the sky.

A quick glance around the ship told him a couple of men had been nicked with flesh wounds, but no one was grievously wounded. All of them grinned wolfishly at him, ready for his next command.

"Bring her around," he shouted. "We're going to shear a few sheep."

Where the pirate dhow captain's strategy had been flight, Erik's would be a surprise attack.

"Ramming speed!" he bellowed from his place at the steering oar. His crew rowed in concert without need of a drummer. Their hearts pounded as one.

"Axes to the ready," Erik yelled.

The dhow plowed the waves toward the eagle figure-head, presenting a small target for arrows as they bore down on the *drommond*'s prow. It must appear to the admiral that the dhow was about to crash into the *drommond* in a suicidal attack.

"Portside, up oars," Erik called at the last possible moment. The crewmen stood their oars on end and shipped them in one fluid movement. The dhow veered away from the snout of the Greek ship and clattered along side the *drommond*. Erik had reinforced the prow of the dhow with a strip of metal. The sharp nose splintered all the *drommond*'s oars on the port side while giving the rowers a nasty jolt.

"Axes to hand." Erik pulled out his double-headed battle-ax and sliced away at every rope and rigging that passed within his reach. The *drommond*'s sails went slack, dangling limply from the spars.

Some of the Greek sailors offered stunned resistance, but most watched in horror as the smaller ship disabled their proud vessel. As Erik expected, the admiral had salted his crew with noblemen and courtiers who wanted to bask in the glory of a prearranged naval conquest. The sight of Varangian *barbaroi* wielding battle-axes in earnest took them aback.

But just before the dhow won clear of the *drommond*, Erik was forced to duck beneath the swipe of an Imperial gladius. He felt the rush of air as the blade swept over his head. He turned in time to see a man with iron-gray hair and a fierce, deeply lined face leaning over the side of the ruined *drommond*, still brandishing the gladius and shouting imprecations after the retreating dhow. He was arrayed in a white linen robe, studded with gems and shot with purple.

The Bulgar-Slayer himself.

Even as the dhow's crew cheered their leader's cunning, Erik's gut churned. He'd just led an attack on the ruler of the Byzantine Empire. Why had no one told him the Lord of All the Earth would be aboard the *drommond?*

He was a dead man.

"They are as good as becalmed," his lieutenant said. "Shall we fire a volley of arrows first or do you wish to board her, captain?"

Erik sank to his knees. In his arrogance, he'd killed his crew as well. They didn't realize it yet, but to a man, they'd all be hanged from the city walls before the sun sank behind the hills.

His dreams of glory and winning a life with Valdis, his honor secure, sank into the depths of the harbor like an anchor stone. He'd condemned the woman he loved to live out the rest of her days behind the zenana walls, the plaything of a vicious tyrant.

"What's wrong, captain?" his lieutenant asked. "Are you injured?"

Before Erik could rise and give an answer, a member of his crew shouted, "Look! Another *drommond.*"

The second Greek ship had slipped her moorings and was rushing to the center of the harbor. It was fitted out with the same Imperial eagles as the first, but from the top of the mast, a pennant with a lion stood out stiffly in the breeze.

A ship loyal to Leo Porphyrogenito was coming to the aid of his beleaguered uncle. Erik had been duped by the Greeks again. This whole scenario was designed to make Leo look strong and the Emperor weak and ineffectual.

The sight stiffened Erik's spine. If they wanted to take him in battle, so much the better. At least, he'd give his crew a chance to win a seat in the Hall of the Slain.

But to his surprise, the ship didn't swing toward the

dhow. The *drommond* bearing the lion's standard bore down on the crippled Eagle. A black cloud of arrows, a few of them tipped with flame, rose up from the lion bound toward the emperor's vessel.

This was no political trickery. This was a coup in the making. With the emperor dead, Leo might well be named the new ruler.

Erik leaped to his feet. "Man the oars! The Bulgar-Slayer is aboard the first ship. We're sworn to protect the emperor and by the gods, that's what we'll do."

Erik grasped the steering oar and muscled the dhow into a tight turn, heading back toward the eagle. Perhaps there was yet a way to seize honor from this day of deception.

The admiral had pulled rowers from the starboard side and spread them thinly on both sides of the Imperial *drommond,* but the ship still moved sluggishly toward its berth. He marshaled a return volley of arrows toward the lion, but Erik saw that the counterattack didn't slow the advance of the other *drommond* by a single oar stroke.

He maneuvered the dhow into the path of the oncoming *drommond* and called to the emperor's craft. "Row for all you're worth! We'll be your rearguard."

The emperor, who'd recently tried to separate Erik's head from his shoulders, nodded gravely to him, then took charge of the *drommond's* escape. Erik's spirit lifted despite the desperateness of his situation.

Then Erik bellowed to his crew. "Bend your bows, men."

The Varangians sent a hail of arrows toward the lion ship and screams carried across the water when some of them found a mark. A thin trail of smoke rose from Leo's *drommond* as its crew scurried about like ants on an upset hill.

"Look, Captain. She's on fire."

"No," Erik said as his last hope withered and died. "She's preparing to make fire."

Valdis watched from the top of the seawall as flames belched from the lion toward the dhow. Greek Fire danced across the waves, snaking ever closer to the small craft. The dhow writhed on the water, tacking and reefing to steer clear of the deadly flames. Behind Erik's ship, the Imperial vessel had won clear of the fight. Another fiery blast issued from the lion, and this time the dhow's sail flared up like a candle. Smoke engulfed the harbor and Erik's vessel was lost to her sight.

But the sulfurous wind carried the screams of the dying to her ears.

Valdis covered her mouth with her hand to keep from crying out. No, it couldn't be so. Erik could not be dead. Surely the sun would cease sparkling on the water in a world where Erik was no more. Iron bands tightened around her ribs and she couldn't draw a breath.

It was her evil dream, come to life. The lion and the eagle sparred with each other. Then when the dragon appeared to separate them, the lion roared fire on him and the dragon sank in the boiling sea.

Her vision tunneled and before the darkness consumed her, one coherent thought raced through her brainpan.

She had the Sight, after all.

"A man's heart is unpredictable. Who can know it?"
—from the secret journal of Damian Aristarchus

CHAPTER TWENTY-SEVEN

News of the disastrous reenactment swept like a fire-storm through the great city. The tale was on every pair of lips and it grew larger and gorier with each telling. Those who'd been unable to secure a place on the sea-wall to watch would lament it for years.

Everyone agreed it was the most realistic battle specta-cle every produced, and though there were casualties—pity about the Varangians, but they did deviate from the original battle plan, didn't they?—at least the emperor and his valiant nephew escaped unhurt.

There was confusion in some quarters for a time. The leader of the cotton-mongers guild insisted it seemed Leo Porphyrogenito was attacking the emperor's flag-ship at first instead of the *barbaroi* dhow. But Habib Ibn Mahomet, powerful magnate of the silk guild, put the lie to that notion.

"The eye can play tricks on a man. The emperor lives and the crewmen of the dhow are dead," he said, spreading his hands in a self-effacing shrug. "If the emperor had been the target—May Allah the Merciful forbid!—then he would have joined the Varangian crew at the bottom of the harbor. When does the mighty Byzantine navy incinerate a ship by mistake?"

Meanwhile, the emperor made discreet inquiries about the intentions of his nephew. Even Basil II had to tread softly, for his nephew was gaining popularity by the week as he continued to give bread to the multitudes at the Hippodrome on a regular basis. The Imperial investigators found that Leo was not in command of the lion ship, as the citizenry supposed. According to reliable sources, he watched in fascinated horror from the rooftop of the palace with his clique of courtiers as his uncle battled for his life in the Harbor of Theodosius. To a man, they all swore that Leo wrung his hands in despair over the fact that he wasn't in a position to come to the Bulgar-Slayer's aid.

In fact, if Leo could only locate the captain of his flagship, he'd happily turn the man over to the untender mercies of the Imperial Ministers of Truth for interrogation in the bowels of the Studion prison. The captain was nowhere to be found.

Some said they'd seen him lowered over the landwall in a basket near the church of the Virgin of Blanchernai.

But they didn't say it very loudly.

Valdis longed to stop the whispering voices altogether. The cataclysmic scene played over in her head often enough without hearing someone else's recollection of the events. She tormented herself with her own knife-sharp memories.

And with guilt.

If only she hadn't told Mahomet that there would be a surprise at the reenactment, perhaps the evil plot would never have been hatched. Erik would be out of her reach, but at least he'd still be alive.

She had no recollection of returning to the Arab's house after the disaster. Once the darkness of her sickness claimed her; no one had been able to wrest her from its grip. She learned that in the confusion, no sedan chairs could be found and Haukon, Erik's friend, had borne her home in his arms.

Concerned for his oracle, Mahomet called for Damian Aristarchus to come with his herbs and revive her. The chief eunuch stood watch over her bedside as her spirit wandered in deep darkness. When Valdis finally emerged from the fit, she couldn't speak at first and Damian counseled her not to try till she should gain her composure.

As if such a thing were possible.

She staggered through the days following that terrible one as if sleepwalking. Chloe had taught her to seize joy from every day, but there was none to be found. No light, no color, no sound could rouse her soul. All food and drink was bland and tasteless and every aromatic smell an affront to her senses.

How could she feel if Erik could not?

The one dim spot of hope was the fact that against all expectation, Mahomet not only allowed her to return to the Hagia Sophia, he encouraged it. After all, it was the site of her most recent vision. He reasoned that more would follow.

Every day, escorted by a gaggle of eunuchs, Valdis made the pilgrimage to her own personal shrine. She would pad softly through the massive basilica and up the ochre staircase to the gallery. There, with her forehead pressed against the runes Erik had carved, she wept till there were no more tears in her. Then she returned to the house of Mahomet, grateful to the once-hated burka she was forced to don for the way it covered her tear-washed face.

A spate of weeks passed, each day exactly like its predecessor. Every day, Mahomet would ask if she had received a new message and, despite Damian's warnings that she must think of something to satisfy her master, she reported that the spirit realm was silent. Damian dangled the promise of freedom before her, but that candle had dimmed to a mere glow in the distant future.

Besides, what would she do with freedom now?

There was still an hourglass of light left in this tedious day when she passed through the large gate of her master's home.

"The chief eunuch awaits your return," the porter told her. "You'll find him on the roof. He's most anxious to see you. Seems he has a new herb for you to try."

Valdis was too weary to protest, so she dutifully mounted the circular staircase that led to the lavish roof garden. She didn't particularly wish to see her old master. But slaves, even well-treated and coddled ones like herself, ultimately had no choices.

Except to choose joy, Chloe whispered in her mind.

No, there is no joy to choose, Valdis thought.

Chloe's sparkling eyes and rasping laugh came back to taunt her. *Then you are not as strong as you look.* Her teacher's sibilant tones were clearly audible.

Valdis shook her head. She was hearing voices now. Perhaps she was sliding into madness. She was nearly past caring. Even the call of freedom seemed muted.

The roof garden at the top of Mahomet's splendid house covered one entire side of the square. There the silent gardeners coaxed orchids and hibiscus into perpetual bloom. Poppies nodded in clumps and several trees in gigantic pots graced the garden with shade and provided a home for the bright canaries that roosted in their limbs. It was calm and orderly and the only place in her palatial prison where Valdis cared to spend time.

Usually, she had to share the space with all of Mahomet's other women, listening to their gossip and vicious backbiting. The fact that Landina had yet to be found was a source of constant irritation. None of them sympathized with the unhappy Frank in the least.

Valdis noticed only Fatima, she of toothless fame, refrained from joining the chorus of praise for their master.

Valdis took comfort in Landina's continued freedom, but she feared it would be short-lived. Not only were Publius's henchmen still prowling by every city gate and harbor, she'd heard him tell Mahomet that riders had been dispatched on every trade route with descriptions of the missing girl, along with the offer of a lavish reward for information leading to her return.

Mahomet didn't need Landina. He had more women than days in the month and, if Valdis could credit the rumors, the silk merchant kept other harems in the many cities where he did business. Landina's escape wasn't a wound to his heart, but it was an affront to his authority. He wouldn't rest until she was once again in his power.

Valdis looked around the roof garden, pleased to see it deserted. She should have expected as much. As evening drew near, all the women engaged in beautification regimens in the hope of being chosen by the master.

It was an honor Valdis hoped never to win again.

She found Damian seated on one of the marble benches that dotted the garden. His olive skin was stippled by the shade of a tamarind tree. He must have visited Valdis's chambers, for he had her slim volume of poetry in his hand. Damian was straining to read by the fading light of the setting sun. He glanced up and then slid over to make room for her beside him.

"Excellent poet, this Dionysus," he commented before reading a passage aloud.

The delights of a thousand dreams await within,
Yet I stand rooted outside your window,
trembling like a tamarind in the breeze.
Unable to move,
Unable to breathe,
Hoping for one flutter of your curtain.

Valdis bit her lower lip. Erik had recited those words for her.

"There is great longing in this verse," Damian said. "How perfectly the poet has captured the way a heart strains toward an unobtainable prize."

As her heart still strained toward Erik. Valdis thought her cup of tears drained dry, but a fresh spring welled up. She tried to hold them in, but once the first drop tumbled over her lower lid, the floodgates were opened.

The crimson sun hurt her eyes and Valdis squeezed them shut, but the tears still flowed. Convulsing sobs started in her chest, but she swallowed back the cry that clawed at the back of her throat. Only a tiny moan escaped her lips.

Then all at once Damian's arms were around her, cradling her head to his chest and patting her shoulder softly. All the while he murmured soft words that must have been meant to comfort her, but her mind refused to make sense of the sound. Finally, she stilled in his arms.

"For the pain you bear," he said in a whisper, "I am more sorry than I can say."

She was surprised to hear sympathy in his voice. Damian's dislike of Erik and the bristling antipathy between them had been obvious almost from the first. Now in an unguarded moment, her old master shared her grief.

"It wasn't your fault," she said, feeling strangely comforted by his embrace. "The blame is mine. I should never have mentioned the spectacle to Mahomet."

"No, Valdis, you mustn't reproach yourself, because it proved that your master and Leo are in collusion. Still, it's a pity about the Varangian."

A tremor shuddered through her. To her amazement, he slid a finger under her chin and tipped her head back. Then he did something she least expected from her former master.

Damian kissed her.

"If I allowed myself to feel guilt over the things I have done in defense of the Empire, I should never accomplish anything."
—from the secret journal of Damian Aristarchus

CHAPTER TWENTY-EIGHT

On the rickety rooftop of the poorest monastery in the Studion, the foulest section of the great city, the Varangian growled in disgust. He lowered the ocular device that allowed him to watch the couple on the rooftop several blocks away, wincing at the pain the sudden movement cost him.

"Careful, my brother," the toothless monk at his side said. "Your burns are not yet healed. The skin is fragile at this stage, but God is good. It appears you will live."

"But I'll never look like anything again," he said softly.

The monk smiled at him, the expression one of almost childlike sweetness. "It doesn't matter, Air-ryck." He struggled to force the percussive foreign name through his inwardly curved lips. "In the eyes of the Almighty, we all look the same."

Erik glanced once more toward Habib Ibn Mahomet's rooftop. Even without the looking glass, he could see that Valdis and the eunuch were no longer there.

It was just as well. Seeing the woman he loved in another's arms would only eat away at his heart the way the cursed Greek Fire had gnawed his flesh. Memories of the spectacle-turned-disaster churned in his gut.

Once he saw the dhow couldn't outrun the flames, he did the only thing he could do. Erik bellowed to his crew to abandon ship.

Better to die by water than fire.

Erik filled his lungs with a precious gasp just before the scorching breath of the Greek weapon filled the air around him with cinders. He hit the water like a stone, his shining armor bearing him into the depths of the harbor. He struggled to rid himself of the greaves and breastplate, clawing at the leather bindings. Panic wrapped its tentacles around his throat. Then he remembered his knife. He pulled out the horn-handled dirk and slashed the remaining leather to free himself.

His ears ached as the water pressure mounted, but even so he heard the muffled shrieks of those caught in the fire. Around him, his crew floundered, trying in vain to flee from the sickly orange glow illuminating the surface above them. In the ghastly light, he saw several men give up the struggle, their frenetic movements winding down like the clockwork birds surrounding the emperor's throne.

Once Erik freed himself of the weight of armor, he kicked toward the surface. His path was still blocked by flames. Part of the truly diabolical nature of Greek Fire was its affinity to water. It spread across the surface without abating one whit, as if water were its natural fuel.

Erik allowed a few bubbles of air to escape the corners of his mouth as he searched for an opening, any place he could grab a quick breath. He spotted a patch of open water above the foundering dhow and he swam through the charred wreckage as she sank in pieces.

He surfaced and dragged in a deep breath. The smoke

seared his lungs and the fire ringing the space closed on him with lightening speed, bubbling the skin on one side of his face with heat. He dived for safety.

His ability to hold his breath for long periods of time had won him several bets in the Northlands. Now it was his salvation. How many times Erik repeated the process of snagging a quick breath and submerging again, he couldn't remember. He only knew he wasn't always able to avoid the glowing Greek monster.

His right shoulder was burned. Scarred flesh pebbled up his neck and across one cheek. Fire claimed one ear, sizzled away his beard and much of his hair on the right side, but at least it left both his eyes intact.

Finally, Erik dragged himself up on the spit of land near the mouth of the harbor and lay there panting for what seemed like an eternity. Pain screamed to his brainpan as he staggered to his feet. All the attention in the harbor was on the safe recovery of the emperor, so no one spared him a second glance until Brother Nestor came alongside him. The monk saw his stunned agony and took him by the hand as if he were a little boy.

Erik didn't ask any questions. He just followed the monk, putting one weary foot before the other in mute suffering. The delirium of fever descended on him and he couldn't remember reaching the monastery where he now resided. Erik suspected he lost consciousness somewhere along the way and Nestor and some of his fellow monks carried his dead weight the rest of the distance.

"Your thoughts are troubled, brother," the monk said. "A peaceful heart will help your flesh mend sooner."

"Believe me, Nestor, my flesh will be whole ahead of my heart."

The monk cast a glance toward the silk merchant's grand house. "The woman is beautiful, without doubt.

But be warned by the story of King David. No good can come of gazing at a woman on another man's rooftop."

Erik smiled wryly. Almost as soon as Erik had regained consciousness, Nestor began telling him stories to help the time pass more quickly. It eased his suffering to listen to the monk's lisping voice as he related tales of wise kings who behaved foolishly and pillars of fire and sons who squandered their inheritance in a far country before finally deciding to come home.

Lately, Erik suspected Nestor told him stories not to keep him amused and distracted from the pain, but to woo him gently into the monk's faith. There was little chance of that. The Christian's god was weak and powerless. What kind of god let himself be killed without lifting a finger in protest? A god that puny, who couldn't even save himself, couldn't be counted on to come to the aid of his devotees either.

"Who is Olaf?" Nestor asked.

Erik looked at him sharply. He was sure he'd never mentioned his brother to Nestor. "What are you? Some kind of diviner?"

"No, just one who listens, friend." Nestor stood and began pruning the vines growing on the monastery roof. The grapes produced there weren't the best quality, but they served for making the homely house's communion wine. "When you were in the throes of fever, you called out the name. Many times. It seemed to give you as much pain as the burn."

Erik had only nightmarish flashes of the time he languished on the cusp between this world and the next. Rising from the icy mists of *Hel*, the shade of his brother came to reproach him.

Or to drag Erik back to that cold hall with him.

"It's a long tale," Erik said.

"Then I'd better get comfortable." Nestor settled next

to Erik, splaying his gnarled fingers on his knees and looking at him with expectation.

In a flat voice, Erik told Nestor of his wife's faithlessness and his brother's betrayal. Then with more difficulty, he relived the killing, or at least as much of it as he could remember through the black *berserkr* haze.

"So, you have done murder," Nestor said thoughtfully. "And yet, he was your brother and you loved him, so the memory pains you."

Against Erik's will, tears pressed against his eyes. He blinked them back. He never cried. Not at the funeral biers of his parents. Not even when Olaf's body was burned before Erik was sentenced to banishment. Not over the men he'd led to their deaths in the Harbor of Theodosius. A warrior didn't weep. Still, a tear slid down his cheek, scalding a salty path over his abraded skin. He swiped it away, heedless of the extra agony the rough touch cost him.

"Bah! Pain has made me womanish."

"No," Nestor corrected. "Do not be afraid to shed tears. You have earned them. The evidence of your remorse gives me hope for your soul. Even our Lord wept. Better men than you have let grief seep from their eyes."

"I have no doubt of that," Erik said sourly.

"You were banished for your crime and yet your punishment has brought you no peace." Nestor seemed to be mulling over the problem as if he were a physic diagnosing a patient. "In ancient times, a murderer might be condemned to drag the body of his victim with him as punishment. Bound wrist to wrist and ankle to ankle with the decaying corpse, the killer would bear a constant reminder of the wrong done. No one could remove it till the bones loosed from their sockets and fell away of their own accord. I cannot see your brother's body on your back, Erik, and yet you bear it just the same. O wretched man, who will deliver you from the body of this death?"

The image of his brother's moldering corpse made him want to retch. Nestor was right. Erik bore the load of his crime in his own heart. He'd never really believed in the Christian idea of sin, but he felt the weight of his guilt bearing down on him anyway.

"There is only one thing you can do," Nestor went on. "You must forgive your brother."

Erik couldn't have been more surprised if Nestor had slapped him. "No, you're wrong. Olaf is dead. Surely there's no going back now." Erik stood and paced toward the parapet. "Even if such a thing were possible, I'm the one who needs forgiveness."

"You're right in that," Nestor said agreeably. "Yet it is a principle woven into the fabric of the universe. In the measure that we forgive others, we ourselves find pardon. Release Olaf from the wrong he did you and you release yourself."

Olaf's face rose up in Erik's mind again, as he was as a boy. A sob fought its way out of Erik's throat and this time, not a single tear, but a torrent poured from his eyes. He buried his face in his hands and wept like a lost child. From his heart, he forgave Olaf for sleeping with his wife. He wiped the offense from his mind. He buried the hurt as a dog might bury a bone and resolved not to take it out and worry it again. The knot of bitterness in his chest dissolved into tiny pieces and washed away with the salty river of his tears.

He felt Nestor's bony, spatulate fingers on his shoulder, easing the shudder that coursed through him.

"Yes, my brother," the little monk said. "Now you have tasted the most terrifying power of Love. The power to forgive."

As his soul quieted in heartbroken peace, Erik decided maybe the Christian's god wasn't as weak as he thought.

> *"Novices to intrigue sometimes regard intelligence-gathering as a game. It is, a most deadly game."*
> —from the secret journal of Damian Aristarchus

CHAPTER TWENTY-NINE

Valdis was too stunned at first to protest Damian's kiss. She had seen Christians at the basilica share what they called "a kiss of peace" and assumed this was what her former master offered, a simple expression of comfort. But when he drove his tongue between her teeth, it was clear there was nothing sympathetic in his embrace. She shoved against his chest with both palms.

"What are you doing?" she demanded. "You endanger us both. Or do you suppose being a gelding will shield you from Mahomet's jealous eye?"

It was the wrong thing to say. Damian's dark brows lowered and his face hardened like marble. Valdis regretted throwing his debility in his teeth. After all, in a world where her family had cast her out and the man she loved was no more, Damian was the only one who seemed to care for her even a little.

And she hurt him to the core.

Yet he was the one who had always urged her to discretion. Whatever possessed him to kiss her like that?

"Forgive me." She stood and walked to the nearby potted roses to put more distance between them. "I shouldn't have said it like that. I only meant—"

"No, you're right." Damian's expression went unreadable as he waved her apology off. "It was a mistake to kiss you. It just seemed you needed something and I was caught up in the moment. We will not speak of it again."

Valdis nodded, but she felt a tingle at the small of her back. From the beginning of her enslavement, Damian felt safe. The kiss shattered that safety forever. Erik's instincts were right. Damian did want her, though the kiss didn't smack of passion. It was more like a test, in which she or he had failed. She'd heard the zenana gossip about late-made eunuchs and their unnatural sexual stamina. If she thwarted Damian's advances, would he still honor his pledge to set her free?

She would always be on her guard with him from now on.

"You usually visit me at daybreak," she said, hoping to bring some normalcy to their conversation. "What brings you at twilight?"

Before Damian could answer, the sound of commotion rose to her ear. Valdis leaned over the balustrade to peer down into the inner courtyard. Guards were dragging two people toward the pergola in the center of the garden.

Valdis saw that it was a man and a woman, though both had been whipped so badly, their clothing hung in bloody ribbons down their backs. They were forced to their knees while the guards bound their hands behind them. The woman raised her heart-shaped face to the fading sunlight.

It was Landina and Bernard.

"Assemble in the courtyard," Publius screeched, his

unnatural alto straying upward in pitch in his excitement. "Witness the terrible wrath and justice of our lord!"

Valdis flew down the staircase, jostling the squealing women of the zenana in her haste to hurry to her friend. The day she and Landina were sold as slaves off the docks, she'd offered mute comfort to the Frankish girl. Once again, all she could do was stand with Landina in silent support.

Landina's gaze darted over the gathering mob, obviously looking for Valdis. When she found her, the Frank's face broke into a sad smile. It was the only good-bye she could offer without endangering Valdis as well, but it spoke volumes—sorrow for her deception, thanks for Valdis's friendship and finally, farewell.

Then the Frankish girl turned her eyes toward her lover, and no matter how the pitiless lash fell on them both, she would not look away.

"I have failed you," Bernard gasped between stinging blows. "I am sorry, beloved."

"I am not," Landina said with fierceness. "We have known love, you and I. I would not trade one moment with you for the span of a hundred lifetimes."

"Silence!" Mahomet strutted forward, hands on his hips. His dark eyes snapped and his white teeth glinted like a wolf about to attack a helpless kid. In his rage, he was terrifying. "You have led my agents on quite a chase. Shall I give you over to them for sport to make up for their trouble? It will give me pleasure to see your living entrails wrapped about your own throats."

The guard wielding the whip threw it down and pulled out a wickedly curved knife.

"Master, a thousand pardons, but I must speak," Publius interrupted with a groveling bow. "Such things are not fitting for the women of the zenana to see. At least five are bearing now and we do not want to blight the children by allowing the mothers an evil sight."

When Mahomet held up his hand to halt the guard's action, Valdis felt a surge of hope. Was it possible that her master possessed a shred of mercy?

"You are right, Publius," he finally said as he held out his hand. "Bring my sword."

Hushed expectancy fell over the assembly. Valdis forced herself to breathe as Publius hauled his bulk up onto the raised pergola. He offered the curved scimitar to Mahomet, jewel-encrusted hilt first.

"Hold still, Frankman," he said to Bernard. "And I will give you a cleaner death than you deserve."

Valdis saw Bernard's mouth move, but couldn't make out the words. Landina didn't turn away as the blade sliced through the air, taking Bernard's head with it. His blood spattered her with a warm shower.

"I will see you soon, love," Landina said to the disembodied head. When Mahomet raised his sword again, she actually gave him a tremulous smile.

Landina's little head rolled to a stop in the grass at Valdis's feet. It lay there blinking up at her for the space of several heartbeats. Then the bright eyes dulled and her smiling lips went slack.

"Behold the mercy of our lord and master," Publius began chanting. The cry was soon taken up by the women around her.

Valdis did not join them.

When she looked up, Mahomet was standing directly in front of her. He kicked the Frankish girl's head away and studied Valdis for a few moments.

"You will dine with me this night," he declared.

Valdis swallowed the gorge that rose in the back of

her throat and bared her teeth at him, hoping he would take the expression for a smile.

He seemed satisfied and moved on.

Valdis bored a hole in his back with her gaze. She understood why Landina smiled before the blade fell. She had known love and the knowledge freed her from fear, even fear of death.

Valdis had known love too—love that unseats reason and drives all other passions before its unassailable tide. There was nothing Mahomet could do to her that would wound her more than the loss of Erik. She was untouchable. She was beyond the reach of her master's cruelty. Death would be welcome when it came for her.

But before I leave this Middle Realm, she promised herself, *I will kill Habib Ibn Mahomet.*

"It is said God is pleased to give us the desire of our hearts. Somehow, I don't believe the Almighty had my heart in mind."
—from the secret journal of Damian Aristarchus

CHAPTER THIRTY

Valdis wandered slowly through Hagia Sophia's arcade and under the huge floating dome with its enigmatic *Kristr* gazing down. Perhaps the god of this great city looked graciously on her in her grief. Last night she'd escaped Mahomet's bed once again.

Damian had been Mahomet's other dinner guest. Thanks to his surreptitious signals, she managed to satisfy Mahomet with vague predictions about silk prices and the coming chariot races. Her gift triumphed over his lust.

Her master was pleased enough by her prognostications that he called for another odalisque to service his body's needs later that evening. Valdis was grateful, but she was even more relieved he allowed her to continue her daily outings to the Hagia Sophia. Though it drained her emotionally to visit Erik's runes in the church gallery, it also anchored her to this world for another day.

Her steps slowed as she mounted the marble staircase. She liked this time of day with the mellow golden quality of light shafting through the windows. It was between worship services, so there were few people around. The basilica was quiet enough that she sometimes fancied she heard sibilant voices floating on the air currents soughing through the man-made cavern. She never caught any actual words, but the sound was restful, and if her heart needed anything, it needed rest.

Usually she was alone in the upper gallery, but today she saw a hooded figure at the top of the staircase. He turned away as she approached and disappeared into the shadows. That suited her purpose. She preferred solitude.

Valdis found her seat and settled into her ritual of mourning. She pushed back the burka so she could see the runes more clearly. A gasp escaped her throat.

Instead of just the first two letters, someone had finished Erik's name. Then the rune writer had carved the most astonishing word.

Alive.

Valdis covered her mouth with both hands to keep from crying out. She wanted to laugh hysterically, to dance till her feet bled, to run screaming his name at the top of her lungs.

Erik is alive.

She whispered her thanks to the solemn mosaic on the dome. Then she dropped to her knees and pressed her lips against the runes. If Erik were alive, then the world was put on its head. The sunlight was brighter streaming in the circle of windows along the base of the dome. The colors of the mosaic tiles were crisp and vital. The scent of incense tickled her nostrils for the first time and it seemed as if the half-heard voices that whispered through the vaulting space were laughing softly with her.

She stood to go and nearly ran into the man with the hood.

"Your pardon," she said as she slid past him to the stairway.

"Valdis," he said so softly she barely heard him.

She stopped dead. There was no mistake. It was Erik's voice. She turned to him, but his face was still hidden. Her hand crept to her breast to make sure her heart was still beating. Then she slowly walked toward him.

His gray eyes flashed in the shadows.

"It is you?" She scarcely dared believe it.

"Almost," was the cryptic answer. The man threw back his hood.

Valdis's eyes widened. But for the fact that he was clean shaven, the left half of his face was the same—the angular strong lines of his jaw and cheekbone, his high broad forehead. She'd never seen him without a beard and mustache. He looked years younger.

But the right side of his face had been ravaged by fire. The angry red skin boiled across his cheek and down his neck, disappearing under his clothing. Valdis wondered how far the river of melted flesh flowed. There was only a blackened nub where his ear should have been and what remained of his hair hung in wisps on that side of his head.

He was like the defunct two-headed deity Janus. Seen in profile, he might have been taken for either a handsome young god or a monster.

But he was still Erik.

And she loved him more than her next breath.

She lifted a tentative hand and touched his cheek. His jaw tensed and she drew back, fearing she had caused him more pain.

"Oh, my love," she said with a sob. "What have they done to you?"

"If you can't bear me, I hold you blameless. I will leave this city and never trouble you again. Erik the Varangian is dead. His oath to the emperor died with him," he said, his voice still husky from smoke. "But if you think you can stand the sight of me, I would take you with me, Valdis."

"And I would go," she said without hesitation.

He drew her into his arms and with great gentleness, he kissed her. For a moment, Valdis wondered if she were having one of her spells and this was only a vivid dream. Surely this couldn't be real, and yet his lips were warm. She slipped her hands under the folds of his cloak and his firm flesh met her touch. His big hands slid down her back and cupped her bottom. When he pressed her against him, she felt his groin harden with unsatisfied desire.

This was no shade, no phantom. It was Erik back from the dead. Wonder and joy expanded in her chest as her body responded to his with warm moistness. As their kiss deepened, tears coursed down her cheeks, washing away the last of her grief. When he finally released her mouth, she laid her head on the expanse of his chest, breathing in his dear masculine scent and listening to the rioting thump of his heart.

"I have booked passage on a ship bound for Italy," he said. "It doesn't leave until next week, but I don't think I can wait till then to have you."

Though she wanted him with a fierce yawning ache that caught her by surprise, Landina and Bernard's death was freshly scored on her mind. Now that Erik was alive, she had every reason to go on living.

And everything to lose.

"We must be wise. I cannot go missing until the ship is ready to sail or Mahomet will set his hounds on my trail," she counseled as she planted a kiss at the base of his throat. "And I have a debt to pay before I can leave this city."

She told him of Landina's end and her vow to bring Mahomet to his grave. To her relief, he nodded in agreement.

"I will help you," he said. "If everything I have learned is true, your master and his confederate were behind the attack of the lion on the emperor's ship and on my crew. I may not be oath-bound to the Bulgar-Slayer any longer, but I owe Mahomet a taste of the agony he gave my pledge-men who died in the harbor."

"Then let us plan, beloved," she said.

"Try to find out what new scheme your master is hatching and I will do the same," he promised. "And once we have finished with this cursed place, we shall drink deep from the horn of love for all our days."

She kissed him once more and forced herself to pull away, promising to come at the same time on the morrow.

As she walked back to her waiting escort, Erik's words played in her head like a half-remembered song.

"We shall drink deep from the horn of love all our days."

She only hoped the number of those days would be more than the fates had allotted poor Landina and Bernard.

"People change. Sometimes right when you're look-ing at them."
—*from the secret journal of Damian Aristarchus*

CHAPTER THIRTY-ONE

"Valdis, my oracle, the worthy chief eunuch's wine bowl is empty," Mahomet said. "And that serving girl has made herself scarce again."

Valdis couldn't blame the child. She was no more than twelve, her tiny breasts mere buds, and yet each time she refilled Mahomet's glass of pomegranate juice, he made a point of fondling her. Once he even joked about checking to see if the figs were ripe enough to be plucked. Damian smiled politely, but refused to join in her master's laughter.

She liked Damian better for it.

"Run down to the kitchen and scare her up," Ma-homet said with a sly grin. "Aristarchus looks parched and dry as a stick."

A dry stick. Was that not the new derogatory term for a eunuch she'd heard only last week? Damian's lips thinned slightly at his host's wit. She marveled at his forbearance.

"A good jest," she heard him say sardonically as she glided from the room. "Isn't it a pity we dry sticks run everything in this Empire?"

Once she reached the kitchen she found the serving girl sobbing in a corner. Valdis bent to whisper to her. "Get you to your bed, child. I will tell the master you are ill."

The girl swiped her cheeks with her small fists. "He'll have me beaten."

"No, he detests malady of any kind in his servants." Valdis winked at the girl in a conspiratorial manner. "Why do you think I've escaped his attentions? It's my falling sickness that turns him from me. Stick your finger down your throat and purge your stomach. You'll be safe for a few days."

The girl's face brightened, then fell in mock illness. She grabbed at her gut and moaned.

"Good girl," Valdis whispered and then went to fetch the wine Mahomet kept for his non-Muslim guests. With any luck at all, she and Erik would successfully rid the world of her child-mongering master before the girl's "illness" passed. She hadn't thought of a plan yet, but she was determined.

She climbed the stairs back up to Mahomet's ornate dining room and paused before the door. Damian was speaking, but she could hardly believe the words coming from his mouth.

"I've arranged for the guard to be negligent the night before the race," the chief eunuch was saying. "Your hired courtesan should be able to slip in and drug Heracles with no problem. He should be incapacitated for several days. The Greens may be the finest examples of horseflesh ever to grace the oval track, but without their driver to make them run as one, the Blues will take them without trouble."

Damian was planning to fix a chariot race. What devilment was this?

"As you requested, I have placed the word on the street that the Blues anchor, the Arabian mare that runs on the inside, has turned up lame. She assuredly is not, but even her trainer has been paid handsomely to say so," Mahomet said. "Because the Greens are so heavily favored, no one will back the Blues against them."

"No one but our purple-born friend," Damian said.

Purple-born? Was the emperor betting against his own team? From Mahomet's words, it seemed as if the chief eunuch and not her current master were the author of this plan. Valdis pressed her ear to the crack in the door.

"This will ruin the aristocracy and most of the high-ranking guild members, who will bet lavishly on the Greens, because to do so will show their support for the old Bulgar-Slayer without risk," Mahomet said with relish. "Leo Porphyrogenito will own them after the race turns the economy on its ear. They will be unable to extricate themselves from crushing debt unless they support the lion's claim."

Leo. As Damian had intimated, Leo was looking to hurry his uncle off the throne. The only surprise was that Damian seemed to be helping him.

The chief eunuch wasn't trying to flush out the emperor's enemies. He was trying to join them, even to lead them, if she could credit her own ears.

"That is why we should also plan to storm the Imperial box after the race, to press our advantage," Mahomet said. "While those in power are still reeling from their losses, we strike. Cut off the head of the serpent and its body may writhe for a while, but it has no way to spread its poison."

Poison. There was an idea with merit. If she could slip

poison into her master's drink, she would be free. She and Erik could leave the city without fear of pursuit. Let the Byzantines intrigue among themselves.

But Damian's duplicity troubled her. Lies, if such they were, fell from his lips as easily as if their conversation were about the weather instead of unseating the emperor. Valdis could trust no one. Her hand shook as she pushed open the dining room door. A tingle ran from her fingertips up her arm to her spine. Her vision tunneled. If Loki were with her instead of shut up in her chambers, the little dog would be growling now. She recognized the beginning of her sickness, but she was powerless to stop the Raven from descending to claim her. The wineskin slipped from her hand.

"Stand back. Give her some air," she heard Damian's voice say through the murk. Valdis followed the sound back to the waking world. "She's coming around."

Valdis's eyes fluttered open and she found she was lying in a sticky red pool of wine. She started to rise, but Damian held her down, his dark brows drawn with concern.

"Not so fast," he cautioned as he pressed his own drinking vessel to her lips. "Here, take some of this."

"Will she speak now?" Mahomet asked from across the room. Damian didn't have to warn him twice to keep his distance when her malady was upon her. Habib Ibn Mahomet was pressed against the far wall, a combination of horror and fascination twisting his features.

"Give her a moment. The spirits have disordered her mind," Damian said. "You've not seen the sickness in full flower before. Now you know the gift of Sight comes with a price. Her strength is sapped. Valdis will need to retire in order to reflect on what she has seen. I will escort her to her chambers."

Valdis suspected Damian wanted a chance to coach her. But she'd heard enough to know of his plans and if she could rattle him with her knowledge, so much the better.

"No." She sat up, putting a hand to her forehead. "Let me speak while the vision is fresh."

In truth, she'd seen nothing at all that she could remember while her spirit wandered between the nine worlds. But Mahomet didn't know that. And perhaps when she was finished, neither would Damian.

"I saw a mighty team of horses, even finer steeds than Sleipnir, Odin the All-Father's six-legged beast. Faster than thought, they surged around an oval. The horses were blue as the summer sky, fleet as clouds racing to cover the sun. None could catch them, certainly not the grass green team, rooted to earth and sluggish."

As Valdis spoke, Mahomet's face changed. He seemed to lap up her words like honey, and against his will, he was drawn toward her. Damian's brows arched in surprise.

"And as I watched the horses, I saw what made them so fast. A lion burst forth from the underworld and chased the team around the track. An eagle swooped from the heavens, trying to stop him, but with a mighty leap, the lion plucked the eagle from the sky."

Both Mahomet and Damian's mouths were gaping. As an afterthought she added, "And as the vision faded, a silk banner fluttered to the ground to be tramped underfoot by a great multitude."

She closed her eyes and sighed. "I leave it to you, my master, to unravel the meaning of these portents. Already the vision recedes from my mind."

A pointed look passed between the two men, and for a moment she feared she'd overplayed her hand. Then

Mahomet walked over, extended his jeweled fingers to her, and raised her to her feet.

"I had not realized the price you must bear for this gift," he said. "The power of the sickness is truly terrible, but the vision is one of equal strength. Once these events come to fruition, I will make sure you are never seized by the spirits again. Even though I will be giving up my oracle, if taking your virginity will release you from their grip, I will see you free of your malady."

Valdis gulped. This was an unlooked for reaction. The last thing she wanted was her master's libidinous attention—especially since Mahomet would surely discover her lack of a maidenhead. Images of Chloe's noseless face and Landina's severed head wavered unsteadily in her mind.

"My master is kind, but I am prepared to bear this burden in order to continue to offer you my gift," she said. "Has the prediction failed to please you?"

"If it be true, it will satisfy my highest desire," he said. "But this power of yours, it is surely too much for a woman to wield. However, if you could pass such an ability to a son, I would make you my fourth wife." His lips drew up into the lazy smile of a dedicated voluptuary. "Once this vision has come to pass, I will devote myself to the pleasant task of getting you with child and we shall see if it is possible for the gift to pass to my son."

The offer left Valdis speechless. So it wasn't concern for her burden that prompted his solicitousness; it was greed for power. Even if she were able to swallow her repugnance and feign virginity convincingly, a child would tie her to this cursed house like an anchor stone.

If such a thing happened, she'd never be free.

"I wonder if it is possible for a spider to become tangled in his own web."
—*from the secret journal of Damian Aristarchus*

CHAPTER THIRTY-TWO

Huddled in the shadows of the Hagia Sophia gallery, Valdis told Erik of the overheard conversation between Mahomet and Damian, the devastating spell and her master's unexpected reaction to her malady.

"What we do, we must do quickly," Erik said, tugging her into his protective embrace. "I will not let that jackal have you. There are many doors leading from this place and countless holes in this city to hide in till our ship sails. Come with me now, love."

"I dare not," Valdis said, remembering the net spread for Landina and her Bernard. "Mahomet has eyes everywhere and Damian would be after us as well because I know of his plans. We'd never leave Miklagard alive."

"Then I'll have to kill them both," Erik said without malice.

"You'd never get close enough," Valdis said. "You know what kind of security surrounds them."

Erik smiled grimly. "You're talking to a Varangian, remember. I helped devise that security. I'll find a way to breach it."

Valdis laid her head on his shoulder, wishing the world would dissolve around her and she could fade into the next one with this man she loved.

"There are so many unanswered questions," she said with a sigh. "Damian is chief eunuch. He's risen high in the Byzantine court thanks to the emperor's favor, and yet Damian betrays him. Why should he turn on the one who has so elevated and empowered him?"

Erik removed his arm from around her shoulders and leaned forward, elbows on his knees as he studied his laced fingers. "I've done a bit of digging and found it was the emperor's order that gelded Damian Aristarchus. If this is your old master's way of paying the Bulgar-Slayer back for the loss of his manhood, I can't say I blame him for that." Erik unclasped his hands and clenched them into fists. "But I do blame him for using you to do it."

Erik's brow furrowed in thought. He'd made it a point to seat himself so the undamaged side of his face was toward her at all times. Valdis noticed he rarely looked at her full on, stealing quick glances at her in an attempt to shield his deformity from her gaze. How could she show him that she still loved all of him when they had only these stolen moments in a public place?

"If we don't stop their plans for the race, the city will be thrown into turmoil. There was an uprising at the Hippodrome once before, and the emperor at that time was nearly killed. Since then, contingencies have been put in place," Erik explained. "There is a decurion-led force assigned to spirit the Bulgar-Slayer from the scene at the first hint of trouble, but if Aristarchus is involved, we have to assume those troops are compromised. If there is civil war, the signal fire will be lit. The city gates would be shut and the harbor closed so no conspirators can escape."

"And our ship trapped with them," Valdis said. "But if the signal for the attack on the emperor is the unexpected win by the Blues—"

"We have to change the outcome of the race," Erik said, finishing her thought. "Even without Heracles, their regular driver, the Greens must win."

"We know Heracles will be drugged by a courtesan the night before," Valdis said. "Why not stop her from visiting him?"

"Because then Heracles would lead the uprising himself," Erik said with a soft chuckle. "The oval track is dangerous. No man is promised survival in a race of that sort. A last night with a highly skilled whore is a given in his profession. And if we stop her from coming to Heracles, Aristarchus and Mahomet will know someone is interfering with their plans. They'd suspect you immediately and I'm not willing to place you in that kind of danger."

"Then what can we do?"

"Leave the race to me," Erik said. "Make your trip to the church as usual that day. It's become enough a habit no one will question it. But be ready to leave quickly when I come for you."

"That won't work." She shook her head. "Mahomet plans for me to attend the race in the Hippodrome, to be with him in his moment of triumph." She didn't add that her master planned to end her tenure as his virgin oracle immediately after the race by taking her to his bed. That prospect was her own private *Hel* and she'd already decided how to deal with it. "I will be in Mahomet's box in the Hippodrome."

Erik put his arm around her again and pressed a kiss against her temple. "Then I will come for you there."

*   *   *

Damian stood on the far side of the street in the shadow of a doorway watching Valdis exit the Hagia Sophia. She minced along, her long legs restricted in her narrow burka, over to the waiting sedan chair, picked up the little dog that still accompanied her almost everywhere and seated herself for transport back to the house of Mahomet.

"Shall I follow the woman, Excellency?" the thin-faced weasel of a man at Damian's elbow asked.

The chief eunuch almost nodded when another figure striding from the church caught his eye. There was something in the man's stance—broad shoulders squared, his weight on the balls of his feet as if ready for action—that seemed vaguely familiar to Damian. Wind caught the man's hood and his face was bared for a moment. The hideous scar marring his features made Damian's lip curl in distaste. Then the man turned and loped away in the opposite direction of Valdis's chair. The other side of the man's face was undamaged. Damian sucked in his breath in surprise.

"So, you are alive, Varangian," he murmured. "But not the man you used to be. Well, are any of us?"

"Excellency, please," the informant's voice wheezed. "If I don't start now, I will lose her in the city streets."

"No, Bemus," he said. "I'll see to the woman. Follow that Northman for the rest of the day and report back to me this evening."

Damian pulled up his own hood and walked after Valdis's sedan chair, sure enough of her route to be able to hang back far enough not to be seen. She stopped in the market long enough to buy a portion of *pastfeli* for Publius. The fat eunuch was quite addicted to the sweet concoction of sesame seeds and honey. Valdis cultivated his compulsion whenever she had opportunity.

The way to Publius's tiny heart was indeed through his ponderous belly.

Valdis paused at a fruit seller's stall, haggling with the merchant over some oranges and pomegranates. So far, she had not deviated from her normal route and Damian almost regretted not following the Varangian himself.

But then Valdis made another stop, this time at an apothecary. Damian was puzzled by her choice. He was certain she wasn't ailing. Didn't he bring the herbs she needed each morning? True, she'd had an unexpected bout with her illness, but he'd boosted the dosage of mint for her since the last attack.

Damian lounged in the shade of the fruit seller's awning while he waited for her to emerge. The shadow of the stall crawled the length of a whole paving stone before Valdis reappeared with a small package.

"What are you up to, clever girl?" Damian wondered as Valdis's chair moved down the narrow street. She was close enough to home; he could let her continue without observation. He ducked into the apothecary shop instead.

The interior was dimly lit with a smoking oil lamp. The grimy walls felt close, the air stuffy, thick with incense and spices and the vaguely sweet smell of putrefaction wafting from behind the curtained back room.

"What can I do for you?" The shopkeeper was seated in a corner, all but invisible till he spoke. He took a pull on a bubbling hookah and looked at Damian quizzically.

"The woman who was just here," Damian said. "Did she seem ill to you? What did she want?"

"Are you the lady's husband?" the druggist asked, his dark eyes unblinking.

"No," he said as he fished out a bezant to offer the man. "I'm . . . I'm her friend."

The bezant disappeared readily enough, but the apothecary just cocked his head and narrowed his eyes at Damian in silent appraisal. He still didn't answer the question. "If you are her friend, why ask me? Ask her. Perhaps she will tell you what business brings her to my shop."

Damian took out another coin, this time rolling it through his fingers instead of extending it within the man's reach. "I appreciate your discretion. Perhaps you will also appreciate mine." He parted his cloak to allow the man a glimpse of his imperial palla. "Caius Augustus, the tax gatherer for this district, is a particular friend of mine. As quickly as you claimed my bezant, it makes me wonder if you sell more information than drugs in this shop. Are you sure all your tax payments are current?"

The man took another tug on the hookah. "The lady wished to buy a quantity of spotted corobane."

"Poison?"

"Most deadly," he assured Damian. "And undetectable when mixed in any liquid, either to the tongue or the nose."

"Little fool," Damian muttered. "Did she seem distraught? As if she was preparing to harm herself?"

The man's smile spread unpleasantly across his face. "When a person wishes to do away with themselves, they always ask me the same questions. 'Is it quick?' they want to know. 'Will it hurt?' These things are important to the soul who wishes his deeper pain to end. I am glad to be of service to such sufferers."

The bezant in Damian's hand caught the lamplight and sent a golden shadow dancing on the low ceiling.

"But when a person asks if a poison can be tasted or smelled . . ." The man shrugged eloquently. "That is why I asked if you were the lady's husband."

Damian flipped the bezant into the air and the druggist caught it in his clawed hand. As Damian wheeled to exit the shop, the man called after him.

"If you are the husband's friend also, perhaps you'd do well to warn him."

> *"When one ventures into an unknown country it is imperative to have a guide."*
> —from the secret journal of Damian Aristarchus

CHAPTER THIRTY-THREE

Damian put down his quill and studied the document before him. He shook sand onto the parchment to set the ink. There it was, to the naked eye all perfectly legal. He was satisfied the forgery would stand up in any court of law. He'd let it dry tonight so it would be ready to take with him on the morrow.

Tomorrow.

So much depended on everything working in concert. He went over the plan once more, checking to be sure he'd covered every contingency. It was a good thing he'd unearthed Valdis's little plot. So far, she had no idea he suspected a thing. And the fact that the Varangian yet lived, well, even that could be useful when the time came. . . .

But in the meanwhile, Damian had an appointment to keep. He glanced at the small water clock in the corner of his office. He'd have to step lively or be late.

Damian threw on his cloak, taking care to bring along the mask he'd ordered especially for this night.

The last thing he wanted was for either party to know his true identity. Once he cleared the Imperial grounds, he slipped the mask over his face and hurried to meet his guide for the evening.

Damian was going on a sybaritic exploration. He meant to test the limits of what was possible for a man in his state and what better way than to watch a similarly afflicted member of the third sex in action. Alexander Lucanus was a late-made eunuch with an exclusive clientele of well-born women whom he saw by appointment only.

Women whose husbands traveled frequently on business.

Alexander was waiting for him in the Forum of the Ox, at the base of the statue of Theodosius.

"There you are," Lucanus said pleasantly. "I was ready to give up on you. The lady we are visiting tonight does not like to be kept waiting."

"She knows someone is coming with you?"

"Eudora was enchanted with the idea of an audience." Alexander smiled, his fine even teeth flashing in the darkness. He led the way down a street that angled off the forum. "As you will soon discover, the lady is not shy."

"To be honest," Damian said as the hobnails in their sandals clacked on the cobbles. "I'm more interested in you."

Alexander's smile disappeared. "You've mistaken me. I am indeed an expert in pleasuring women. I have no interest in pleasuring men."

Damian felt his cheeks burn. "I only meant I want to know what you can do. Like you, I am a late-made eunuch. I want to know if I can . . ."

His voice trailed off. How could he put into words the longing he felt? It seemed like forever since he'd held a woman naked in his arms, since he'd felt the shudder of her release around his swollen cock, so long since he'd thought himself a real man. Even with the anonymity of his mask, Damian couldn't voice these desires to this paid lover of women.

"I see," Alexander said, his long-lidded eyes half-closed in speculation. "Let me get an idea of what we're dealing with then. How long since you were gelded?"

"Ten years."

"Did they take just your testicles or was your penis removed as well?"

"I've still got my cock." Damian bristled under his prying. "And it still stands on its own."

"Good," he said. "That was my next question. Don't get testy. I'm here to help, you know. Even if they'd fixed you so you have to pee like a girl, there are still methods of pleasuring you could try."

"I don't want to try," Damian interrupted. "I want to succeed."

"Duly noted," Alexander said. "Now about these cock-stands you're so justifiably proud of—only in the morning or are you able to be roused by a woman?"

Damian remembered kissing Valdis on the rooftop. When he plunged his tongue into her mouth, his groin hardened quickly enough. But when she pushed him away, he shriveled in a moment. "I am roused, but I don't know for how long."

"An honest answer," Alexander said with a compassionate glance. He turned down an alley so the back sides of a number of great houses were facing them. "So you haven't tried—"

"No."

"Not with a serving girl?"

Damian shook his head.

"I know a very discreet woman of pleasure who enjoys a challenge. She could—"

"I don't want to be someone's challenge," Damian said. "I just want to know what's possible. If you can do it, I can do it."

"Fair enough," Alexander said as they entered a walled garden and walked up to a dark door. "I will show you what's possible." He wrapped twice on the portal. "And after we're done here, I'll tell you what isn't."

Damian looked around as they waited for the door to open. This moon-kissed garden seemed familiar to him, but he'd been so absorbed in his conversation with Lucanus, he neglected to keep his wits about him and watch where he was going. When the door opened, he was grateful for the mask he wore. It hid his surprise.

The woman who greeted them was the fresh-faced young wife of Sergius Regulus, the aging ambassador to Crete. Damian had dined with the ambassador and his wife in this very house a number of times. Eudora—'Dora' to her clearly smitten older husband—was a model hostess, soft-spoken and apt to blush when Damian complimented her. Damian would have sworn she was the soul of modesty and propriety.

As soon as the door was closed, she pulled Alexander's head down and kissed him hungrily. Then she released him and delivered a ringing slap across his cheek.

"You're late," Eudora accused, her sweetly dimpled cheek taut with fury.

"I'm sorry, Dora. I came as soon as I could."

"So did I." She grinned wickedly at him. "You made me start without you."

He took her hand and sniffed it. "The smell of a freshly satisfied woman is one of the wonders of the world." He licked her fingers one by one. "No wonder you taste so delicious, my little tart."

"That's what I love most about you, Zander," she all but purred as his lips traveled over her wrist and up to the crook of her elbow. "No matter how bad I am, I know you're worse."

"Infinitely, my pet," he agreed. Then he grabbed her and pulled her in front of him, her spine pressed against his chest. He reached around and ripped open her palla to bare her breasts to Damian's view. They were golden globes tipped with crimson-tinted nipples. She squealed in mock alarm.

"Here you are, Excellency," he said to Damian. "Meet the breasts of Eudora Regulus. Sweetest tits in the Empire, and if they don't raise your standard, my friend, your flag will not fly."

Damian didn't dare say a word lest Eudora recognize him by his voice. Her breath came in shudders, causing her breasts to waver before him. His cock stiffened at the sight.

"Don't you want to play?" She slid out of her palla and let it pool at her small neat feet. Eudora pouted prettily at him.

"He's just here to watch, remember?" Alexander whispered into her ear as he cupped her luscious breasts and delivered a trail of baby kisses down her neck. "But I'm not."

Lucanus turned her around and lifted her so she could hitch her legs around his waist while arching her back to present her breasts to his lips. He took one of her nipples between his teeth and pulled back on it till she cried out. When he released it, the little minx put the other one into his mouth.

"More," she ordered.

He suckled noisily on the fresh pap as Eudora, the staid wife of the respected ambassador, threw her head back and growled with pleasure.

When Alexander finally came up for air, he looked back at Damian. "Time to go to the playroom," he said, and turned to walk with Eudora still wrapped around him like a Varangian's breastplate.

Damian followed the couple, half envious, half embarrassed by their whispered giggles as they led him through the ambassador's stately home. The Thessalian marble corridors were empty, the open doors leading into dark chambers. Obviously, the ambassador's gaggle of servants had all been given the night off.

"Eudora's very inventive," Alexander said over his shoulder. "What are we doing tonight, sweet?" he asked her as he set her lightly on her bare feet.

"You are the wicked Roman conqueror and I am Boadecia, the pagan queen of Britain," she explained as she led him to a wall where shackles hung in wait of a willing victim. Eudora clapped his wrists in the restraints, letting her bare breasts tease across his chest. She brandished a willow switch. "You raped my daughters, you fiend, and now I'm going to punish you."

The punishment consisted of undressing him slowly, pulling his robe up over his head and letting the garment further bind him since it couldn't be completely removed. Eudora used the switch more to tickle than whip him, and Alexander's bared member swelled to an impressive size.

"Now for the slave collar," she said as she opened a small casket on an ebony table. Eudora removed an ivory ring, yellow with age. She held it up for Damian to see. "A little trinket from the East," she explained.

The ring was smooth as glass and Eudora put it to her mouth and ran her tongue around the inside of the circle. "Zander has amazing stamina on his own, but when he wears this, I swear, the man could go all night."

Eudora slid the ring over her lover's purple head all the way to the base of his erection. "Now it's your turn to punish me, Roman," she said to Alexander.

A low growl issued from his throat. He tore the manacles from his wrists and Damian realized they were theatrical props, designed to be destroyed. Alexander grabbed "Bodecia," bent her over and took her savagely from behind.

Eudora was ecstatic. "Deeper," she urged before losing the power of speech as a rolling orgasm made her body buck with its force.

So, it is possible to bring a woman to completion, Damian thought, even though the earthy Eudora seemed easily moved.

From one feat of sexual athleticism to another, Alexander Lucanus and his client took turns being the aggressor. Though there was occasional submission, nothing remotely like tenderness passed between them. At one point in a standing position, while Lucanus was pumping away furiously, Eudora looked back over her shoulder at Damian, cupped her own buttocks and spread them.

"Come, my silent friend," she invited. "I've always wanted to be taken both ways at the same time."

Damian looked at the tight little sphincter winking in her crevice and shook his head. He was here to learn, not to experiment. Despite the erection aching under his robe, he still questioned his potency. When he was ready to take a chance, it would be with a woman who wouldn't flay him for a failure. Eudora stuck her tongue out at him and turned her attention back to Alexander.

When Eudora finally declared herself too sore to continue, Lucanus removed the ivory ring and handed it back to her. Only then did his prodigious erection subside.

"Same time, next week," she said as she handed her

lover a leather pouch that emitted a satisfying jingle. Eudora sent a glare in Damian's direction. "And if you're going to bring someone with you again, make sure they want to do more than watch." She yawned hugely. "Let yourself out, would you, Zander? I'm going to bed."

Damian and Alexander walked in silence back toward the Forum of the Ox.

"Well, now you know what's possible," Lucanus said when they reached the statue of Theodosius. "Do you have any questions?"

"Just one," Damian said as he reached for his purse. Alexander waved away payment.

"Eudora is more than generous," he said. "What do you want to know?"

Damian pressed the bezants into his hand anyway. "You've shown me what's possible for a eunuch. You said you'd also tell me what isn't."

Alexander sighed and studied the paving stones for a long moment. "It is possible for men like us to give pleasure, but we cannot receive it. Oh, the feel of a woman's skin is fine under a man's fingers, and what man can suck enough tits? But you saw for yourself, however many times I bring Eudora to the fields of Elysium, I never arrive at that blissful country myself."

"Never?"

"Never." He shook his head. "I hope each time that I'll pass a barrier of some kind and find a measure of release, but it never happens." His face hardened in the pale silver moonlight. "The worst thing is, I've begun to despise the women I service—all of them. The selfish cows take and take and not one of them can give me more than a handful of coin in exchange."

Damian felt despair emanating from Alexander Lucanus, the self-proclaimed king of late-made eunuchs. "Do you think it would be different if you loved the lady?"

Alexander shrugged. "I don't know. My heart has never been thus engaged." Then his sensual mouth lifted in a mocking half-smile. "So you love a woman?"

Damian nodded.

"Perhaps it would be different then," Lucanus conceded charitably. "Let me know when you find out."

If I find out, Damian amended in silence.

"The Devil indeed is in the details."
—from the secret journal of Damian Aristarchus

CHAPTER THIRTY-FOUR

"What do you think you're doing here?" Agrippina demanded. The round-faced slave ruled Mahomet's kitchen with the same high-handedness Publius reigned with in the harem. She snatched the knife from Valdis's hand. "Odalisques serve the master elsewhere. Let me see to the needs of his belly. You can tend to what hangs beneath it." She cackled at her own wit.

By coming early while the rest of the household was breaking their fast, Valdis had hoped to have the kitchen to herself to put her concoction together. She should have known Agrippina wouldn't stray too far from her domain. She turned a forced smile on the old woman. "What you say is true, Agrippina, and I could never hope to rival your reputation as a cook" —the woman grunted in agreement—"but I wanted to make something special for the master, to take with us to the races today," Valdis said.

"I already have a hamper of food packed and ready to go." Agrippina pointed to a wicker casket. "The master doesn't trust the food sellers at the Hippodrome and well he shouldn't. Filthy swine, the lot of them. He'll have leeks, olives and cold chicken curry just as he requested."

"But you haven't packed a drink," Valdis said with hope. "The Hippodrome is dusty and if the sun isn't hidden by clouds, it'll be hot as well. I have fruit here—oranges and pomegranates fresh from the market that I thought to mix for a refreshing juice. Please, Agrippina, I only want to make something special for him."

Agrippina frowned. Clearly Valdis had thought of something she hadn't. "You can help me then," she conceded, "but don't get in my way."

Valdis watched as Agrippina sliced the fruit and ran the pieces through a press to squeeze out the juice. She poured the liquid into a bowl.

"Here," she said, handing Valdis a long-handled spatula. "You can stir while I add some spices. Bet you didn't think of that. Any fool can mix juice, but only a cook can add the right flavorings to make it something special." Agrippina cast an appraising gaze at Valdis. "Not one of those others has ever thought to darken my kitchen to make something for the master. They don't seem to realize men like it when you fix them a special dish with your own hand. Keep this up and you'll be a favorite in no time."

Valdis smiled as if the status of harem favorite were her sole aim in life, while Agrippina added a pinch of ground cloves and a dash of nutmeg to the swirling juice. Then the cook dipped a finger into the bowl and sucked the liquid off to taste her creation.

She grimaced. "Needs honey." Agrippina took the honey pot from the top shelf and ladled in a generous dollop.

Valdis continued to stir, wondering how she'd be able

to add the vital ingredient she'd brought in the vial se-
creted within the folds of her palla without arousing
Agrippina's suspicion, or worse yet, insisting on a taste
of the finished product.

Agrippina dipped out a swallow of the drink in a
small cup. She rolled the liquid around her mouth for a
moment like a true connoisseur.

"Nectar," she pronounced.

"How about adding ice?" Valdis asked, hoping to distract the cook.

Agrippina's lips pursed tightly together. She obviously wasn't accustomed to receiving or taking suggestions in her own kitchen. She shook her head. "No, he
doesn't favor ice chips in his drinks, but this mix might
taste better cold. Now do you think you can pour it into
that amphora without spilling it? Good. I'll just go shave
some ice to pack around it and it'll be cool by the time
the race starts."

Valdis could scarcely believe her good fortune as
Agrippina waddled away to the cold room, where precious blocks of ice were kept. Her hand shook as she
emptied the powder from the vial into the amphora.
Then, holding the amphora steady as she could, she ladled the juice in a little at a time. Every other dipperful,
she cast an anxious glance over her shoulder and
shook the amphora a bit to mix the spotted corobane
thoroughly. She was fitting the bung into the mouth of
the vessel when Agrippina returned with a small crate
filled with ice in which to nest the amphora.

"That should do nicely," Agrippina said, rubbing her
thick-fingered hands together to warm them. She gave
Valdis an approving nod. "Serve the master as well in his
chambers as you've served him here, and I'll not be surprised to see you elevated to wife if you give him a son."

Valdis's stomach curdled at the thought, but she

thanked Agrippina for her well-wishes and her help. As she climbed the stairs back to her suite, Valdis wondered what would become of the cook and Publius and the women of the zenana once Habib Ibn Mahomet was no more.

It was a delicate business, this taking of another life; she had never even thought about it, much less considered carrying it out. Now that she was committed to it, she realized that her act would affect many more lives than just her intended victim. Had Mahomet arranged for his women and servants to be provided for upon his death?

Valdis doubted it.

And yet, even if she stayed her hand, Erik would not stay his. When he came for her at the Hippodrome, after whatever he did to undo the skullduggery already afoot for the race, Erik's sense of honor would oblige him to kill Mahomet to insure he didn't again try to help Leo Porphyrogenito unseat the emperor.

Mahomet was reputed to be a master in the use of his curved scimitar. He certainly handled the wicked blade with ease when he lopped off poor Landina and Bernard's heads. Valdis tried to tell herself she was bringing justice to her friend's memory, but her heart condemned her as a liar.

She was afraid. Erik was a blooded warrior, but how much had his injury changed his abilities? At any rate, a contest of blades was a risky, noisy affair, sure to bring unwanted attention at a time when she hoped to slip the leash of her master's control. Valdis didn't want to take any chances.

With any luck at all, by the time Erik came for her in Mahomet's private box, her master's body would be cooling in his ornately carved chair.

* * *

The beautiful horses known as the Blues were stabled in subterranean stalls beneath the massive Hippodrome. The flooring may have been sawdust and sand, but the walls enclosing the pampered equines were smooth, azure-veined marble.

Erik stole a glance around the corner and down the corridor where the Blues were housed. He saw only one guard stationed before the stables. Erik turned back to his friend, Hauk.

"Are you ready?"

"When someone back from Hel gives the order, what choice do I have but to obey? But I'm in no hurry to visit that Cold Hall myself, so what you're about to do, do quickly." Hauk opened the skin of date palm wine and sloshed half the contents over himself. Then he took a long tug at the mouth of the skin, the excess liquid dribbling down his russet beard. "Point me toward the guard before this rot-gut strikes me blind."

Erik watched from the shadows as Hauk stumbled toward the *tagmata* on duty, singing a ribald drinking song at the top of his lungs. Badly.

The horses snorted their displeasure at Hauk's growling voice, but the guard eyed the supposedly drunken Varangian with amusement.

"Look, friend," the *tagmata* said. "You're not supposed to be down here."

"Where's the privy?" Hauk slurred, all but running into the hapless guard. "Don't tell me they don't have one, a fancy tavern like this."

The guard tried to wave him off and argue with him about where he was, but Haukon was a huge man, head and shoulders taller than the Greek. And he lived up to the Northmen's reputation for stubbornness by refusing to believe he wasn't in an ale house. Hauk also provided admirable cover for Erik to slip unnoticed into the stable area while the guard tried to give him directions to the nearest privy.

"All right," Hauk said amiably between prodigious belches. "I go down this corridor, then up two flights of stairs—"

"Only one flight," the man corrected.

"Make up your mind," Erik heard Hauk demand. "Tell me again and talk slower this time."

Good man. Hope he doesn't overdo it, Erik thought. He and Hauk had seen each other through some tight spots in the past, but this scheme required more delicacy than any other they'd attempted. If Erik were caught meddling with the Blues, he expected to be drawn, quartered and fed to the great cats who were also housed beneath the Hippodrome in the emperor's menagerie.

Hauk had argued for killing the guard, but that would alert the grooms that the team had been tampered with. In order for Erik's plan to succeed, the Blues incapacitation had to be taken for dumb bad luck.

The horses whickered softly at his approach, tossing their arched necks and casting him inquisitive looks. The boldest one came and leaned his head over the stall, sniffing at Erik's offered palm and rolling his large liquid eyes. The stallion nosed him, the velvet nostrils aquiver. Erik reached into the pouch at his waist and drew out a handful of oats, salted with a noxious herb that horses seemed to find irresistible. The weed would reduce the animals to drooling sluggishness, but the effects would wear off by the time the sun found its bed. When Erik first told Hauk what he intended, his friend counseled him to hamstring this magnificent team to insure a lost race. After seeing them up close, Erik was glad he'd chosen a different path.

When Erik made his way out of the darkened stable

area, Hauk had managed to lead the guard a good ten paces away from the entrance. He was still trying to get directions to the privy. Erik advanced toward them, abandoning stealth.

"There you are, cousin," he said loud enough to make the horses stamp and blow in their stalls. "I wondered where you'd gotten off to." He turned to the guard and lowered his voice. "He wasn't bothering you, was he? Got kicked in the head last week, trying to stand up to a cavalry charge. He hasn't been right since." Erik sniffed the air and curled his lip at his friend. "Or sober."

A thunderous roar made the stones above their heads reverberate in sympathy. The games in the Hippodrome had begun.

"No, no harm done, but all the same, you'd better get him out of here," the guard said. "The driver and the grooms will be coming before long and they don't want anyone hanging about the stables."

"I didn't do no hanging," Hauk protested as Erik dragged him in the direction the guard had pointed. "I just got to take a piss."

Once they rounded a sharp corner, Hauk's frame straightened and he threw off his drunken disguise. He slapped a ham-sized hand on Eric's shoulder. "I guess this is where we part company. Even though I'm doubting I'll be needed after your bit of trickery, I'll hie myself to the emperor's box. I'm one of the guards for the Bulgar-Slayer this afternoon."

Erik stopped in his tracks and clasped forearms with his friend. "I haven't thanked you——"

"When was there need between the two of us?" Hauk said.

Erik's mouth wouldn't form the words. His heart was full for this friend who'd stuck by him through his disgrace and even traveled with him to Miklagard, this bizarre city of the Christians.

"Who knows if we shall ever meet again in this Middle Realm?" he finally managed to spit out.

"Then look for me in the Shining Lands," Hauk said, looking away lest Erik see his weak eyes. "We'll raise a horn together there. Smooth sailing to you and your lady."

"Strength and honor," Erik offered in return as Hauk stalked away. The words seemed so small a thing for their parting. He and Hauk had saved each other in battle, starved together hunting in the frostlands, and undertaken the greatest journey of their lives when Erik was banished and they ventured down the wild rivers to the Black Sea.

He would miss his friend, but now Erik was beginning a new journey with Valdis. Above him, the crowd roared again.

It was high time he wrested the love of his life from her master.

"When a plan falls apart, one has no choice but to improvise."
—from the secret journal of Damian Aristarchus

CHAPTER THIRTY-FIVE

Damian tried not to let panic force him into an undignified trot. He'd expected to have more time, to be able to make his preparations and join Mahomet and Valdis at his leisure, but the latest scrap of intelligence to reach his keen ear sent him striding out of Leo Porphryogenito's elite box with scant apologies for his untimely departure. He climbed to the farthest reaches of the Hippodrome and made his way along the outer corridor, far from the press of humanity jammed into the rows of seating.

The tigers from beyond the Indus were in the arena, stalking helpless antelope once again. The act was a popular one, and Damian didn't meet a single soul on his circuit of the vast oval. Then he heard the sound of footsteps behind him, a heavy, hobnailed tread moving at a fast pace.

Best to find out if he was being followed, he reasoned. Damian ducked into one of the many alcoves along the curving way, wedging himself between the wall and a statue of the inebriated Dionysus on a waist-high pedestal.

Damian could make out a man advancing steadily down the corridor, the figure appearing and disappearing in the recurring patches of sunshine and shadow peculiar to this hall, half open as it was to the outside. Chain-mail glinted in the light and the man's ice-grey eyes shone in the dark.

The Varangian. Damian almost swore aloud. He would only be in the way. Damian had half a heartbeat to decide what to do about him. As soon as Erik Heimdalsson strode past his place of concealment, Damian pushed the statue and brought it tumbling down on the back of the Northman's neck with all the force he could muster.

The Varangian crumpled to the marble floor with the remains of the sculpture in scattered shards around him. Damian stepped over his inert body to resume his journey to Mahomet's box. He was mildly surprised that Erik had been so easy to subdue. Perhaps the injury he sustained in the fire was even worse than it looked.

Then a grip strong as a crocodile's bite grabbed Damian's ankle and he fell headlong. Before he could collect his wits, the Northman had dragged his body back and plopped astraddle the small of Damian's back. Then the man grasped a handful of Damian's dark curly hair and pulled his head back to bare his throat. Damian felt the sharp kiss of the Varangian's horn-handled blade nick his flesh.

"Let me go," Damian demanded.

"You've used Valdis in your schemes for the last time, eunuch."

"Wait!"

"Give me one reason why you should draw another breath," Erik said.

"Because if you kill me, you kill Valdis," he spit out between clenched teeth. "She's about to give Mahomet a poisoned drink."

"Good," Erik said. "It'll save me the trouble of gutting him."

"You don't understand," Damian said. "I know how he thinks. He has a taster for everything. He won't drink anything unless she drinks first. If she refuses, he'll know something is wrong."

Erik eased the tension of the blade at his throat. "You're certain of this?"

"You should know by now there's very little of import in this city that I am not privy to. If I'm lying, you can kill me at your leisure," Damian suggested. "But if you want Valdis to live another day, release me at once."

Erik clearly didn't believe him, as he still didn't move. Damian tried another tack. "Look, I know what you did to the Blues and I approve. Your plan showed more subtlety than I gave you credit for, but the herbs you used were too strong. The horses are already incapacitated, and it's not yet time for the race," Damian said. "A spy came tattling to Leo Porphyrogenito and the purpleborn's plans have changed. He won't wait for the results of the race to signal his attack. His men will strike as the chariot teams are making their entrance, when all eyes are focused on the long dark tunnel where they'll appear. The emperor is vulnerable."

"That no longer concerns me," Erik said, tightening his grip on Damian's hair with a twist of his wrist. "I'm only here for Valdis. She's all I care about."

"I thought you Varangians held your oaths sacred."

"So we do, but the dead are no longer bound. I died

to the Empire with my pledge-men in the harbor. I suspect you had a hand in the lion's attack that day as well. You've woven your last web, you Byzantine spider."

Damian felt the bite of the blade again.

"And what of your friend, Hauk Gottricksson? He's in the Emperor's detail. Would you wave away his life in your hurry to end mine?"

The knife at his throat again eased a bit.

"You can still aid your friend if you use the back entrance to the emperor's box. Warn them of the attack while there's time, and I swear on the soul of my only son, I will see Valdis comes to no harm."

"Why aren't you warning the emperor yourself?"

"Because saving Valdis from her own trap seemed more important," Damian said, wondering at his own words. The strange Norse woman with mismatched eyes had ceased being a tool to be used for him some time ago. "I know you love her, Northman, but Mahomet is surrounded by his bodyguards. You might kill them all, but can you do it in such close quarters without endangering Valdis? I'm the only one who can save her life. I will send her to you. Trust me."

"It seems I must." The big Varangian helped him to his feet. "But if you've lied to me and she comes to harm, I will kill you. And I'll take my time."

"Fair enough." Damian gave Erik a fisted salute.

The Northman smiled grimly at him, his pale brows raised. "You salute a *barbaroi?*"

"A moment of weakness," Damian said, surprised at the respect he'd come to feel for this *Tauro-Scythian*. "Save the Bulgar-Slayer for the Empire. She is not ready for him to die."

"Save Valdis for me or nothing else matters."

"God speed you, Varangian."

"Luck in battle." Erik grasped Damian's forearm for a

moment, then turned and set off at a dog-trot back
down the corridor.

"Perhaps he deserves her, after all," Damian murmured. Then he hurried down the corridor in the opposite direction. There was one more thing he must do
before he joined Mahomet and Valdis. He only wondered if it could be done in time.

And if it would work.

Valdis squirmed in her seat. Loki must have sensed her
agitation, for the little dog leaped from her lap to sniff
around the corners of Mahomet's private portico. Her
master had instructed her to open the hamper of food
Agrippina had prepared and ordered Valdis to peel
grapes for him as he watched the mock battle being en-
acted on the oval below. When one of the soldiers was
spitted on a pike, he smiled in morbid enjoyment of another man's dying screams, chuckling low in the back
of his throat.

Valdis despised him with terrifying thoroughness. If
ill-wishes could kill, Mahomet should already be dead.
However, he made no move to uncork the amphora of
juice, and Valdis didn't trust her voice to suggest it. Even
though she could think of a hundred reasons why her
master must die, the actual doing of the deed was much
harder than she expected.

"Are you not enjoying the spectacle?" he asked.

"I find no joy in the misery of others," she answered
truthfully.

"That is because you are attuned to the spirits. No
doubt it is disruptive for so many new souls to cross
over to their punishment or reward all at once. For me,
the scene holds a particular charm. Watching the
deaths of others while I am surrounded by luxury and
comfort helps me deny the truth that I am myself mor-

tal," he said with surprising insight as four men with a stretcher ran out onto the blood-soaked sand to gather up the fallen combatant's body. "The delusion of immortality is a vapor, but a pleasant one. Pour us a drink, my oracle."

Valdis's heart lurched against her ribs. Finally, the moment was upon her. She murmured her obedience and stood to do his bidding, praying furiously that her hands would not shake.

Agrippina had packed two delicate Frankish glasses in the food hamper. Valdis unstoppered the amphora and poured the golden liquid into a pale green goblet. The tang of citrus tickled her nostrils. Sunlight sparkled on the cup of death, lending it a glow of false vitality. With utmost care, Valdis knelt to place it in her master's hand.

"Cook tells me you made this drink for me yourself," he said, his dark eyes boring into her. Valdis was sure he must see her soul quaking. She forced herself to smile at him. "I'll not imbibe alone. Pour a glass for yourself as well and let us drink to the time when I no longer require your services as a seeress and can sample you as a woman. I will see you enjoy that time as well. Never let it be said I am not a generous lord."

"None would deny that," she said, feeling her smile go brittle. She had a distinct sense of unreality, as if she were watching herself from outside her body as she poured the last of the poison into an amber goblet.

So this is the God of this city's sense of justice, she thought as she held death before her. *I am allowed to kill him but it will cost me all.*

She could not bear to think of Erik. Instead, Landina's face rose before her. And Fatima, whose teeth had been yanked out to suit her master's comfort. And all the women of the zenana who endured this man's use and abuse. A few professed to love him, but even they feared him. If she could rid the Middle Realm of Habib Ibn Mahomet only by her own death, so mote it be. She decided it was a fair exchange. Valdis lifted the goblet toward Mahomet in silent pledge, then brought the rim to her lips.

Before she could drink, Damian Aristarchus bullied his way past Mahomet's guard and strode into the private box.

"Thank you, Valdis. I'm absolutely parched. I'll take that," Damian said as he swiped the cup from her hand and knocked back the contents in a long swallow that would have done an ale-house patron proud. He belched loudly, the time-honored compliment of pleasing fare, when he finished. "Pure nectar," he declared. "Is there any more?"

"No," Valdis mouthed, shocked to have her poison go so badly astray. Even though she suspected Damian of conspiring with the very men he'd professed to oppose, she never intended to catch him with her toxin. Shock rooted her to the spot.

"Pity," he said with a shrug, and turned back to Mahomet. "Drink up, my friend. I bring word that all our plans are proceeding nicely."

"That indeed is cause for celebration." Mahomet brought the green goblet to his lips and drained the bowl.

Valdis expected to feel jubilation at the sight, but instead her stomach heaved. She'd killed her friend along with her nemesis. How long before they showed signs? Would it be painful? These were questions she hadn't thought to ask the apothecary.

Damian swiped sweat from his forehead. "Hotter today than expected. I don't suppose you thought to ask Agrippina to pack any of that Macedonian wine?"

Mahomet shook his head and leaned forward to get a better view of the carnage on the oval. "Leave the fermented grape alone, my friend, or it will be the death of you."

"Under the circumstances, I'm inclined to risk it," Damian said cheerfully. He tossed a leather pouch to Valdis. "Take this, my dear, and see the vintner by the camel gate. He's hawking a passable Etruscan, and you look like you could do with a glass yourself."

"Valdis cannot wander the Hippodrome alone," Mahomet protested.

"No, of course not," Damian agreed. "My man Lentulus is waiting in the corridor. He'll watch over her for us and see her safely where she's bound." He turned to Valdis and startled her by switching to Norse. "Go quickly and do not return. Everything has happened as it should. Trust me."

"What was that?" Mahomet asked.

Damian laughed. "I just told Valdis that she wasn't the only one who could learn a new tongue. I've been working on a few Norse phrases. Look at the surprise on her face. Hurry and fetch that wineskin for me; there's a good girl." He waved her away and turned back to his host. "You might find this amusing. I was reading a new scientific treatise the other day that proves women don't get as thirsty as men. Just like camels, they store water in . . ." Damian made a breast-shaped gesture on his own chest.

Valdis heard Mahomet's salacious laugh as she walked unhindered out of the sunlight into the dim corridor with Loki at her heels. Lentulus was nowhere to be seen. Valdis picked up the little dog and ran, putting half the distance around the Hippodrome's oval behind her before she stopped.

Everything has happened as it should.

What did he mean? Did Damian know he drank death when he snatched that goblet from her hand?

She looked in the leather pouch and found enough coin to buy an entire shipload of Etruscan wine as well as a document. She unrolled the scroll and ran her gaze over the parchment.

It was a certificate of manumission, signed and witnessed, complete with Mahomet's own seal. It was surely a forgery, but such an artful one, Valdis didn't doubt it would prevail in any court. She'd never seen Mahomet without his signet ring. How Damian managed such a thing, she couldn't begin to guess.

Valdis's knees buckled and she collapsed to the smooth marble with a sob. Damian Aristarchus had kept his word. He'd set her free.

And she'd killed him.

"The endgame is never a dead certainty."
—from the secret journal of Damian Aristarchus

CHAPTER THIRTY-SIX

A guttural roar erupted from the Hippodrome, a wall of sound that roused Valdis from her tears and raised her to her feet. She wobbled to an opening to the arena and looked down at the oval track. The chariot teams burst from the dark tunnel and thundered across the sand, the Blues conspicuously missing from the lineup. Erik had been successful in undoing Mahomet and Leo's trickery.

A fresh growl rose from the crowd as a band of armed men a hundred strong followed the chariots out and turned midway in the field to climb into the stands. Spectators who lingered too long in their seats were cut down as the mob made its way toward the emperor's box.

Swords flashed from the Imperial guard as they prepared to make their stand against a larger force. Panic sent the crowd stampeding to the exits, trampling underfoot those too slow to get out of the way. Valdis pressed herself against the wall as the fleeing populace surged past her.

Over the din, she heard an unearthly sound, a feral

howl bursting from a myriad of masculine throats as if from a single raging beast.

A *berserkr* cry.

Only a troop of Northmen, a decade of Varangians could make that noise. She fought against the tide of people to see what was happening. Jabbing with her sharp elbows, she worked her way further into the stadium.

The armed insurgents reached the defenders and the fight was enjoined in deadly earnest. A man standing in front of the emperor bellowed an order and another ten men threw off their cloaks to reveal the Varangian *byrnnie* beneath.

Valdis's hand flew to her heart.

The man standing in front of the emperor, laying about him with his battle-ax, protecting the Bulgar-Slayer with his own body, was her Erik.

In some ways, every battle was the same—the same dry mouth, the same queasiness that disappeared the moment he first drew his weapon. Erik was acutely aware of the drumbeat of his own heart pounding in his ears. It dulled the sharp cries of injured and dying men around him. A thousand tiny details clamored for his attention: the glint of sunlight on an opponent's blade, the cloying reek of blood and entrails, an occasional whiff of urine, the whoosh as a sword sliced the air near his good ear, the black mole on an enemy fighter's misshapen nose. Each image, scent or sound would haunt him later with knife-sharp clarity, but he dismissed them now while he hacked away in the melee.

Power surged through his limbs. The ax handle became an extension of his arm, its swing a study in deadly grace. He breathed in rhythm with each stroke, not taking time to tally the fallen. Only one thing was necessary in battle: keep moving and make sure your opponent stops.

A *berserkr* roar burst from his lips as another insurgent came within the arc of his ax. A man was never more alive than when he was but a finger-width from death.

But Erik never had so much to lose before. One misstep, one slow turn and not only would he be done for, but he'd miss out on a life with the woman who made breathing worthwhile. He shoved all thought of Valdis away as he ducked beneath a scything blade.

Time expanded and contracted around him as the rebels kept coming. His arm grew heavier, but he kept swinging. Someone yelled that more rebels were coming up the back tunnel, closing off the emperor's escape. From the corner of his eye, he saw that the Bulgar-Slayer had thrown off his jewel-encrusted crown and picked up the sword of one of his fallen guards. The Lord of All the Earth's hair might be iron-gray, but he still had the grit to show men how he'd earned his nickname. Erik pivoted to face the new threat, placing himself between the fresh enemy fighters and the emperor.

The clatter of steel on steel echoed around the emptying arena. The battle flared up to a white-hot inferno, a conflagration from which it seemed none would escape, and then just as suddenly, burned itself out. The last insurgent was stopped by Erik's double-bladed ax.

No more rebels charged up the stadium stairs or out of the dark tunnel. Erik straightened and looked around. Hauk and a handful from his command were still on their feet. Many more were clutching wounds or staring sightlessly into the pitiless sun. Unspeakably weary and bleeding from a dozen flesh wounds, Erik pulled his ax blade from the chest of his last foe with a squelching sound.

The emperor was upright and unhurt. Though his snowy palla was blood-spattered, none of it was his. Erik breathed a sigh of relief.

"Erik!"

He turned to see Valdis running toward him with that silly little dog of her yapping behind her. Fresh life surged through his limbs and he leapt over the fallen bodies to meet her on the steps of the Hippodrome.

"You're alive!" she exclaimed as she threw her arms around him and peppered his jaw with kisses, heedless of the battle grime. Even Loki clamored around his knees, excited to see him for the first time.

He held her close and inhaled in her scent, the cleansing breath an affirmation that there was truth and beauty in the world after all. The eunuch had kept his promise. Valdis was alive and she was his. Her body pressed against him left Erik with an aching erection, but right now it was enough just to hold her and let the world slide by them.

But the world was never content to do anything so benign as that.

"You there, Varangian!" Erik heard the emperor bellow. "Return to us this instant."

Erik trudged back to the carnage in the Imperial box, leading Valdis behind him, loath to release her hand for a moment.

The aging potentate narrowed his eyes at Erik for the space of several heartbeats. "We know you. You captained the pirate dhow in the Harbor of Theodosius."

Erik nodded. "Your Majesty came very close to removing my head from my body that day."

"But not close enough. You crippled my ship," the emperor accused.

Erik hadn't known the Bulgar-Slayer was onboard. He wanted to give the fleet a taste of true battle. A thousand excuses leapt to Erik's lips, but he knew none would satisfy. "Yes, my lord, I crippled your ship," he admitted.

"You deviated from your orders and made us appear

weak before the populace," the emperor continued, his black eyes snapping. "You placed our Majesty in danger from our nephew's minions on the lion ship."

Erik felt as if he was before the lawspeaker, about to be convicted all over again. He hung his head and tightened his grip on Valdis's hand. He never should have stayed to fight this last battle. He should have stolen her away in the confusion and let the Greeks sort things out for themselves.

"Then you placed your craft between us and danger and sacrificed your entire crew to save our royal neck." The emperor's face split into a wide smile. "We thought you dead with the rest of your gallant Northmen. And today you have risked yourself for us again. It is not often we receive loyalty from a man who has already died once in our service. How shall we reward you?"

Erik blinked in surprise. He'd expected punishment, but instead the Lord of the Byzantines was offering him whatever he wanted. He could think of only one thing.

"My lord, I have served you for many years. Let my release from your service be my reward. I have already secured passage to Ravenna on a ship leaving with the evening tide. I desire nothing more than your permission to leave this city with my woman." He turned to Valdis and cupped her cheek. "My wife, if she'll have me."

Tears shimmered in her eyes and she whispered the word he longed to hear: "Yes."

The emperor studied Erik for a moment, chin in hand. Then he shook his head. "We give you permission to leave the Empress City, but not to withdraw from our service. We have even more need of loyal men at the far edges of the Empire than we do here. The garrison at Ravenna is in want of a new prefect. Consider yourself promoted." He turned to the captain of his guard. "Now let us return to the Imperial Palace to consider what must be done with our purple-born nephew. Take a detachment and bring Leo to me with all speed."

"If the worst happens, I instruct Lentulus to deliver this journal to my wife, Calysta, with regrets for the man I was. And even more for the one I have become."
—last entry in the secret journal of Damian Aristarchus

CHAPTER THIRTY-SEVEN

Valdis and Erik stood at the gunwale of the Imperial *drommond*, watching the spiky skyline of Miklagard slide past them. They were still bound for the distant port of Ravenna, but the emperor insisted they go in style to Erik's new position. Lights from the Imperial Palace danced on the choppy waters of the Sea of Marmara, streaks of silver on the purling surf. Erik slipped his arm around Valdis's waist. She shivered.

"You're not sorry to be leaving, are you?" he asked.

"No, there's nothing for me in the city." She cast a quick glance up at him. He was glad he'd made sure to have the good side of his face toward her. Even so, he rarely caught her looking at him. She probably couldn't bear to.

"From what the Bulgar-Slayer tells me, there's plenty waiting for us in Ravenna. Aside from the hefty rise in pay, the prefect's position comes with a fine home in town for winter and a summer villa in the nearby mountains." Now that Valdis was free, nothing stopped her from returning to the North. He hoped she wouldn't regret coming with him to yet another southern city. "Ravenna's not home, but Hauk said the mountains and the narrow sea reminded him a little of the North when he was there last."

She smiled at him. "Anywhere I'm with you, I'll be home. I'm sorry if I seem preoccupied, but I was just thinking about Damian," she said as she continued to stare at the disappearing metropolis. " 'Everything has happened just as it should,' he said. It's still hard for me to believe he willingly took my goblet. He knew he had drunk my death, and he actually smiled at me."

"We made a deal. Damian convinced me he knew how to save you and would do so, if I guarded the emperor. I didn't know exactly what he was planning, but he was driven to protect the Bulgar-Slayer at all costs. And he kept his word to you as well," Erik said with admiration in his tone. "He knew exactly what he wanted to accomplish and he was willing to do whatever it took. He may have lived a eunuch, but he died a man."

"It would have made him happy to hear you say so," Valdis said with a sad smile. Then she turned her gaze on him and the smile changed to a look of unmistakable invitation. The pale brow arched above her dark eye. "Perhaps we can name our first son after him."

"Damian Eriksson," Erik said testing the name on his tongue. "If we're blessed with a son, nothing would make me happier. But that assumes I get you with a son. The sooner the better." He took her hand to lead her to the sumptuous cabin below decks that had been reserved for them.

From the luxurious appointments, Erik guessed this was the cabin the emperor himself used when he sailed on this vessel. A row of windows looked out over the stern, and the room even had its own private head. An oil lamp swung from a hook above an ebony commode fitted with a brass basin for washing.

Loki had already claimed a corner and curled up in Erik's discarded cloak. The little dog finally seemed to accept Erik's place in his mistress's life and had ceased growling at him at every opportunity.

The only complaint Erik had about their quarters was that the space was designed with the much smaller Greeks in mind. The cabin ceiling was so low Erik had to stoop to avoid knocking his head. But the room boasted a fine bed, even if it were somewhat short by Nordic standards. It was a bed Erik hoped would see hard use during this long passage.

A swell made the ship rise suddenly and he narrowly missed banging his forehead on a low beam.

"Sit down," Valdis urged him. "I don't want to spend my wedding night with an unconscious groom."

"Let me douse the lamp first."

"No, leave it," Valdis said with a hand to his forearm. "I want to see you."

Erik sank onto the end of the bed and studied his hands. She was so beautiful. A light-gilded elf maiden could scarcely be fairer. While he'd never thought of himself as a particularly handsome man before, now his injury rendered him ugly as a troll. He shook his head.

"How can you bear to see me?"

She sank to her knees between his legs and forced him to look into her seductively mismatched eyes. "How can you bear to hold me when the Raven comes for my mind and I know not who or what I am?"

"That's different. You can't help your malady."

"And you can't undo the past," she said softly. "Do you have any idea what it was like for me when I thought you dead? I'm so grateful to have you back from the water and the flames, I'll not complain over a few changes."

A few changes. Erik had seen children stare unabashedly at his ruined visage, pointing and nudging each other, till their mothers bundled them out of his sight. Even battle-hardened men had trouble meeting his gaze without wincing. He was hideous and he knew it.

"A wise woman told me once that a life cannot be judged by what is lost, but by what remains," Valdis said, reaching up a tentative hand to touch his ravaged cheek. "Shall I tell you what I see, Erik? I see a man who swears to his own hurt and does not change. I see a man who will not abandon his duty even in the face of death. I see a man of honor and courage."

"You must see what no one else does," he said.

She nodded. "We are not just flesh and bones, you and I. I see your soul, Erik." A single tear coursed down her cheek. "And it is dazzling in its strength and beauty. I see the man I will love with my whole heart till I am but ashes." She lean forward and kissed him.

He tasted the salt of her tear at the corner of her mouth. His tongue slid in to play with hers, a quiet seeking game. Her fingers tightened where she rested them on his shoulders. When he released her mouth, she smiled at him, and for a moment, he saw his reflection in her eyes. His face was whole in the warmth of her love.

They took their time. With unhurried delight, he undressed her and allowed her to tug him out of his clothes as well. He traced every crevice: the crook of her elbows, the hollow between her breasts, every curve of her luscious body with his fingertips. Then when she pressed against his chest, he lay back and surrendered to her exploration. She handled every bit of him, kissing the scarred flesh and touching with love his most unlovely parts. Under her uncritical acceptance, his healing was complete.

Their leisurely loving woke a deep hunger, a raw emptiness that could only be assuaged by one thing. When their bodies finally joined, it was with the sweetness and completeness of a homecoming. The North might be forever barred to him, but he found his home in Valdis's welcoming arms. He buried himself in her, wrapping himself in her love and giving his with equal measure. Not until her body spasmed around him did he allow himself release. He called out her name, cried out his love for her, his longing and loneliness fading in their oneness.

"O my heart," she said, cupping his cheeks with both palms. "Life is a short journey. While we travel it together, let us choose joy."

"Every day," he promised. "Every day."

"Neither let the eunuch say, 'Behold, I am a dry tree.'"
—Isaiah 56:3

CHAPTER THIRTY-EIGHT

The man crested the rise and looked down into the village of Sardica. It seemed smaller than he remembered, shabbier, but tears welled in his eyes anyway. He sank onto the lush grass to catch his breath. The last climb was steep, and for one who had recently cheated death, foot travel was a weary business.

Damian Aristarchus, one-time chief eunuch to the Imperial household, took out his waterskin and brought it to his lips. By mid-morning, he'd refill this skin at the well in the center of his hometown. He couldn't summon up the courage to think further than that.

He was still suffering from the aftereffects of the dose of spotted corobane, but his precaution, the flask of olive oil he'd downed just before joining Mahomet, coated his insides enough to protect him from the full malevolence of the draught. Mahomet was not so lucky. Damian watched him die in agony, shortly before losing consciousness himself.

Even with the oil, it had been a near thing. By the

time Damian recovered enough to ask Lentulus what had transpired while his spirit hovered between worlds, the emperor had already dealt with his nephew. Leo Porphyrogenito was given a choice of punishments— blinding or gelding. Either debility would exclude him from succession to the throne. Leo chose darkness.

Damian thought the choice showed a lack of courage. A blind man was still a man.

Below him, the village was coming to life. A woman came to the well, bearing a clay pot on her shoulder. When she set it down to draw water, Damian caught a clear view of her face—dark laughing eyes, her nose perhaps a shade too long, lips like an angel slightly turned up at the corners by a trick of musculature than gave her a perpetual enigmatic smile. There was no mistaking her. Calysta.

His heart hammered in his chest and though he'd just taken a drink, his mouth went dry. Coming home to his wife seemed a much better idea when he was back in Constantinople than it did now. But despite his trepidation, he wanted his life back. He wanted to know his son. He wanted to love his wife.

Or try to, anyway.

And if Calysta couldn't accept him as he was?

He brushed away his doubts. If he didn't try, he'd never know. Damian shoved the bung back into the waterskin. He raised himself to his feet and started walking down the switchbacked goat track. He picked up his pace.

He'd already died like a man. It was time to start living like one.

AUTHOR'S NOTE

Though *Silk Dreams* is a work of fiction, a few historical personages are named—notably the Emperor Basil II. His nephew, Leo Porphyrogenito, is a product of my imagination, but his niece, Zoë is not. Zoë succeeded her Uncle Basil to the Byzantine throne and was married to no less than three of the subsequent emperors. Rumor has it she helped more than one to an early grave, but that is fodder for another story.

The use of Northmen as the Emperor's elite guard is well documented. The Varangians were the unlikely watchdogs of the most sophisticated court of its time. The veneer of civilization didn't rub off on the displaced Northmen though. Visitors to the Hagia Sophia today can see runic graffiti carved into the fifth-century church's fine wood—a sort of Viking version of "Kilroy was here."

Sufferers of the "falling sickness" have been alternately reviled as demon possessed or exalted as kissed by the gods throughout history. I'd like to give a special word of thanks to my friend, Angie Sumoski, who battles her epilepsy with a cheerful spirit and was open-hearted enough to share some of her experience with Valdis and me. Angie's a true heroine.

I love to hear from my readers. Please visit my website at www.dianagroe.com and drop me an e-mail.

Wishing you the Mighty Passion,
Diana